Deep in the Heart of Madison

Book 3 of the Heart of Madison Series

Jennifer,
Enjoy!

Happy reading!

sands press
Brockville, Ontario

Deep in the Heart of Madison

Book 3 of the Heart of Madison Series

By Crystal Jackson

sands press

sands press

A Division of 3244601 Canada Inc.
300 Central Avenue West
Brockville, Ontario
K6V 5V2

Toll Free 1-800-563-0911 or 613-345-2687
http://www.sandspress.com

ISBN 978-1-988281-91-9

Publisher's Note

For information on bulk purchases of this book or any book published by Sands Press, please call 1-800-563-0911.

To book an author for your live event, please call: 1-800-563-0911

Sands Press is a literary publisher interested in new and established authors wishing to develop and market their product. For more information please visit our website at www.sandspress.com.

Also by this Author

My Words Are Whiskey

Heart of Madison Series
Left on Main
Right on Walton

To Josh and Amanda, for being #relationshipgoals

Acknowledgements

With four books out, this section becomes increasingly difficult to write. But I cannot express enough gratitude for the fact that I can say that this is my fourth published book. This has been my dream and so, I'll start with my readers:

Thank you for your encouragement and support. I hope you enjoy this latest trip into Madison with me. And don't forget to come back for the last. If you enjoyed this book or any of my others, please leave a review on Amazon and Goodreads. I cannot express to you how important reviews are to help other readers discover my work. I appreciate you!

I'll keep this short and sweet. To my children, Luna and Linus, with my love and gratitude for just being who you are—and for your patience with my work. To David Baumrind for your ongoing support—and for being both partner and best friend. To Laurie Carter for your editing skills and encouragement. To the wonderful staff of In High Cotton for your continued support of this series. To Madison, Georgia, for the ongoing inspiration. And to Josh and Amanda—for your love and support; you are my favorite family.

"Friendship is certainly the finest balm for the pangs of disappointed love.

—Jane Austen

Chapter 1

"It is a truth universally acknowledged that a single woman over the age of thirty has already met her soul mate. She just wasn't paying attention." Beth Everett grinned at the book club as they settled down and turned their attention her way. A couple of them were already giving her knowing looks. "If you're going to rip off an author, at least let it be the late, great Jane Austen, right? What single woman doesn't identify with Jane?" Beth paused and let her gaze wander the room. She fiddled with the book in her lap. "This is just one of many adaptations of Austen's work, and we'll discuss it in a minute. But I wanted to talk about Mr. Darcy first."

"Mr. Darcy!" Amie, friend and tearoom chef, sighed his name. "The McDreamy of Austen men."

"More like McSteamy," a new group member added. Beth thought her name was Kirsten, but she couldn't see the name tag from her seat to confirm.

"A little of both, right?" Beth continued. "There's only one Mr. Darcy, but generations of women read these books."

"And then go out into the dating world to get disappointed by real men," Vera said wryly to nods around the room.

"Right?" Beth agreed, nodding toward the local innkeeper and family friend.

"I swear, for every one Darcy out there, there are about twenty Wickhams," her Aunt Keely chimed in as the group nodded in agreement. The lone man in the room tentatively held up one finger and indicated himself. They all laughed.

"My cousin Seth," Beth said with a smile, knowing he had only come out because his fiancé couldn't make it for work. He'd fill her in later. It's not that men didn't come to the book clubs, but it wasn't typical. "Definitely a Darcy in a sea of Wickhams."

"Thanks," he said, sitting back in satisfaction and then half-eyeing the dessert table to see if he could justify seconds. Well, thirds would be more accurate. Beth looked at him as if reading his mind, and they both exchanged smiles as he got up and filled up a third plate. She turned back to the group.

"Every woman and most men I know are frustrated by the whole dating scene. We start to think about the one who got away. You know, our chance at love that we missed because we weren't paying attention."

"Or there was a timing issue. Or they were with someone when you were with someone," Amie agreed, as Seth sat down beside her and started in on a variety of petit fours.

"So, I wanted to start out telling you about how I met my own Mr. Darcy, and then we'll pick up with the book," Beth said happily, exchanging looks with Vera and Amie while Seth shook his head knowingly. They were familiar with the story, but most of the group tonight was new and hadn't heard it yet. After all, this was their first Austen-inspired book club pick. "It took a while to find him, and we didn't meet in what anyone would consider a traditional sense. It was most unexpected and right when I'd given up all hope. I feel like I should give you a little basic history.

"My first crush was a few months before my eleventh birthday. His name was Jonah, and he had freckles and a wide smile. He was kind of adorable with his blonde hair always sticking up and his wide, goofy smile." She smiled fondly as she remembered him.

"Me? Well, I don't know if anyone would have called me adorable. Feisty, for sure." Beth brushed her red hair off her shoulders, regretting that it was still straight as a stick no matter how often she'd try to make curls stay. Her blue eyes were covered by horn-rims, and she kept her makeup limited to mascara and colored lipstick most of the time. "But anyway," Beth told them, continuing her story and reigning in her thoughts, "Jonah was a textbook *cute boy*. I had a crush before I even knew what a crush was, and I followed him around until he got sick of me and told me to 'drop dead' or something to that effect. So, I did what any other self-respecting nearly-eleven-year-old girl would do when thwarted by her man: I booby-trapped his treehouse like *The Parent Trap* and hid with my girlfriends to watch it all go down."

Beth made a face and a laugh rippled around the group.

"You did *not*," one of them said.

"She did," Seth told them with glee. "There are pictures. Somewhere."

Beth smiled at him and shrugged. "Well, I was a little sorry when he sprained his wrist falling off the ladder, even if I did laugh at first, but he didn't rat me out, so we were able to eventually resume our friendship. Of course, fast-forward four years and Jonah decided to ask me out, but I just laughed and told him to drop dead and he never asked again. Anyway, when I was single, later on during college, and lonely with it, I thought about Jonah. I wondered if he was the one who got away, you know—the actual *one*—and I had been too proud and—gasp! —prejudiced to pay attention. I would weave these daydreams in my head about how we'd run into each other, and it would all come together. Or I'd think about what would have happened if I hadn't shot him down so thoroughly, how maybe we'd be together even now." A few of the women nodded sagely.

Keely came in from the kitchen with another tray of cookies. The first had disappeared quickly, and Seth had cleared out most of the tray of petit fours, claiming it took about a dozen to make one regular piece of cake. Beth smiled at her aunt and continued. "But the truth is that every single person I know—man or woman—plays that game. We get lonely, and we start to wonder if Mr. (or Mrs.) Right wasn't someone from the past we just overlooked." Beth paused to take a sip of her drink and scanned the group.

"Anyway," she continued, trying to stay on track, "I kept taking myself out on dates, hanging out with friends, enjoying my awesome job, and generally loving my life. I dated a little, but after a few hard knocks, I decided to take a little moratorium and use the extra time that I'd used to focus on dating to volunteer at the animal shelter in town. Mostly, I would take the dogs out for walks. And that's how I met him …

"Yes, him. Mr. Darcy. The love of my life. Handsome, charming, well-mannered with that hint of bad boy persona under the surface. You know the type." Most of the women in the group laughed, and Seth rolled his eyes. Beth let the appreciative murmurs settle before continuing. "Anyway, there I was, being dragged back to the shelter by a lab mix when I saw him. You could say it was love at first sight if you believe in that sort of thing. I just know that I was immediately smitten. There he was, just waiting for me—the most handsome bull terrier you'll ever meet."

Beth caught the groans from the group. "He was so little, and he was only a year old at the time, give or take a few months. He sauntered up to me and gave me what I swear was the biggest doggy smile. And I was sunk. My heart? Gone! He was solid white, my white knight, except for a black nose and one black eye. It was love at first sight and completely mutual—just like all the love stories you've ever heard."

From the back room, Keely emerged with Mr. Darcy, to a chorus of coos and sighs. He went straight to Beth and laid down at her feet. She reached to pet him, continuing her story. "I named him Mr. Darcy because I didn't need any other man. I had my perfect guy, and we were going to be very happy together. At least, if 'the one' had two legs instead of four, I've never met him. Anyway, that's the story of how I came to meet my Mr. Darcy. I'd love to hear your own love stories, and then we'll talk about what we all thought about this particular adaptation." She held up *Pride and Prejudice and Zombies* for the group to see.

Beth sat back and listened as each group member shared a story of finding true love or failing to find it. Then they segued into a heated discussion of the book and how it compared to the classic. Beth was glad that she'd started the book club. For a while, it had floundered, but lately, it was a runaway success.

She considered how much life had changed in the last year. Beth wasn't lonely, and she'd stopped playing the game where she imagined every past lover might have been the one that got away. These days, she wasn't even sure she believed in that for herself. Anyway, Beth thought, reaching down to scoop Mr. Darcy into her lap, it's not like the story was over. She had plenty of time for exciting things to happen.

Chapter 2

Beth reached a hand over to pet Mr. Darcy who was stretched out on the chaise lounge beside her. The book club had gone late the evening before, and then she'd stayed up too late reading the next pick. She was exhausted and hadn't moved out of the chair since she'd woken up hours before, except to grab food from the kitchen. Mr. Darcy snuffled in his sleep but didn't acknowledge her otherwise. She sighed. She thought about the book club discussion. She really was happy with her life. Sure, there were the occasional lonely days, but they didn't come around often. She picked up her phone to text Jamie, her best friend.

"Movies tonight?"

His reply was almost instant. "Seven okay?"

"Seven is fine. Bring pizza." She finished with a series of smiley faces and pizza emojis.

He responded with a smiley face, and that was that. She looked down at her pajamas. They were a very pretty light pink with a pattern of tiny books all over them. She'd gotten them from Aunt Keely for Christmas. They were soft and perfect, probably hand-stitched or something fancy, and she had worn them all day. In fact, first thing in the morning, Beth had proclaimed it Pajama Day. Now she wondered if she should put on something before Jamie came over. Normally, she wouldn't, but things hadn't been exactly normal between them in a while. Well, not since Christmas.

"It was just a kiss," she told Mr. Darcy aloud. He looked thoroughly unimpressed, but he'd heard it before. After all, it had happened around Christmas, and they were already into August now. She wished she could let it go. It didn't mean anything after all. "He's my very best friend. That hasn't changed," she continued, trying to convince herself more than her dog. She leaned back with a sigh, curling her feet underneath her. Mr. Darcy sighed loudly and rolled over, leaning into her leg. She patted him and closed her eyes for a minute.

She thought back to that morning under the mistletoe with Jamie. It really shouldn't have meant anything. It was just a casual kiss between friends, a joke so she could check one last holiday activity off her list. It wasn't even much of a kiss in the grand scheme of things. Close-mouthed and brief, just a brush of lips really. She couldn't even say that it was the best kiss she'd ever experienced. Not that she could fault his technique. It was just so quick, and then it was over.

They'd seen each other tons of times since then. Nothing had really changed. Still, it seemed to mean something that neither had mentioned the kiss since it happened. If it had been nothing, wouldn't it have eventually turned into an inside joke or something? Instead, it was this thing that they didn't even talk about, like it had never happened. But it had happened alright, and months later, Beth couldn't quite forget that it had. She wanted things to go back to the way they were before when she wouldn't have thought twice of staying in her pajamas. She sighed and got up to go change.

***

"When you see Beth later, will you tell her I left Libby's copy of the book at the store?" Jamie Radford looked up from the box he was sorting in the back room to Seth who was crouched over another.

"How'd you know it was Beth?" he asked, putting his phone down and eyeing Seth with suspicion. He wasn't close enough to actually read his messages, but he'd known anyway.

"Your face," Seth said shortly, holding up what was quite possibly the scariest doll Jamie had ever seen. "I'm not putting this out. It's like a freak show."

"Save it for Halloween. What about my face?"

"When it's Beth, I can tell. You have no poker face," Seth told him absently, digging through another box of estate sale items they'd been recently "gifted." When the real estate agent had dropped the haul, they'd been excited to score so many finds for the antique store for free until they'd started paintstakingly going through the boxes. They'd found a couple of treasures that made the dig worth it, but most of what they'd found was junk.

"I don't even know what that's supposed to mean," Jamie said, turning back to a cigar box that had caught his eye. He was distracted. He loved movie night with Beth, always had. He was just tired, and he'd thought about canceling with Beth and calling it an early night. But of course, he hadn't, he thought in disgust. He'd go over there and pretend that he didn't want more than exactly what they had. It had been easy to pretend before Christmas. He'd meant the mistletoe as a joke, but he'd also been curious. Well, curiosity killed the damn cat, he reminded himself irritably.

"That one's a keeper," Seth said suddenly.

"What?"

"The cigar box you're scowling at? Put it in the Keep pile. I've got a customer who will want it."

"Right," Jamie told him, putting it in the Keep pile and pulling out a new box.

"Something else on your mind?" Seth asked, as he added a set of vintage salt and pepper shakers to the Keep box. "Everything okay with Beth?"

"She's good. I was just thinking about signing up for one of those dating apps. It's a pain in the ass, but maybe it's easier than heading to the bars in Athens every time I want to meet someone new."

"That's how I met Charlie," Seth said with a shake of his head.

Jamie laughed. "So you wouldn't recommend it?"

Seth pointed what might have been the ugliest dust catcher they'd seen yet in his direction. "Hey, if going through that bullshit with Charlie got me to Libby, I'd do it all again."

Jamie shook his head. "Everyone in relationships says that when they're found the right person. But would you seriously go through the whole thing and get cheated on? You'd have met Libby either way, right?"

"Maybe. We'll never know. But I think we've both made peace with the past now. We're right where we want to be. Maybe online dating is how it happens for you," he said with a shrug, tossing the ugly tchotchke into the Pass pile.

"Maybe," he said absently. He'd been hoping that Beth would bring up the kiss, and they could finally transition from friends to something more. But she didn't, and the more they didn't talk about it, the more certain Jamie felt that Beth didn't feel the same way. But he was no masochist. It wasn't healthy to sit around thinking about someone who only had platonic feelings for him. "I hate online dating."

"Everyone hates it. Anyone who doesn't hate it is probably what's wrong with it in the first place," Seth said, standing up to pull a new box down.

"That's some interesting logic."

"Probably true though."

He thought he'd work on a dating profile later, mentally cringing even as he thought it. After hearing Beth regale him with some of the hilarious photos she'd seen with online dating, he was sure to avoid putting pictures of himself fishing (which he did occasionally), working out (he went to the gym every day but never photographed the process), standing at the bathroom mirror with a shirt off (who does that?), and posing with someone else's kid (although maybe Lindy would let him borrow Maya? Probably not). He'd keep it simple and try to find pictures of himself that didn't include Beth in them. That would just be weird.

They both looked up as the door to the back room swung open unceremoniously. Seth's thick wavy hair contrasted with Jamie's bald one as they turned toward the figure standing dramatically in the doorway. Not that Farrah was trying to be dramatic, but the sixties era jumpsuit she was wearing with sparkly hoop earrings, winged eyeliner, and a bouffant kind of made her entrance less than ordinary. Her love for all things vintage made her a perfect—if surprising— fit for their store.

"Well, you're both deep in it now," she told them with a raised eyebrow and quirk of her bubblegum pink lips.

"We're making progress," Jamie said with a shrug. He'd stripped down to a T-shirt in the back. Although it was perfectly air- conditioned, he'd been moving around boxes most of the morning. He could see Farrah eyeing one of his tattoos and waited for the inevitable questions to follow. Her eyes moved over him casually, not like she was checking him out but more like he was a bug under a microscope.

"I need your personal trainer," she said flippantly with a nod to his body before turning back to Seth who was waiting patiently. "We've got a customer who wants the history on every item he picks up. One of you want to do the honors? I need to run the cash register."

Jamie reached for his shirt, but Seth held up a hand. "I've got this. If it's who I think it is, it's going to take a while, and I've already put an item away to distract him. You go ahead and work on this."

They left, and Jamie turned back to the box. Farrah's entrance had distracted him from thinking about Beth, but in the silence they left behind, he tried to get himself in the mood for movie night. If he just treated her like he always had, they'd get back to normal. He was probably just being awkward about it, which made her feel awkward about it. He'd try to relax, and then they could get back to where they'd been before. Maybe she could even look over his dating profile and tell him if it was stupid. She wouldn't pull any punches, that's for sure.

Chapter 3

Libby Reynolds was just finishing up her morning run. She'd gotten in five miles in well under an hour, which was an improvement. She'd been thinking about adding in a speed training day to her workout, or maybe just cross-training. While she was cooling down and heading toward home, she heard the unmistakable sounds of Beth and Mr. Darcy. She smiled. Beth was infamous for carrying on full conversations with her dog on their walks.

As Beth rounded the corner, she jolted when she saw Libby. "Hey, you. Say hi, Mr. Darcy." The dog obediently sat and put out a paw to shake. Libby took it with a laugh and patted his head.

"I meant to wake up early to run before it got this hot. I can already feel the humidity," Libby said with a grimace, pulling her tank top away from her skin where it was already sticky with sweat.

"Mr. Darcy and I were just talking about going on a lake adventure soon. He likes to swim as much as I do. How's the wedding planning coming?"

"I've got a few ideas. I just need to run them by Seth and see." It still felt strange to be talking weddings when she felt like she'd only just got divorced, though in truth, it was closer to two years ago now.

"He'll do whatever you want," Beth said, watching as Mr. Darcy took an interest in a butterfly that had landed on a flower. He plopped down and tried to do a belly crawl to get closer, but the butterfly flew away. Beth and Libby exchanged a smile.

"I need to talk to Lindy, too, and make sure that our plans don't overlap. They have Maya to consider, after all, so we'll work around that," Libby said, referring to Seth's sister Lindy and her upcoming wedding plans. That was still a surprise, although not an unpleasant one. They had all been so pleased to see Lindy fall in love. Maybe they'd been a little surprised that she'd decided on Dean. After all, he had a reputation that preceded him, although he'd retired it once he started seeing her.

"I'm getting some Maya time tomorrow. Jamie's coming over later for movie night, or I'd sneak over and cuddle her today."

"Is movie night a date?" Beth looked at her quickly, and if Libby wasn't mistaken, there was a blush. Of course, it could just be the heat.

"Not at all. It's just our regular thing." Mr. Darcy wandered back over on his leash, and Beth gave him a quick rub. "This is my guy," she said proudly.

"He is handsome." Libby thought about getting a dog. They had so much going on that she didn't want to suggest it yet. But Madison was a great town for a dog. The local businesses put out treats and bowls of water. There was a groomer's right in town; the vet was close by; and they even had an organic dog food company a stone's throw from the historic district. The city enforced leash law and had built an expansive dog park. She'd been eyeing possibilities on an adoption site online, but she had only just moved in with Seth. She wasn't sure that it was time to suggest such a big change.

"He's great. You should get one," Beth said knowingly, watching Libby make doe eyes at her dog.

"Maybe one day."

"Well, you're welcome to occasionally borrow mine if you need a fix."

"Thanks. I think I'm going to head home and shower. Want to have lunch later this week?"

"At the tearoom, or were you thinking somewhere else?"

"If you're tired of the tearoom, we can grab something else."

"No, I never get tired of it. You'd think I would, but I pop out for lunch most days or bring my own. Besides, we can ask Aunt Keely to join us if she has time. Is it weird that she's going to be your mother-in-law?"

"Not at all. It's actually kind of great. My last mother-in-law hated me. I mean, really despised me," she explained, when Beth let out a short laugh. "Keely's wonderful. She hasn't even weighed in on the wedding plans yet. She's just letting me decide. It would almost be weird if it wasn't such a relief."

"Well, tell Seth hi for me. I'm going to finish this one's walk so I can get back before it gets too hot."

***

Keely Westerman looked around the house she'd called home for most of her life. She'd only moved out at the beginning of the year, and it still felt strange to call the farm she shared with her new husband home. She was glad Lindy had moved in though. There was a peaceful symmetry in having been raised in this house, bringing up her babies here, and then passing it on to Lindy. Maya would grow up here, and it would stay in the family for a little longer.

Lindy had lived in the carriage house on the same property before Keely had moved out to the farm. Over the last few months, Dean had moved in, too, and they were making the big house their home and talking about turning the carriage house at back into a rental property. Keely sipped her coffee and noticed small changes they'd made. It didn't bother her at all, but it was strange to be visiting the home she'd always thought of as her own.

Lindy Carver came back into the room holding Maya in her arms. "I knew I'd heard her on the monitor. She was hungry." Lindy kissed the top of Maya's head and smiled. Keely smiled, too, knowing that Lindy was doing the thing that all mothers before her had— breathing in that scent so particular to newborns.

"Did you wake her up just to cuddle?" Dean Walton demanded as he came into the room. "She hardly ever puts her down even to sleep," he told Keely in exasperation.

"He's one to talk," Lindy said with a sardonic smile, as Dean went to pour a cup of coffee. "I heard him on the monitor in the middle of the night talking to her. Then he picked her up and brought her back to bed with us." She rolled her eyes in his direction. "I thought it would be good to let her sleep in her own room from time to time, but he's not having it."

"I can't help she's irresistible," Dean said, dropping a kiss on to Maya's head as he passed and then pressing one to Lindy's forehead.

Keely smiled into her coffee, lowering her eyes to give them a moment. She hadn't been exactly surprised when Dean and Lindy discovered their interest for each other. She'd wondered over the years when it would happen. Dean had been coming around the house since he was just a boy to play with Seth. He'd always been a rascal but a charming one. She'd welcomed him and even considered him like a second son. He would be one soon enough, and the thought of it pleased her.

Keely had been watching the two of them dance around this for years. Lindy had first reacted with annoyance to having another boy in the house, particularly a younger one who made as much if not more noise than her little brother. Then they'd gotten older. Keely had known about Dean's teenage crush on Lindy from the start. If Lindy had noticed, she'd treated him with even more disdain. Eventually, they'd gone their separate ways. Lindy, to art school and to a business she would love. Dean, to a long list of lady friends he'd charm and a career as a firefighter, which only helped him add more women to that list.

She wasn't sure when exactly it had changed, but it seemed like the last few years had been inching them slowly toward each other. She'd wondered idly if anything would come of it, but then she'd seen the signs before they had. Their arguments had always had heat in them, but this was something else. Something that might, to an observer like Keely, have indicated desire more than irritation.

She put her coffee down and reached out. "Now you two have this baby all the time. Stop hogging her."

Lindy laughed softly and gently put her still-sleeping baby in Keely's arms. Dean said he was going to go upstairs and shower. They both watched him walk away, Keely with affection and Lindy with undisguised lust that tickled Keely. Dean had been a handsome boy who'd grown up into what even she could admit was a sexy man. She sometimes wondered what had taken Lindy so long to see it. Of course, her girl had always been stubborn.

"Has Theodore decided what he wants Maya to call him?" Lindy asked, filling up a large mug with coffee. She leaned back against the counter and admired the picture that her beautiful mother and daughter made sitting at the counter.

"We discussed it," Keely said, admiring Maya's pretty hands and long lashes. "We've decided we like Lolly and Pops."

"That's cute. Dean's parents decided they'd go with Grams and Gramps. Simple enough."

"Have they adjusted to the news yet?" Dean's parents had divorced, and he had one sister who lived on the other side of Atlanta. They weren't very close, so they had almost been the last to hear about the birth and engagement, which had caused some bad feelings.

"Oh, they're fine. Danielle wants to have more of a heads up on the wedding, but she likes the idea of being someone's aunt."

"Have you picked a date yet?"

"Don't you start. Dean asks me that practically every other minute when he's not asking me to hand Maya over. He'd marry me tomorrow if I agreed."

"So why don't you?"

"I don't know. I guess I'd like an actual wedding. Nothing big and fancy but maybe something small and rustic. With a huge party afterwards with all our friends. Maya's too little to leave for a real honeymoon so we may put that off until next year. Go on a cruise or something."

"You know I'll be happy to keep her whenever you want."

"I know. Libby and Beth have said the same thing. We're just not ready to be away from her yet. I thought I would miss work more, but I'm not ready to go back."

"You've got a while yet before you have to. Don't worry about that right now."

"How are things with you and Theodore? How's his recovery going?"

"He's back to normal now. It's like the heart attack never happened, only of course it did. I quite like life on the farm, though I do miss walking in to work."

"Is Layla doing okay?"

While she'd been in active labor with Maya, her family had been embroiled in drama out in the waiting room. Dean and Keely had missed it, since they'd been right by Lindy's side throughout the delivery, but Theodore's family and their own family and friends had all witnessed the drama unfolding. Layla's then-boyfriend had been asked to leave the hospital while Layla stayed behind with her family. Of course, after he'd been asked to leave, Keely had announced the news of Maya's arrival, and the conflict had faded into the background. It was only later that night that Theodore filled them in.

"Layla's getting through it. She was right when she said Noah would destroy her things. He sent some of them back to her shredded, and the rest of it he either sold or threw away. Just goes to show you can't judge a book by its cover."

"I know. He seemed so ordinary. I thought he was kind of an odd match for Layla, but in a good way, you know?"

"We all thought that. How's Dean dealing with it?"

Lindy thought about it. "He's okay. I mean, he was pissed, but he's better now." They'd found out after the fact that Noah had been making damn sure that some of his activities were covered up by casting doubt on Dean. "Is she still bunking with her sister?"

"They've been sharing an apartment over in Athens, but I know both girls want that to be a short-term situation. Theodore's convinced that his girls need each other right now, and I don't think he's wrong. How are you settling in here?"

"We're getting it the way we like it, and I've been thinking we should rent out the carriage house. But not just to anyone. We're not in a hurry though. We can always make it an AirBNB while we figure things out."

"What's Dean going to do with the lake house?"

"We've decided we're going to keep that. It'll be a nice getaway, and we can rent it out when we're not using it. Of course, he's already fixed up a nursery for Maya so we'd be catering to the family set. Whoever thought Dean Walton would be such a good dad?"

"Well, I did, for one," Keely said, snuggling Maya. "I always knew there was a good man lurking under all of that playboy business."

"Hmm ... well, you had more faith than I did."

"Now if we can just get Beth to settle down ..."

"If I know Beth, I think the best thing we can do is leave her be. She won't see it until she's ready."

"See what?" Dean asked, coming in and kissing Lindy in passing.

"Who she's supposed to be with," Lindy told him.

"What, did Beth meet someone? How'd I miss this juicy piece of gossip? Has anyone told Mr. Darcy?"

"Funny. Actually, we weren't thinking of anyone new."

"We were more thinking of someone she already knows well," Keely added, watching to see how long it would take Dean to catch up.

"This would be so much easier if you just told me who you meant," Dean said with a heavy sigh.

"Jamie, of course." Lindy rolled her eyes.

"Jamie? They're just friends."

Keely and Lindy exchanged a quick laugh and expression of disbelief. "If there is anyone out there perfect for Beth, it's Jamie. How do you not see it?"

"Then why hasn't he asked her out?"

"Maybe not everyone has your smooth ways." Lindy looked at him in amusement.

"This is true. I don't recall my charms working with you."

"I figured I was immune. Clearly, I was wrong."

"I did, too. All the way up until you proposed," Dean said, kissing the top of her head.

"Well, I was under the influence of the epidural."

"No take backs," Dean said, reaching over to stroke a finger down Maya's cheek.

"Oh, I'm going to marry you. Just stop asking when. Let's get through Seth and Libby's wedding first," she said with a smile, tilting her head up to kiss him.

"Don't mind me," Keely said. Lindy and Dean broke apart, turning bright smiles in her direction. She laughed and reached over to take the baby back.

"I'm going to be late," Dean said. "I'll see you all later." He waved and walked out the back door.

"I don't think I'll ever get used to it," Lindy said ruefully.

"Which part?" So much had changed in the last couple of years.

"Me and Dean. Our little family. It's like a dream."

"Well, you've always had a practical bent, for an artist. I'm glad, at any rate, that it's Dean. He always felt like a second son to me. Now he'll be one."

"I'll tell him you said so. You know he loves you."

"I know. Now if you'll just marry him already."

"Don't you start." Lindy picked up a wedding magazine Libby had left for her and began flipping through it with a roll of her eyes.

Chapter 4

"Why is there always a pretend engagement in these movies?" Beth asked Jamie, passing him the bucket of popcorn. "I've never had a pretend engagement." She popped a couple of kernels of popcorn in her mouth and chewed thoughtfully. "And why is this whole plot line so satisfying?"

Jamie had arrived at the door of Beth's house carrying pizza and a bottle of wine. Beth had done an impromptu happy dance and informed him that she'd stocked his favorite beer and made apple pie. They found the arrangement mutually satisfying and then settled in to watch Beth's movie selection since it was her turn to pick. She'd gone straight to the Hallmark Channel and settled in with glee. The pizza had disappeared quickly during the first movie, and they'd paused to make popcorn. Beth wasn't even particularly hungry; after all, she was saving room for pie, but she loved the smell of popcorn while watching movies.

"Ah- the mysteries of life and the Hallmark Channel. Want to be pretend engaged?"

"No. You know how this works. If we've learned anything from Hallmark, we know that a pretend engagement inevitably ends in a real wedding," Beth said with a sigh. "It gets complicated." She leaned her head into Jamie's shoulder. He stretched his arm around her and rested his head on top of hers. He thought regretfully of the app on his phone and that profile out there circulating in the dating world. He wished that it could be as simple as this, just staying right where he was with the only woman he wanted to be with. But then he thought, philosophically, that he could at least keep the friendship but find someone new to satisfy his romantic interests. Though he wouldn't have objected to a pretend engagement, had she been interested.

"Complicated is the word for it, alright. But we love it, don't we, Mr. Darcy?" Jamie said, patting the dog's head. Mr. Darcy looked at him quizzically and then put his head down in Jamie's lap and went back to sleep, unimpressed with their banter and skeptical about the Hallmark Channel.

"Thanks for staying in with me tonight. I know you're missing that movie you wanted to see. I just didn't feel like going out," Beth said, snuggling deeper into the blanket she was sharing with Jamie.

She'd changed out of her pajamas into a pink T-shirt and cutoff jeans but left her hair down. It was more basic than her usual eccentric style. She just wanted to be comfortable. She'd tried to style her hair differently and then had given up when it hadn't wanted to do anything but hang there. She might have overthought showing up for movie night in pajamas, but she knew that she didn't have to worry about Jamie seeing her with a fresh face. After all, it would hardly be the first time.

"I don't mind. It'll still be playing later." He pulled Beth in closer and tried not to think about how perfect this seemed. They were just friends after all. That's all this was ever going to be. He stroked her hair and tuned back into the movie. It didn't really matter what they watched. He was always able to relax with Beth. It had been that way from the start. They never ran out of things to say to each other, either. He sometimes thought if he could dream up the perfect girlfriend it would be Beth Everett—but, you know, if she were actually interested in him. Which she wasn't.

"See that? That's another thing I'll never understand!" Beth exclaimed, gesturing at the movie and waking Mr. Darcy in the process who looked at her disgruntled. Jamie reached over and patted his head softly.

"What's that?" Jamie asked in amusement at the indignant tone of her voice. She really got into these movies.

"The angry sex thing."

"The angry what thing?" Jamie asked curiously, pulling back to look at her. "Are we still on the Hallmark Channel?" He wondered how long he'd been lost in his own thoughts.

"You know what I mean," she waved her hand. "That whole thing in movies and romance novels where the main characters get into this big fight, and then the lust just comes through. Well, this is Hallmark so it's attraction and maybe a kiss, but you get it."

"Oh, yeah. That. Sure," Jamie agreed, waiting to see where this was going. "And?"

"Well, I'm sorry, but it works as a plot device, but it's not exactly realistic. I mean, there's not one time in my life where I was in a big argument with some jerk when I all of a sudden realized that I wanted him or ended up making out while in the middle of a fight."

"It would certainly end the fight though."

"Like in the old movies—using kissing as a way of interrupting. It just doesn't sit that well with me. I mean, if I'm interrupted with a kiss, I'm going to finish what I had to say as soon as it's done," Beth said stubbornly.

"Not if it's a good kiss," Jamie pointed out, always entertained at the way Beth's mind worked.

"Well, you have a point there."

"Besides, I know you. You love that part of the movies."

"Hey, I'm not saying that it doesn't work. Just that it's not exactly realistic."

"I can't say I've ever had it happen either. I guess I never really thought about it. I guess it would make for a boring movie if people did in fights what they really do. Like the silent treatment or some kind of passive aggressive shit."

"I guess that's true." Beth settled back into Jamie and rubbed Mr. Darcy's ears.

"What would *Pride and Prejudice* have been like without all the friction and tension?"

"Don't use Jane Austen against me," Beth told him with a smile he could feel without even seeing it. She cuddled in closer, and Mr. Darcy circled around until he found the most comfortable spot by Beth's feet on the couch. He stretched himself out and went back to sleep, and Jamie enjoyed the citrus scent of Beth's hair as they watched the movie play out.

When the second movie ended, Beth headed into the kitchen for pie. She'd even gotten French vanilla ice cream to go on top. While Jamie went to use her restroom, she heated up the pie and scooped out the ice cream on top. She leaned against the counter for a second, wondering if she should have had that second glass of wine. She wasn't usually such a lightweight, but she might have filled up her glass a little more than usual. Relaxing with Jamie used to be effortless, but sometimes she thought too much about a kiss that shouldn't have happened. The wine helped her to relax and treat him like she always had. This wasn't a date so there was no need to have these nerves flip flopping around in her stomach. She pressed a hand to her belly.

"Too full for pie? I'll eat your slice," Jamie volunteered, walking into the room.

"I'm never too full for pie. Besides, I'll walk it all off with Mr. Darcy later." She handed him a plate, and they walked back to the couch to eat it. She sat down, her leg resting next to his, and then she wondered if she shouldn't have given him a little space. But then she overthought that, too, because before the kiss, she would never have thought twice about sitting anywhere in the room, including right in his lap. The thought of doing that now made her dizzy, and she set the plate down on the end table with a thunk.

"Hey, are you okay?" Jamie asked, setting his own plate on the table and reaching out to touch her face. She wanted to tremble, but thanked all the gods and the wine that she didn't.

"I'm fine. Maybe drank too much. I don't know," she said,

closing her eyes a moment. This close, she could smell his cologne. He didn't exactly pour it on the way so many men did, to her everlasting regret. It was subtle and rich, and she wanted to lean in and smell it on his collar, but she knew he was already worried enough. She sat up and tried to pull herself together. Even Mr. Darcy had cocked his head at her, perplexed.

"Are you going to be sick?"

"No, I'm okay. I want to eat this before the ice cream melts." They both picked up their plates, and Beth tried not to notice the worried and slightly amused looks Jamie was sending her. "So tell me something about your week. What have you got planned?" she asked him, needing a distraction.

"There are a few auctions coming up, but mostly I'm reorganizing stock," Jamie said with a shrug. "And I signed up for this online dating thing so I guess I'll see how that goes." He paused, not sure exactly what had motivated him to bring it up. He watched Beth for a reaction, but she didn't as much as tear her eyes away from the slice of pie she was scooping on to her spoon. His heart sank a little. If he'd needed further proof that she didn't care, there it was.

"Well, that should at least be entertaining," she said evenly, keeping her eyes fixed on her plate. The wine had been a mistake. It was making her a tad bit emotional, and she liked to operate on a fairly even keel. Something about the thought of Jamie dating again made her sad when of course she'd be happy for him to find true love. If there was one thing Jamie really enjoyed, it was a steady relationship, and as his friend, she wanted him to have what he wanted. So why didn't she feel the slightest bit happy about the news? "There are a lot of weirdos out there so be careful with that," she said with an attempt at lightness.

"You'll always be my favorite weirdo," Jamie said affectionately, and Beth looked up at him suddenly with a smile.

"How's the pie?" she asked him sweetly.

"It's great. Thanks for making it," he returned, looking at her with suspicion. "What do you want?"

"Nothing. Really," she began, looking up at him innocently. He groaned. "So maybe just a little help later this week. But only if you have time."

"Fine. What is it?" Jamie asked, wondering what she was up to.

"I kind of want to move some furniture around. I mean, not all of it, obviously. But I could use a little help."

"What's in it for me?" Jamie asked with a laugh.

"Well, I thought afterwards we could head over to Dean and Lindy's cabin for burgers, beer, and swimming in the lake. I'd buy the beer and be your designated driver back home after."

"That doesn't sound like a bad offer. Sure, I can help. It's really good pie."

"Want to stay for another movie?" Beth asked him, putting down her plate and leaning on his shoulder.

"I think I should probably get home. But I'll walk with you and Mr. Darcy if you want the company," Jamie offered, knowing Beth would take the dog for an extensive evening walk before bed. Mr. Darcy heard his own name and the word *walk* and had headed to the door to wait for his leash.

"We'd love it, thanks." She put her hand on his thigh to push herself to standing and then hated that she overthought that, too. She swayed a little, more dizzy at her own thoughts than any intoxication.

"Are you sure you're up for walking? I could take him out before I go. It's no trouble," Jamie told her, looking into her eyes. They were standing closer than they usually did. In fact, the only time they'd stood this close was for a kiss that neither would talk about.

"No, I'm okay," Beth said softly, wondering what would happen if she leaned in just a little.

"Want me to grab his leash while you find your shoes?" Jamie asked, prolonging the moment. He liked being this close to her. She had the lightest lashes, but they were still long and framed the prettiest blue eyes. He could count her freckles if he wanted to, but he kept being distracted by her mouth. Still, if she'd wanted to kiss him, she'd had plenty of opportunity. And apparently, she'd been unimpressed with their kiss and wasn't likely to want to repeat the experience. At that thought, he stepped back, turning away from the leash and didn't see Beth inch closer to him and then rock back in surprise when he moved.

"Yes, the leash, please. I'll just go get my shoes." She rushed into the bedroom, trying to compose herself. Well, that was the answer she needed. She'd moved in, and he'd turned away. Of course, he probably hadn't even been aware of her intentions, but maybe he had been and was just trying to avoid straight-out rejecting her.

Besides, he'd just told her he was going to be dating other people so it's not like she had any illusions about their relationship. She was committed to being single for the rest of her life, wasn't she? She shook her head briskly trying to snap out of this funk she'd fallen into. She slipped on her shoes and took a minute to just breathe. This was Jamie, her best friend. Everything was fine. She'd just had too much to drink and was being weird.

She came out of the room with an over-bright smile, which Jamie didn't really notice because he was busy trying to get his own thoughts in order. He thought maybe he'd skip the next movie night. He'd still help her move furniture, but then he needed a little space. It was just too tough to be around her and know that they didn't want the same thing. Besides, he really hoped he'd have a date lined up soon.

He put the leash on Mr. Darcy and passed it over to Beth who seemed like her normal self. They headed out to walk the neighborhood with Mr. Darcy doing his version of a happy dance at the end of the leash. Jamie smiled, and Beth returned it easily. They both breathed a sigh of relief that things could go back to normal between them. Beth nearly laughed to herself when she thought of how anxious she'd made herself over nothing. This was Jamie, after all. Nothing had changed.

Chapter 5

Seth Carver walked through the store one last time. He'd spent the morning making notes on the displays. He'd found a couple of broken items he'd moved to the back. He'd have to figure out if they could be repaired or not. If not, he could write them off for being damaged. He'd also made notes on what he wanted to change and what stock they might want to rotate in from storage.

He enjoyed these early mornings when the store was empty. At times like these, he thought back to the years he'd spent in the store with his grandfather and then with his mother. His grandmother had been ill more often than not, and none of Seth's memories with her included the store. But he'd sat quietly on the floor and played with a box of tin soldiers his grandfather had given him. He'd sat under a table reading comic books. So much of his childhood had played out right here.

He heard the back door open and looked up to see Jamie coming in from the storage room. He waved and indicated the back office, where he would undoubtedly acquire coffee. Seth always started a pot when he came in each morning. He was lucky to have Jamie. He'd gotten him full-time when Jamie had lost his job during the recession and wanted to turn his part-time hours into full-time ones. Seth had taken him on, realizing that he was invaluable to the business. When the economy started to recover, Seth had fully expected to lose Jamie to a higher paying job, one with the potential for upward mobility. Jamie had surprised him by wanting to stay. He'd even begun taking accounting and bookkeeping courses to take that part of the business off Seth's shoulders.

"Was the gym crowded?" Seth asked, as Jamie came in.

"Not this early in the day. I saw your fiancé heading in as I was leaving."

"Yeah, Libby isn't a fan of running in this heat. She's got a yoga class this morning, and then I'm sure she'll put in a few miles. I should go, but I get so bored."

"It's not for the faint of heart. But Libby's going to leave you in the dust if you don't try to keep up."

"I think I got enough exercise in working on Dean's house this last year. I get muscle cramps just driving by the home improvement store now."

"How's the house coming?"

"It's great now. It was a beast when we started though. They're thinking about renting it out to tourists, so we got everything ready. It looks good."

"How's the wedding planning coming?" Jamie asked, taking a sip of his coffee and looking over Seth's notes from the morning.

"Libby's still considering our options. She'll let me know what she wants, and that's what we'll do. She made this so easy."

"You're a lucky man."

"I know I am."

"Beth likes a good wedding. She is interested in what kind of cake you're having. Be prepared for an interrogation," Jamie warned with a laugh.

"Thanks for the heads-up. Did you call that real estate agent back?"

"Yeah, we've got an appointment today." They'd gotten the referral a week ago from a client. A new real estate agent in town wanted to discuss estate sales. The stock they acquired from auctions and estate sales was essential to the business.

"Let me know how it goes," Seth said as he headed to flip the Open sign on the door.

***

Across town, Beth was doing a little inventory of her own. Naomi was stocking the shelves with her earbuds in and occasionally sang along to one of the songs out loud. Beth was pretty amused, but more than that, she was glad Naomi seemed to be feeling better lately. There had been a time when she'd been nervy and anxious. She'd spent months dealing with an abusive relationship and had only confided in Beth when it had escalated to assault.

What made it infinitely worse was that Beth had known the assailant—and was actually acquainted with his girlfriend, Layla, and her family, too. Layla's father had married her Aunt Keely, who also happened to be her boss. It was that way in small towns sometimes. Everyone knew everyone. The knowledge had weighed on Beth until she'd been able to unload it on Presley, Layla's sister. Together, they'd helped Layla confront her boyfriend and put an end to it.

As Beth made notes on inventory, Naomi finished stocking the new release section and pulled out her earbuds. Her dark hair was pulled up in a ponytail, and she'd used a light hand with makeup today. Beth admired her skill there and thought about asking her for tips before deciding that she honestly didn't care enough to really learn. "I'm having lunch with Layla today. Did you want to join us?"

"I would love to another time, but I'm going to sit down with Libby and Aunt Keely and go over the wedding plans."

"I bet Libby's so happy. Has she chosen her bridesmaids yet?"

"She's having her sister, Rose, and me. But get this: Seth's having Dean, Jamie, and *Lindy*."

"Wait—his sister's going to be his best *man?*" Naomi asked, perplexed.

"Seth and Libby both wanted her in the wedding. And you know they're thick as thieves anyway, always have been. She said she's going to wear a suit and everything."

"And she'll be standing up by her fiancé. That'll be interesting."

"Does that bother you?" Beth asked. Naomi had dated Dean briefly before Lindy. She'd had a hard time getting over it.

"Not anymore. It did at first. I've gotten used to it."

"Dean's broken a lot more hearts than just yours," Beth said dryly, thinking of the one time she'd gone out with him herself. That had been a disaster she was glad to leave in the distant past.

"Well, to be fair, he told me how it was going to be upfront. I just thought I'd be the one to change him."

Beth thought about that. "Isn't it funny that we want to change the people we say we love rather than loving them for who they are?"

"I think he's good with Lindy," Naomi said quietly, straightening a few books on the shelves.

"I know, right? With everything that's happened in the last year, I think I've had enough change to last a lifetime," Beth said with a sigh as she made a final check to the inventory and placed her next order.

***

Ansley McKellar did a quick walk-through of the home. She had a few minutes before meeting the representative from the antique store. Her colleagues spoke well of Jamie, and she'd arranged a meeting on those recommendations. She'd already had a few phone conversations with him, and he'd seemed short and taciturn, although friendly enough not to be off-putting. She wasn't sure what she was expecting, but it wasn't who arrived at the door. She saw him approach the porch and stand hesitating by the open door. While she was unobserved, she took the time to check him out.

He was tall, bald, and muscular with a number of tattoos peeking out of the sleeves of his shirt. He looked like he should be astride a motorcycle or something, not surveying his notes carefully while assessing the open door. Saving him the trouble of deciding whether or not to knock, she stepped out from the hallway so he could see her.

"Hi. Are you Jamie?"

"I am. Ansley McKellar?" he asked, returning the smile with a wide one of his own. He seemed to look at her approvingly, as if he liked what he saw.

Ansley was glad she'd made an effort this morning to appear as professional as possible. She'd paired a casual blue silk blouse with a navy skirt that flared out mid-calf. She'd slipped on low heels with a peep toe. Her blond hair was down, straight and cut in a short inverted bob. She was the slightest bit freckled, although it was barely visible with a light layer of makeup. Her brown eyes were long-lashed and inquisitive as she stood there with her hand on the open door.

"Guilty," she said, reaching out her hand to shake his. "Why don't you come in and tell me what you can do to help with this mess?"

She stood back, ushering him inside. While it was far from the most cluttered home that Jamie had seen in his work, nearly every surface was covered with collectibles. Even the sofa was loaded with crocheted pillows and knit blankets. "As you can see, staging would be difficult as it is. We can't quite put it on the market as-is, and the couple selling isn't up to the task of getting it ready."

"Illness?" Jamie asked absently, picking up a figurine and examining it more closely.

"Not exactly." Ansley said, watching him walk around the room carefully. "They're moving to Florida to be closer to one of their kids. They're actually already living down there so they aren't here often enough to properly address what's left behind."

"Didn't they take any of their things with them?" Jamie asked, looking up in bemusement.

"Apparently, they did. Just imagine," Ansley said with a little awe in her voice.

"Are they interested in selling what's left, or are they coming back for some of it?" Jamie asked, taking out his notebook.

"They've set aside a few boxes in the garage to come pick up, but the rest they'd like sold—either with the house or in a separate auction. I might be able to sell it at least partially furnished, but I can't even list it with the rest of—this." She indicated the collections.

"You'd think they would take their collectibles at least," Jamie commented, sitting gingerly down on a couch after moving a few pillows out of the way.

Ansley sat across from him in a chair chosen more for comfort than looks and crossed her legs slowly, taking out her own notebook from the tote she carried. "Apparently, they weren't collecting exactly." When Jamie's lips quirked and he reassessed the room, she continued. "Most of these were gifts from their grandchildren who seemed to think that their grandparents would like nothing better than figurines for every occasion."

"That's kind of cute."

"They said it was cute. At first. It grew less cute over the years and more into something of a joke. They're using the move as an excuse to sell the lot of them. They're claiming they don't have the room in their new digs for the collection. In fact, I'd bet dollars to donuts that they chose a place small enough that they could make that claim," she said, her lips quirking into an amused smile.

"Can't say I blame them. Let me just go through what we typically do and how it all works, and you can let the client know and see what they think."

He began to go over the basic process and to give a few options. He seemed to think they might have some clients who would be interested in a few of the collectibles, but the rest could be sold at an estate sale or auction, depending on which the client preferred. While he spoke, Ansley took notes, but she also observed him. No wedding ring. He looked to be in his mid- to late-twenties. Ansley had just turned twenty-six herself. She was currently single and looking. Her last relationship had gone out with a fizzle more than a bang, and that had been just over a year ago. Of course, Jamie wasn't exactly her type, but she wondered absently if he was seeing anyone.

After they walked around and he made a few more notes, Ansley took out her new business card. "I'll talk to my client and get back to you about which way they want to handle this," she said, as she flipped the card over and wrote her cell phone number on the back. "I'll follow up with you, and we can take the next step. I have a few other properties coming on the market soon, and I'd love to go over those with you, too." She passed him the card, and his eyebrows quirked a little at the number on the back. "That's my office number on the front, but mostly, I'm available on my cell phone. I'm not in the office as often."

Jamie looked down at it and up again to meet her eyes. He'd probably stayed longer than strictly necessary, but she was attractive and he'd enjoyed talking to her. "I should probably get back to the store. I'm glad we got a chance to meet. Just give me a call if you have any questions or figure out which way you want to handle this. I'll give our clients a call and see if there's any interest in those collections."

Ansley stood on the veranda and watched him go. She had to admit it was a nice view and wondered if he'd call her for anything other than business. She sighed. She was rusty at this. She wondered if she should have been more obvious flirting with him, but then she reminded herself that it just wasn't her style. She walked back inside, looked at the over-crowded room, and breathed a sigh of relief that she wasn't going to have to deal with it alone.

Chapter 6

Jamie walked back into the store with his notes and found Seth looking through a display in the back. He'd passed a few customers and had waved at Farrah who was manning the counter, her new smooth bob out of place in the store when they'd just grown accustomed to her high beehive.

"What's with Farrah, now?" Jamie asked as Seth looked up. They'd just gotten used to her hair looking more normal, for lack of a better word, when she'd gone and changed the color again.

"She's decided that she feels more like a brunette these days. Hey, at least she didn't go pink again. How was the meeting? What's the new realtor like?"

"It went well. I think we'll be able to work something out. In fact, we've got a boatload of figurines someone might be interested in. You know the client lists better than I do so I took a few notes. I'll go back and get a more thorough inventory after she's talked to her clients."

"Sounds good," Seth said absently, stepping back and assessing the display.

"She's going to call me later after she's talked to them."

"Huh," Seth said noncommittally. He looked at Jamie more closely. "So, what's she like?"

"She seems nice enough."

"Okay, spill. Pretty lady?" He'd had it on good authority from the client who'd referred them that she was pretty, available, and just around Jamie's age. He didn't tell Jamie the referral had come from Vera who may or may not have had a little matchmaking in mind when she'd made the suggestion.

"Yeah, she's attractive."

"But too old for you?"

"No. About my age, I guess. Maybe a little younger."

"But married, right?"

"No, I don't think so." Jamie said, looking curiously at Seth. "You know you're engaged, right? Why the interrogation?"

"You know you're not, right? So, let me see if I've got this straight. Pretty, young, unmarried woman you find attractive. Did you even get her number?"

"She gave me her card. Seth, it was a business meeting." Jamie said as Seth rolled his eyes.

"Let me see the card," Seth demanded. He took one look at it and smiled. "I see she's written another number on the back. You'd be an idiot not to give her a call."

"You're my boss. Aren't you supposed to be advising against mixing business with pleasure?"

"You must be thinking of some other boss. You're allowed to have a life."

"I have a life."

"I'm sorry, but the gym, work, and your weird platonic thing with Beth doesn't count."

"What's weird about having friends? You're just doing that weird thing people do in relationships. You think everyone should have one."

"I highly recommend it. And here's the reason," he continued. "Speak of the devil."

"I hope I'm not interrupting, and I don't know how I feel about being called the devil," Libby said with a smile as she walked over. "Hey, Jamie."

"Hey." Jamie had to admit that Seth and Libby made relationships look good. Not that they made it look easy. He'd seen what had happened when they had struggled. Seth had barely been able to function when he thought he'd screwed everything up.

Jamie smiled at the picture they made, his tall, dark-haired boss in his casual business attire and Libby with her bright blue dress with the wide white belt. Her hair was nearly as dark as Seth's but with more red tones. She leaned in to kiss his cheek, and Jamie noticed the picnic basket.

"Did you find that in the store?" he asked curiously. It was old fashioned and a red checked blanket peeked from the corner.

"No. Seth gave it to me when we first started dating. I'm going to steal this one for lunch, if you don't mind."

"I'll just get out of your hair."

"Call her," Seth called out as he was walking away. Jamie waved the words away with a laugh as he headed into the store.

"Call who?" he heard Libby ask as he walked away.

***

Libby and Seth walked out the door of Lost Horizon Antiques and headed toward the park in the center of town.

"Jamie met a pretty new realtor today."

"And you told him to call her?" Seth reached to take the picnic basket from her and then reached for her hand as they walked. She looked down at their joined hands and smiled. Her engagement ring winked in the light, and she couldn't quite get over the thrill of it. Not the ring as much as this relationship with this man.

"She gave him her cell number. She probably told him she's interested, and he wasn't paying attention. You know how Jamie is."

"You know my opinion on the subject. I don't think you should push him."

"I think you're going to have to give up on that. They're just friends."

"I just think there's something more there. They can both say they're friends all they want, but Beth and Jamie were made for each other."

47

"I don't disagree. But if they aren't going to do anything about it ..."

"I know," Libby said with a sigh. "I know she's your cousin, but she has a stubborn streak."

"Family trait."

"I'm well-aware."

They walked into the park, and Libby stood back while Seth spread the blanket on the ground. They could have sat at one of the picnic tables or under the gazebo, but they always returned to the spot where they'd had that first picnic. She sat down carefully, spreading the skirt of her dress around her. She reached for the picnic basket, slowly unpacking it. Seth was actually the cook and baker of the two of them, but Libby was capable of arranging a decent picnic. She'd chosen dessert from the sweet shop in town, but the rest of the meal consisted of charcuterie, a selection of cheeses, and fresh fruit. She'd tucked in little bottles of water and the bakery box of sweets.

"How are the wedding plans coming?"

"Ours or Lindy's?"

"Either. Both. Does it bother you at all that our weddings might overlap?"

"Not at all. It's nice to see them happy," Libby said with a smile, reaching for a slice of watermelon. "I've been thinking about the wedding. Ours, I mean."

"So have I."

"I know you haven't been married before so I don't want this to be all about me."

"That's kind of the bride's prerogative."

"It's just that I've had a big splashy wedding, and I wondered if we could do something different."

"What were you thinking? Paint me a picture," Seth encouraged, leaning back on his arm and looking up at Libby and the picture she made already with her pretty dress and the picnic basket at her side. He smiled as he watched her. Their relationship hadn't always been as smooth as this. It had taken some work. They were still working on it, but he watched her and knew it was worth it.

"Okay." She took a deep breath. "There's a farmhouse near here that does weddings. They have the sweetest oak tree outside. So I thought maybe an outdoor morning wedding in the fall followed by brunch with our friends and family. We could still have the colors we like and the attendants we've chosen. I just thought maybe we could keep it to close friends and family."

"This fall?"

"I know it doesn't give us a lot of time," Libby began as Seth sat up from where he was reclining. She stopped talking when he took her face in his hands and pulled her in his direction.

"It's perfect," he murmured, leaning in for a kiss. It spun out, leaving them both a little breathless. He pulled back just a little, his lips still close enough that she could feel the heat of them on her own. "Let's do it."

"Really?" she asked, her mouth quirking up in a smile. "We're talking a couple of months."

"Okay," Seth said, sitting back and reaching for the bakery box.

"Okay," she agreed with a smile.

Chapter 7

Jamie grabbed another burger and loaded it up with toppings from the makeshift bar they'd set up on the screened-in porch. He took it outside and sat down beside Dean on one of the lawn chairs looking out over the lake. He was looking forward to a free day to relax and not think about anything. Working with Seth was usually a pleasure, but he'd spent the last couple of days annoying him about his love life, to the other staff's amusement. He let out a long sigh as he scanned the stretch of shore along the lake.

"This is the life," Jamie told Dean with a smile.

"It's not bad," Dean smiled back, looking over as Lindy came outside with Maya. Beth followed close behind, carrying a six-pack. She handed Jamie and Dean each a beer and then settled herself in a chair beside Jamie. Lindy was headed for a seat when Dean grabbed her hand. Setting his burger down unceremoniously on the table, he pulled Lindy into his lap where she readjusted Maya carefully.

"Hey," she said to him with a smile, her mouth inches from his own. "I need to eat so she can eat," Lindy reminded him, her tone warm rather than abrasive. Dean wasn't quite used to it, but he liked it. Of course, he liked it when she was sharp and sarcastic, too. That's how he knew he was crazy about her, or maybe just plain crazy.

"A minute," Dean said, moving in to kiss her. On the other side of them, Jamie and Beth exchanged an awkward smile. It was a long minute. He pulled back and just grinned. "Now give me the baby, and go make a plate."

"You just want to hold her."

"Yes, I do. Now go away," he said with a laugh, carefully taking Maya from her arms.

"I'll come with you," Beth offered. "I'm starved!"

"You are?" Jamie returned. "Dean, you will not believe how much furniture she had me moving. 'A little help,' she told me." He rolled his eyes in exasperation.

"And it's appreciated," Beth called from the screened-in porch.

"You should get one of these," Dean told Jamie, nodding to the baby. "I highly recommend them," he said, kissing Maya's sleeping lips. "Isn't she the best?"

"She's pretty great."

"You going to have kids?"

"Well, not right this minute. Kind of missing an important ingredient for that plan," he joked, taking a bite out of his burger.

"Not necessarily. Does pretty real estate lady want kids?"

Jamie almost choked on his burger.

Beth and Lindy walked over, and Beth thumped Jamie helpfully on his back. "What's wrong with him?"

"Does Seth tell you everything? What's a person got to do to get a little privacy here?"

"Move somewhere else," Lindy suggested helpfully, sending him a sympathetic look. She wasn't going to bring it up, but she'd heard about the new interest, too. She eyed Dean suspiciously. She had a feeling he knew exactly what he was doing.

"What's Seth got on you?" Beth asked curiously, raising her hamburger up to take a large bite.

"Nothing," Jamie began just as Dean cut in with, "Jamie met someone."

Beth paused before taking a bite, chewing carefully. When she swallowed, she took a drink of the beer she was glad she'd grabbed from the kitchen. She was allowing herself one before she was strictly in Designated Driver mode. "You didn't mention anything. Who is she? What's she like? We need details."

She hoped she sounded interested and normal, but she wondered if she did because she caught the look Lindy sent her way.

She put a smile on her face and wondered why it felt so strange. They were friends, after all. They always had been. It was just weird that he hadn't said anything. This is the kind of thing you tell your best friend.

"It's not like that. I had a meeting with a real estate agent, and Seth has blown it all out of proportion," Jamie explained uncomfortably. He'd never felt weird talking to Beth about dating before. It was that damn kiss that had screwed everything up!

"Did you get her number?" Beth asked curiously.

"I mean, she gave me her number. But I have to have that for work."

"Okay, new question," Beth said gamely, taking it more in stride. "Have you called her?"

"Well, yeah, but only to respond to some texts she sent."

Beth and Lindy exchanged a look. "He's totally clueless," Beth lamented. "So do you like her?"

Jamie sighed heavily. "I don't even know her. Now can I eat my burger in peace?" he asked with a long-suffering look at the group.

"Fine. But we're not done," Beth warned him. She leaned back in her chair and enjoyed the hot sun on her face. She was going to go for a swim in a little while so she didn't mind the heat. She'd liberaly applied sunscreen so that her sensitive skin wouldn't fry in the hot Georgia sun, and she'd pulled her red hair up into a messy bun on the top of her head. She enjoyed her burger and the cold beer and relaxed. It didn't even sound like he was that interested in this person. Seth was probably just trying to set him up. It was clear he was embarrassed about it.

On the far side of the circle, Lindy leaned in close to Dean to shift Maya out of his arms to feed her. "I see what you did there," she breathed softly.

"Nothing gets by you," he murmured back.

"Get a room," Jamie called out lazily, taking a drink. They smiled and ignored him, moving closer to each other. Dean stroked a hand down Lindy's hair and then grabbed a handful of it to pull her in for a kiss, which she eagerly returned.

"A little push couldn't hurt," he murmured against her lips.

She pulled back and looked at him while reaching down to shift Maya into position. The baby was starting to wake up, and she tended to wake up hungry. Lindy could feel the pull in her body, the cue that coincided with Maya's own appetite. "They'll figure it out. But you might have lit a fire there."

"I'd like to light one here," Dean said, reaching to pull her back in.

"Later." Lindy settled back to feed Maya and wondered how her life could have changed so much in such a short amount of time. She'd pictured her life as a single mother in such exquisite detail, but she'd never made the slightest preparation for a significant other. The fact that it was Dean only added to it. They'd gone from annoying the hell out of each other to falling into bed to falling in love. She still wasn't quite used to it.

Jamie rolled his eyes and settled back, thankful he'd deflected the conversation about his love life. He'd not only been talking to Ansley regularly over the last few days, they also had a date scheduled. He was a little nervous. She was attractive, smart, and sweet, but he wasn't sure he was ready for another relationship. He looked over at Beth who was watching the lake absently and petting Mr. Darcy, who was sleeping under her chair, with her free hand. The other hand held the beer bottle, tipped precariously close to spilling in her lap. He reached over and righted it.

"Daydreaming?" he asked, as she focused on him.

"Something like that."

"You look a little sad. Is everything okay?"

"Do you think we'll still be friends when you start dating someone?" She hadn't intended to ask and almost wished she hadn't the second it was out of her mouth. She'd wondered how the dynamic would change once Jamie started dating again. She knew he was a serial monogamist, and it was only a matter of time.

"Why wouldn't we be?" Jamie asked, his eyebrows drawing together. Beth shrugged. "You're my best friend," Jamie reminded her. "That's not going to change."

"That's really not a promise you can make," Beth said, closing her eyes against the heat of the sun. She opened them slowly and looked at him, curling into the wide chair. Mr. Darcy lifted his head up curiously and then settled back into the grass. "So much has changed in the last year. Seth and Libby are getting married, and no one could have predicted this whole thing with the two of them." She nodded toward Dean and Lindy. "Even Keely got remarried. It happened so fast. I guess I just worry sometimes that things will change when you meet someone."

"How about when you meet someone? Maybe your boyfriend wouldn't want you hanging out with me," Jamie said evenly, wondering where this had come from.

"Well, we know that's not going to happen. I'm fine with Mr. Darcy. But you really like relationships."

"You might, too, if you'd had a good one," Jamie returned, watching her carefully.

"I don't know. I like my life."

"It's a good one." She wasn't interested in relationships, he reminded himself. It was okay that he'd asked Ansley to dinner. Or she'd asked him. He wasn't quite sure how they'd gotten there, but he was curious about her. Beth was right anyway; he did like relationships. "We've always been friends. There's no reason that should change."

"I'm sure you're right," Beth said, secretly doubting that. It should have made her feel better, but instead it just made her feel kind of sad. Maybe she wanted things to change. She shook off the mood and decided she was going to enjoy the day. "What do you think about all that?" she asked him, indicating Dean and Lindy where they were currently caught up watching each other and Maya.

"It's good to see. It's pretty sweet, if sometimes annoying." He said the last words loudly, catching a grin from Dean.

"You're just jealous," Dean threw back. "Anyone up for a swim?"

"In a little while," Beth said. "I'm going to walk Mr. Darcy and then lay in your hammock before I jump in."

"I'll walk with you," Jamie said, standing as Mr. Darcy jumped to his feet. They walked around the lake house following the happy jaunt of the dog while Dean and Lindy watched.

"See?" Dean asked in a normal voice. Lindy rolled her eyes and shifted Maya to the other side.

"I don't see anything yet. Don't get cocky."

"Too late. Think they even have a clue?"

"Well, we didn't."

"I did," Dean said with a smile. "I just had to talk you into giving me a chance."

"I don't think that's quite how it went," Lindy argued.

Chapter 8

On the other side of the lake house, Mr. Darcy was exploring every blade of grass and flower within reach. Jamie was walking with Beth. They were both quiet, lost in their own thoughts when Beth blurted out, "I don't think you should mention the kiss."

"What?" Jamie asked perplexed. "Are you having a heat stroke?"

"No," she said with an exasperated sigh. "I just think if you start dating someone you shouldn't mention the kiss. You know. The mistletoe? It might make someone uncomfortable," she said in a rush, looking everywhere but at Jamie. "Then we can stay friends."

The silence stretched so long that Beth darted a look over at him, her face suffused with a pink that she attributed to the sun but was more likely due to the blush that was creeping up her face. "I mean, it's not a lie exactly. It's just that it might confuse things," she finished awkwardly, regretting that she'd brought up the thing they didn't talk about.

"Oh," Jamie said carefully, surprised into silence. "I thought we weren't talking about that."

"Well," Beth replied, taking a deep breath. "I know we haven't. It's just that if you're going to date someone, it might come up. I mean, there's no reason for it to come up. But if it did, it might make things hard to stay friends." She was rambling, and she took a deep breath to stop.

"And you just want to stay friends," Jamie said uncertainly, unsure if he was making a statement or asking a question.

"Yes," she said, thinking she'd finally made her point. She let out the breath she was holding. She had no reason to worry. They were friends, and they could stay that way. She could even make friends with whoever he dated, although she couldn't quite see how that would work. She tried to picture it, but couldn't quite make the image come clear.

"Okay," Jamie said. He felt disappointed, but he thought he should probably feel relieved. It was out in the open now. "Why haven't we talked about it?"

"I don't know," she said awkwardly. "I guess I was afraid it would make everything weird." she replied, watching Mr. Darcy to avoid looking at Jamie.

"That bad, huh?" Jamie asked with a joking tone, trying to insert a little levity into the conversation.

"Not at all," she said, turning around quickly and looking up at him. She hadn't realized he was standing so close. They were about as far apart as they'd been when they stood under the mistletoe, and she could see him remembering that, too. Neither one of them moved.

"It was just a kiss," Jamie murmured, afraid to speak at a normal volume in case it broke whatever moment they were having.

"It doesn't have to mean anything," she breathed out.

Mr. Darcy knocked into her from behind, and she stumbled a little toward Jamie. He reached out an arm and caught her, and then he left his hand there, holding her elbow. They both froze, and then Jamie stepped back. Beth shook her head a bit, trying to clear it.

"Thanks for the save," she told him. "What's your deal?" she asked Mr. Darcy who was sniffing around a bush on the property. He looked up at her innocently.

"No problem," Jamie answered, looking out toward the lake. "It's going to be another hot one."

"It was hot when I woke up this morning," Beth agreed. Summers in Georgia could be brutal. She was glad they could talk about the weather while she cleared her head. In a Hallmark movie, that moment would have gone straight into a kiss. She thought for a minute ... but, of course, she was being silly.

"So we stay friends?" Jamie asked, getting back to the subject they'd been discussing.

Beth tried to find her bearings. She reminded herself that the whole point of this conversation was to protect their friendship in case he started dating someone new. She looked at him, trying and failing to read in his expression if that moment had meant anything to him at all.

"We stay friends," she confirmed, sure that she'd just misread the moment. Well, at least she hadn't embarrassed herself by betraying her thoughts to him. Usually, he could read her so well. She turned her attention to Mr. Darcy, trying to orient herself.

Jamie watched her turn her attention to Mr. Darcy. For a moment, he'd thought that something was going to happen there. Then, he realized that he was just kidding himself. She had just said she wanted to stay friends, and he'd always respected what she wanted. It's why he'd never asked her out. He tried not to feel disappointed, but he had to admit that he'd hoped things might change. Still, he was happy to be her friend, even if he was interested in more. He decided it was time to stop feeling guilty about the date he'd made. "Ready to head to the hammock?"

"Actually, I think I'm ready for that swim now," she said, feeling hot from more than just the sun. They walked around the house and she let Mr. Darcy off the leash so he could swim. She laughed when she saw him run to the small beach that formed on the edge of the lake. Then, carefully, she reached down and slowly pulled off her bathing suit cover-up. It was a white sheath that skimmed her thighs and could even be mistaken for a casual summer dress. She could feel Jamie's eyes on her from behind, and she turned to lay it over the back of her chair.

If she was honest with herself, she might have pulled it off a little more slowly than usual, knowing he was watching. She was glad it was hot enough outside to cover up the blush that was still staining her pale skin. She glanced back at him where he was standing as if frozen.

"Coming?" she asked with a slow smile. She'd only ever thought of Jamie as a friend, but she had to admit there was something there, like a buzz under her skin. She'd felt that spark when he'd caught her. Of course, he'd touched her casually so many times, but she'd never felt anything but comfort. This wasn't exactly comfortable, she thought.

"Nice swimsuit," Lindy called out from her chair where she was applying another layer of sunscreen on Maya.

"Thanks," Beth acknowledged with a smile. She'd found the vintage, polka-dot one piece in an antique shop and had spent more on it than she normally would have. It fit like a glove on her petite body, but it was flattering. The waist tucked in, and the top gave her the boost that provided ample cleavage, which was impressive given her petite figure. Admittedly, she considered this her sexy swimsuit and had packed it anyway. She tried not to think of her own motivations for doing so. She was afraid that she was going to overthink everything now.

Jamie smiled at her and took off his own shirt, and Beth didn't even bother to pretend she wasn't watching. Lindy let out a wolf whistle, and they laughed. "Now you're just showing off," Dean called from the porch where he was coming out with a few towels. He was already shirtless, and both Beth and Lindy exchanged an admiring glance.

"Well, you were right about the view," Beth tossed out casually as she headed for the lake. Lindy's laugh followed her as she joined Jamie in the water.

Chapter 9

Jamie smiled across the table at Ansley who was leaned back letting loose a long easy laugh. He was glad he'd chosen a comedy club for the first date. They'd gotten there before the show was scheduled to start and had a drink at the bar. He figured that if either of them felt uncomfortable, the comedy routine would ease the tension and allow them to go their separate ways afterwards. He'd made sure to vet the comedian first to make sure her act was appropriate for a first date. He laughed aloud himself and exchanged an amused glance with Ansley who looked like a flame in her yellow dress and matching heels.

The show wrapped up to applause, and they made their way slowly out of the comedy club and out onto the street. They stepped closer to the building instinctively to get out of the way of the foot traffic that was always busy in Athens, Georgia, on a Saturday night.

"Would you like to go for a walk?" Jamie offered. He didn't want the evening to end quite yet. They'd met at the comedy club, since Ansley lived in Athens, and Jamie had driven over from Madison.

"I would love to," she said happily, adjusting the strap of the small purse she carried on her shoulder. "I didn't even know there was a comedy club here."

"A friend tipped me off." Dean had given him a handful of first date ideas when he'd stopped by the shop to meet Seth for lunch. Jamie had told him that he didn't need dating advice, but the comedy club had sounded interesting. "He said he'd come up here a couple of times, and they've always had solid acts."

"Well, he was right," Ansley said, stepping aside as a large group of college students came around the corner. Jamie reached out a hand to steady her as they stood on the edge of the curb.

"They always seem to travel in a pack," Jamie joked, nodding toward the group loudly moving in the direction of the bar down the street.

"Didn't you at their age?"

"Not really. I worked while I went to school so I didn't have a lot of time for that." He watched them go, a few of them stumbling along. He wondered absently how many bars they'd frequented already. "I don't know that I was ever *that* young."

"You're not exactly an old man," she said sardonically, arching one perfect eyebrow.

He laughed and let her lead the way. He enjoyed dating, that easy back and forth of conversation when there was chemistry present. He rarely experienced nerves during the date. He simply looked at dating as an opportunity to get to know someone new. He tried not to have any expectations outside of that. He kept up his side of the conversation and watched Ansley. He liked how animated she was as she talked. Her emotions flitted across her face, and he found himself smiling in response. He was glad he'd asked her. When her Uber arrived to take her home, he didn't hesitate and leaned in to kiss her.

"Let me know when you get home safe?"

"Of course. Thank you for this, Jamie."

"This?"

"This whole night," she said with a smile as she climbed into the back of the car.

***

Back in Madison, Beth was curled up in a chair at Lindy's house. She'd always loved this chair. As Lindy's cousin, Beth had been in and out of this house her whole life. She looked up as Lindy walked into the room.

"Gimme," she demanded, stretching up her arms. Lindy handed

Maya over with a smile and then sat down on the couch next to Libby who was flipping through another wedding magazine. Maya looked up at her with big sleepy eyes.

"She's irresistible, isn't she?" Libby asked. "I don't think you're going to have a problem finding babysitters."

Lindy replied smugly, "We did make a pretty baby."

"You couldn't have designed a prettier one if you tried," Keely commented, coming into the room with another bottle of wine. They all remembered how Lindy had planned to select a sperm donor in order to start a family. She'd even decided on one and prepared herself for the process before finding out she'd gotten pregnant by Dean. Even though they'd used protection, Lindy suspected that the fertility drugs she'd started taking had contributed to the quick conception. She certainly hadn't planned it, especially since she didn't view Dean as anything more than a casual fling.,

"She's perfect," Beth cooed at Maya. "One of these days, I may get the name of your clinic though. I may not care for a relationship, but I wouldn't mind a family," she told Lindy with a smile.

"Girl, be careful what you wish for. Best laid plans and all that."

"She's right. I never anticipated Theodore. After their father left," Keely said nodding to Lindy. "I thought I was done with relationships. I dated, but I just never quite had that spark with anyone else."

"And in walks the sexy gentleman farmer-slash-novelist," Lindy picked up on the story.

"That's your stepfather you're talking about," Keely reminded Lindy wryly.

"That's still so weird. I mean, I have stepsisters now."

"How are they doing anyway?" Libby asked. She' d met Theodore's daughters Presley and Layla a handful of times now, but she hadn't seen either of them for more than a few minutes since Maya's birth.

"They're adjusting. It's not easy for siblings to live together," Keely commented.

"I love mine, but I wouldn't live with either one of them," Libby said with a laugh, thinking of Rachel and Faith. Faith was off on yet another cruise, where she worked as a masseuse. Rachel was a stay-at-home mom and met up with Libby at least once a week for a kid-free lunch. She thought of Faith's perpetually messy rooms growing up and Rachel's tendency to over-organize and obsessively clean. She guessed she fell somewhere in the middle of that.

"Who'd have thought I'd get remarried?" Keely continued, looking over at Maya. "Or that you'd end up with Dean."

"The elopement was a surprise," Beth said, remembering how Keely had sprung the news of her marriage without as much as mentioning an engagement beforehand.

"Understatement of the century," Lindy murmured. "Do I get my baby back?"

"Wait your turn," Libby told her, gently picking up Maya from Beth's arms. "I called dibs." She kissed the top of Maya's soft head with her full head of dark hair and closed her eyes. In her first marriage, she'd tried without success to get pregnant. Now that she and Seth were planning a future together, she wondered how being a mom would fit in. He'd already said they'd adopt if they needed to. She settled on to the couch with a sigh, as the sleeping baby nestled closer.

"I think what she's saying is that it could happen to you, too," Lindy told Beth bluntly. "So don't make too many plans."

"I've got my guy," Beth said with a smile, reaching down to pat Mr. Darcy's head where he was stretched out on the carpet.

"I'm sorry, but you can't possibly get everything you need from the dog," Lindy said wryly. "What happened to sex?"

"I have sex," Beth said, affronted.

"With who?" Lindy demanded, as Beth darted a look over at

Keely who was listening in amusement.

"I mean, I have casual sex when I feel like it. There's an occasional friend with benefits."

"Do you know what that means?" Lindy asked Keely.

"Well, I'm not dead. I'm quite familiar with the term as I've had a few myself pre-Theodore," she said with a smug look, as Lindy eyed her curiously.

"Al-right," Lindy said, turning her attention back to Beth. "Like Jamie?"

"No, not Jamie," Beth said, rolling her eyes to the ceiling and keeping them there. "No one lately, no one you'd know, and there's an entire toy industry to help single women out," she said flushing.

"Nothing wrong with that," Libby said supportively, shooting Lindy a warning look as Beth headed to the restroom. "Careful there," she cautioned Lindy quietly.

"She's young, and she's happy. I don't think she needs the push," Keely reminded her. "And if she's anything like you, it wouldn't work anyway."

"Well, we'll never know," Lindy said smugly.

"Oh, we know," Libby said, exchanging a smile with Keely.

"We wondered if there might be something between you and Dean," Keely admitted. "I might have given you a push or two, inviting him over so often. But you didn't seem to take the hint."

"I guess it must have been disappointing when we sat around and argued instead," Lindy said with a wry laugh. "Well, Dean decided he's on board with this whole idea and might have given the two of them a push the other day at the lake. Nothing happened though, so maybe we're wrong."

"We're not wrong," Libby said confidently.

"What are y'all talking about?" Beth asked suspiciously when she came back into the room.

"Lindy and Dean," Libby told her.

"Ah. That," Beth said with a nod of her head. "Personally, I thought you were crazy."

"For the record, I thought it was sweet," Libby inserted.

"Of course you did," Beth said, rolling her eyes. "That's because you didn't have a lifetime of watching Dean on the prowl."

"Well, those days are done," Lindy said smugly.

"You've certainly got me now," Dean said from the doorway. He had been upstairs changing for work when he came down to catch the end of ladies' night. "Decide on a dress yet, Libby?" he asked, leaning over to kiss his baby.

"She distracted me," Libby admitted, as she passed Maya over to Dean and reached for a magazine.

"She does that. If I'm not careful, I'll be late for work. Who gets the baby next?"

"That would be me," Keely said, getting up to take the little one. "Now kiss the girl, and get out," she said, shooing him away. "No men."

"That's what I keep saying," Beth said with a laugh.

"And I used to be her favorite guy," Dean said jokingly.

"You're still my favorite soon to be son-in-law."

"Only. Only son-in-law. But I'll take it." He kissed Lindy and sauntered out the door with all the women watching him.

"Pretty, isn't he?" Lindy asked.

"I heard that," Dean called out, as the door shut behind him. The women laughed, and Beth reached for the bottle of wine to refill everyone's glasses, except Lindy who waved it away.

"We just need to go out and let you try some on," Beth suggested to Libby.

"That's probably a good idea. I need to decide soon. After all, we don't have a lot of time," Libby sighed. "I need to find bridesmaid dresses, too."

"Don't worry. We'll find everything you need," Keely said calmly, looking at Libby warmly. "I've already picked out my mother of the groom outfit, but I want you to look at it and make sure it'll suit."

"You have impeccable taste. I'm not worried. I'm a little worried about what my parents will show up in, if they'll even remember there's a wedding at all." Libby's parents were traveling the country in an RV, and family functions weren't their forte.

"Still, take a look."

"Oh, no. There has to be a fashion show," Beth insisted.

"Agreed," Lindy said, looking over at her mother. They were nearly identical, except for Lindy's eyes, which she shared with her absentee father. "I'm going to model my tux when I get it. I'm going out with Seth and Dean tomorrow so pick a different day so I can come with you, too."

"I'll see what works for everyone. You'll come, Beth?"

"I wouldn't miss it. Just work around book club night, and I'm in. Although I could really let Naomi handle that if it came down to it."

"How's Naomi doing?" Lindy asked. Naomi had once made her life a nightmare. A former paramour of Dean's, she'd been none too happy when Lindy and Dean had started dating. Then, she'd been distracted with another romantic entanglement that had become steadily abusive. Lindy didn't consider her a friend, but the bad blood was gone.

"She's good. Better," Beth added. "She's not dating or anything, but she's doing well at the shop. She's a natural with groups, too. She's helping with some of the catering jobs at the tea room, too."

"I love that she and Layla have become friends, of sorts," Libby commented. "I'm sure it's good to have someone else to talk with about what it was like."

"And it's nice to see her and Presley trying to reconnect," Keely said in agreement. "It's good for sisters to be close. Of course, it's a struggle since they're like night and day."

"I'm just glad they're getting along since they'll both be at the wedding. I'd hate to have any awkwardness," Libby said uncomfortably. So far, the guest list extended to only close friends and family. "Of course, we invited Marnie so you'd think that would be awkward," Libby said, referring to Seth's high school girlfriend who had stayed a family friend.

"Well, she's bringing that handsome husband so I don't think you have anything to worry about." Lindy smiled, knowing full well that Libby wasn't the least bit worried. After all, she and Marnie were on good terms when Marnie came to town to visit. They'd even gone out to dinner as a group with Marnie's husband Patrick.

"I just appreciate all the eye candy," Beth piped up. "I may not be dating, but I can look." She took a sip of wine and picked up a wedding magazine to help Libby look. "Should I just circle the ones I like? Can I put a big X through the ugly ones?"

"Feel free." Libby offered, holding up one she'd written a large black NO over.

***

Later, Beth walked home with Mr. Darcy, promising to call as soon as she made it inside. She only lived up the street, but she had drunk a few glasses of wine. She made it into the house and slipped off her shoes by the door. She took off Mr. Darcy's leash and headed into the living room. She went into the bathroom and turned on the bath water as she sent Aunt Keely a text saying she was home. She noticed she had a message from Jamie and smiled.

"How was ladies' night?"

She texted back as she climbed carefully into the bath. "Always fun. No dress yet. What have you been up to?" she replied, setting down the phone a safe distance away from the bubbles rising in the water.

"Nothing much," came the response. Beth eased into the bath

and wondered why she and Jamie hadn't crossed that line into friends with benefits. In a way, she wouldn't have minded, but then she'd decided it might ruin the friendship. She didn't want to lose that, and she'd never managed to remain friends with anyone she'd gotten involved with, however casually. She texted him back idly and wondered why things couldn't just stay the same.

Across town, Jamie looked at his phone and wondered why he'd said that. Usually, he'd tell her all about a date, and they'd discuss it. It was getting late. He made up his mind to tell her about it tomorrow instead.

Chapter 10

Beth finished setting up for the book club meeting and stood back with a smile of satisfaction. She had to admit that Naomi was much better with the presentation than she was. She'd been relegated to organizing the arrangement of the chairs while Naomi set up the book display and the evening's refreshments. She looked over at Naomi who was adjusting the book display one last time. Hiring her had been a risk. She'd done it partly as a favor to Elle at Brews and Blues and partly because she believed in second chances. Naomi hadn't been a model employee at Brews, but Beth had decided to take the chance. She was glad now that she had.

"It looks good," Beth said admiringly.

"It's not bad." She stood up and stepped back to look it over.

While she did, Beth looked Naomi over. She'd pulled her chestnut hair back into a French braid, and even though she still wore makeup, she seemed to go for a less-is-more look these days. Beth feared at first that she was trying to make herself less noticeable after all she'd been through, but then it just seemed like she wasn't trying quite so hard anymore. She seemed like she was finally comfortable in her own skin, although she'd confided in Beth that she'd been seeing a counselor for the last few months.

"Do we have a headcount yet?"

"We should have a pretty full house tonight. I know of about fifteen people who said they'd make it, but I planned for a few more, just in case. The author event next week will be packed out though," Beth added.

"When is Keely's husband coming back in?" Naomi asked. He always drew a crowd, partly because he was a local author but also because the book had been so successful.

"He's busy working on the second book now. I don't think we'll be able to get him in for a while. Presley might be joining us tonight though. Do you know if Layla is coming?"

"She has to work, I think. I'm glad that she's not angry with me. About Noah, I mean. It wasn't anyone's fault. Well, if it was anyone's fault, it was mine," she corrected herself firmly. After all, she thought, she'd known Noah was in a relationship when she'd gotten involved with him.

"If it's anyone's fault, it was his."

"I have to learn to take responsibility for my part in it. I'm just relieved that Layla could forgive my part. Some women wouldn't."

"I think she understands better than anyone how easy it would have been to have been taken in by him."

"True. We're just ready to move past it."

"Have either of you heard from him since ... " Beth let the sentence trail off. She didn't really need to elaborate.

"I blocked his number, to be honest. He bothered Layla for a while. I told her she ought to get a restraining order, but I don't know if she did."

"I hope that's the end of it," Beth said fervently. She'd met Noah a few times and hadn't gotten any negative vibes from him. Apparently, he'd hidden that side of himself well enough.

Within a few minutes, the book club members started trickling in to the store. They all made a beeline for the refreshments before finding a seat in the circle Beth had set up. Presley was one of the last to arrive, and she headed straight over to Beth when she came in.

"Almost didn't make it. I had a patient come in as I was leaving. At least, it was a false alarm." Presley was a midwife at a hospital in Athens and had said she'd make it to book club night if she could after her shift.

"How's Layla doing?"

"She's good. Working tonight. She picks up a lot of extra shifts, but I think it helps her to stay busy."

"That's understandable. But I hope she doesn't work herself too hard."

"So I've told her. But she never listens to me. She's just so stubborn."

"Unlike anyone else in her family."

"Touche. How's Jamie?"

"He's good. Busy with work, but good."

As Beth chatted with Presley and greeted a few customers who had become friends, she remembered that he hadn't heard much from Jamie this week. They usually talked most days. Dean had mentioned that he'd had a date, but Jamie hadn't said a word. Beth tried not to feel bothered about the omission, but as the days went by without contact, she worried that their relationship was changing already—and not in a good way. She turned her attention to the group, calling their attention to get started.

When Beth walked in from book club, Mr. Darcy came to the door to greet her. She immediately headed for the leash she kept on a hook nearby and decided that a long walk was in order, despite the fact that it would be getting dark soon. She tucked a flashlight into her pocket and headed out with Mr. Darcy on her heels. They walked through the streets, and she told him all about book club. This month's selection had been a page turner, filled with so many unexpected twists that they had all been riveted. She'd already chosen a steamy romance for the next month, just to keep it fresh. She wanted to introduce the club to a variety of genres, and she was hoping to schedule more regular author events. It helped with sales, but for Beth, it was always more about the books than the sales in the end.

She made it around a few blocks and back to her door, ready to pour a glass of wine. She was on the porch patting her pockets when she realized that she'd left her keys on the counter and then locked the door behind her. She sighed and walked around to the back yard, where she kept a key hidden under a garden gnome that she kept near the model of Pemberley that Mr. Darcy used for a dog house outside. She looked under it and then remembered that she'd left the extra key inside, too. She'd left it there the last time she'd locked herself out, even though Jamie had reminded her twice to put it back before she forgot. She got out her phone and called him.

***

Jamie's phone rang, and he almost sent it to voice mail when he saw Beth's name pop up. "Sorry," Jamie told Ansley. "Do you mind if I get this?"

"Go ahead. I'm just going to use your restroom."

He answered the phone and grinned when Beth skipped the customary greeting. "I locked myself out again," she said without preamble.

"You didn't put the key back outside, did you?" he asked with a smile, already knowing the answer.

"Never mind that. Can you come let me in? It's getting dark."

"Sure. Give me a few minutes." They hung up just as Ansley came out of the restroom. "Beth locked herself out of the house. Do you mind a quick drive?"

"Not at all. Is it far from here?"

"No, we could walk, but it would be dark coming back."

"Let's take my car since I'm parked behind you."

"Thanks. It shouldn't take but a minute."

"So, you have a key to Beth's house?" Ansley asked in curiosity, feeling a twinge of unease.

"She makes a habit of locking herself out. But this way you can say hello and finally meet her."

"That'll be nice," Ansley said, wondering if it would be. She wasn't sure what to make of his friendship with Beth. She believed men and women could be friends, but she'd also had an ex-boyfriend who had broken up with her once to date a friend of his that he'd always sworn was *just a friend.* It made her a little uncomfortable now when she was confronted with this sort of close friendship. "How long have you known each other?"

"Maybe five or six years now?" Jamie said, a question in his voice. "I've been working at Lost Horizon for six, and she's always been in and out of there, but our schedules didn't cross for a while. Not until I started working there full-time."

Ansley tried to think of how to ask if Beth had a significant other. It was an awkward question, one that would most certainly showcase her own insecurity. She couldn't think of a way to ask that wasn't intrusive. She decided she'd just meet Beth for herself and see.

They pulled up at the little house and parked on the street. Beth was sitting outside on the porch with the cutest little white dog. They got out, and Beth called out, "Did you steal a car?"

"Nope. I had company. Beth, Ansley. Ansley, Beth," he said quickly, as he leaned down to greet the dog. "And this is Mr. Darcy."

"It's so nice to meet you both," Ansley said sincerely. She shook Beth's hand and leaned down to pat Mr. Darcy's head. "Isn't he handsome?"

"He is," Beth enthused. The compliment to her dog instantly warmed her. Beth started explaining to Ansley the way they'd found each other when she was volunteering at an animal shelter while Jamie went to unlock the door. "Why don't you two come in and have a glass of wine with me?"

Jamie looked at Ansley who answered, "That would be nice. Thank you." She was curious, after all. They headed into Beth's house, which was decorated in a funky, eclectic style that somehow managed to pull off a cozy vibe.

"I'm going to go put your extra key out back before you forget again," Jamie told her, grabbing the key from the bowl on a shelf and heading to the backyard. "Gnome or Buddha?"

"Buddha," she called back to him as she poured the wine. "I move around my key," Beth explained with a shrug. "Sorry to interrupt your evening." She was curious about Ansley. Jamie hadn't even said he was dating anyone new. If Dean hadn't spilled the beans, she would have been completely blindsided.

"It's okay. It's nice that you have someone nearby who can help out," Ansley offered, taking the glass of wine that Beth held out. "Thank you."

Jamie came back in and went straight over to sit down by Ansley, picking up Mr. Darcy and putting him in his lap. "Want a beer instead?"

"No, I'll let Ansley drink, and I can drive us back. How was book club?"

"We had a good turnout and sold a pile of books for next month. I called the library earlier and made sure they have some copies available there, too, for whoever wants to borrow them instead. Everyone seemed to like it. A couple groused about doing a romance next, but I think they'll be pleasantly surprised."

"They usually are. Beth runs a book club at the bookstore in town." They talked books for a few minutes, and then Jamie suggested that they head home.

"It was nice finally meeting you," Beth told Ansley, turning to Jamie and giving him a significant look that Ansley couldn't see. He shifted uncomfortably. The fact that he hadn't mentioned Ansley made it more uncomfortable than it should have been, but Beth hadn't let on that she'd been surprised. Of course, she might have heard already that he was dating someone, but in fairness, she should have heard it from him. "You should come join the book club sometime. It's a great group, if I do say so myself."

"I'd like that," Ansley said sincerely. "It was nice to meet you, too." She bent down to pet Mr. Darcy again. "And you," she added.

Chapter 11

Jamie set the coffee holder down on Beth's porch and shifted the box of pastries in his hands as he knocked again. It was early, but it wasn't unreasonably so. He shifted impatiently and wondered what was taking her so long. He looked around the porch and noticed that her hanging plants were starting to droop. The summer heat had been particularly brutal, and they really could use a good rain about now. He set down the pastries and moved to find the water can she kept out beside the porch swing. He was watering the plants that looked particularly distressed when he heard the door open behind him.

"I was going to do that," Beth told him, one hand on her hip and the other holding firmly to the dog's leash.

"I know. They just looked so sad. Are you heading out for a walk?" he asked, nodding toward Mr. Darcy. He saw the dog's interest turn toward the pastries and rushed over to scoop the box up.

"No, we were out back. I just didn't want him to make a break for it when I heard all the knocking on the door," she looked at him pointedly. "What brings you here so early?" she asked, as she turned and headed into the house without waiting to issue an invitation for him to enter. They had known each other too long to stand on ceremony, and she hadn't even had time for coffee yet.

"Brought coffee. And breakfast," Jamie added, setting both the drink carrier and pastry box down on the counter.

"Coffee," Beth breathed out. She snatched one up and inhaled the aroma with her eyes shut tight and a smile on her face. Jamie watched her with a smile and a quick roll of his eyes toward Mr. Darcy who looked puzzled. She opened her eyes and moved to the pastry box, which she opened without hesitation. "Not bad," she said as she examined the scones, donuts, and coffee cake assortment. "What do you want?" she asked him baldly, as she selected a cream-filled donut from the box. "You need to borrow money?" she asked, her lips quirking up into a smile.

"Sorry about last night. Springing Ansley on you and all that. I should have told you she was with me when you called," Jamie said, by way of explanation, and reached over to take his own coffee from the carrier.

"What I'm wondering is why you didn't mention her at all."

"I don't know. I didn't know if it would even go beyond the first date, and then when it did, it felt weird that I hadn't told you about the first date."

"Yeah, it was weird. Dean told me though. So it's not like I didn't know."

"But you didn't say anything to me. Why didn't you tell me you knew?"

"Why didn't you? I figured if you wanted me to know, I'd hear it from you. Otherwise, it's called minding your business," she said as she took out a scone. "So is it a serious thing?"

"It's too early to be a serious thing. But I like her," Jamie replied, reaching to get a piece of coffee cake. He walked over to sit in the breakfast nook she'd installed in a window of her tiny kitchen.

She'd insisted on finding a booth rather than a traditional table, but it had been Jamie that had found the retro fitting at an estate sale and gotten it for her. Of course, he remembered, then she'd talked him into installing it, too. It had been a perfect fit, which had pleased them both. Now, he sat drinking his coffee in the window, and he heard Mr. Darcy head his way as Beth released him from the leash. He reached down to stroke the dog's head as he looked up at Beth who was walking over to join him, the box of pastries in her hand.

"She seemed sweet."

"She is."

"So, are we just not going to talk about things now? Should I just wait to hear the news from someone else? I didn't think you'd stay single forever, but I'm a little surprised you just didn't tell me."

"Which is why I brought apology coffee." He gestured magnanimously to the coffee and pastries on the table, which made her laugh.

"Appreciated. Next time, just don't be so weird."

"So noted. So what are you doing today?"

"It's wedding dress day," Beth enthused. When Jamie looked at her blankly, she continued. "For Libby? Drink your coffee. You're clearly not quite awake yet. We're shopping today for dresses and then doing a little wedding planning after. You want to do a movie night later this week?"

"Sure. Let me just see what's going on and let you know."

"Uh-huh," Beth said with a roll of her eyes. "Check with the girlfriend first."

"It's not like that."

"Well, it's a little like that," Beth reminded him with a shrug. "Just let me know."

***

Beth was grateful for the coffee by the time they were sitting down for lunch. Keely, Lindy, and Libby sank into chairs around the table. Libby's sister Rachel had darted outside to take a phone call from her in-laws who were watching her kids.

"I am exhausted," Beth said with a groan. "And starved!"

"You are?" Libby asked her with a laugh. "You've been sipping champagne and watching me try on dresses. *I'm* exhausted."

"I didn't think we were going to get you out of that one," Keely commented with a shake of head. "Now who picked out that ugly thing anyway?"

"No one's admitting it yet. I've never seen so many frills and flounces in my life. It was ugly on the hanger and uglier on. I'd like to go on record and say that I wouldn't have touched that dress with a ten-foot pole."

"I thought one of you liked it and didn't want to hurt anyone's feelings. But, oh, it was ugly! And when the zipper got stuck, I was sure I was going to have to keep it."

"At least Rachel was able to pry you out. All those years of sewing kids' costumes made her the resident expert," Beth reminded them. "I was impressed."

"Impressed about what?" Rachel asked, as she slid into her seat. She'd cut her hair boy short the year before, and it had only grown out just a little. She looked completely put together and poised, which was impressive for a full-time mother of three.

"Your skills in getting Libby out of that ugly dress," Beth explained.

"Oh, that. Well, it's one thing if she picks out an ugly bridesmaid's dress, but I'm not having my sister get married in anything that awful."

"The bridesmaid dresses aren't ugly," Libby insisted.

"No, they're actually not bad," Lindy admitted, reluctantly. "I honestly thought they'd be terrible, but you did okay."

"When you said lilac, I thought it was going to be terrible," Rachel said honestly.

"So did Rose," Libby admitted. Rose had to be in court for the day. As Libby's best friend, she'd wanted Rose to be there, but she'd insisted they go without her and send her pictures instead. She'd been texting pictures all morning and getting replies while she waited for her turn in court. As a social worker, it was a part of the job she didn't love, although she liked it better now that she was dating one of the family attorneys. They never worked the same cases, but they would make time for lunch when their court schedules overlapped.

"It was a few shades lighter than plum, but maybe darker than lavender. What was it called again? Wisteria?" Keely spoke up. "And I thought they were lovely."

"They're beautiful," Beth assured her. "Is Seth going with a black tux?"

"No, he's going to be in a charcoal suit with a matching vest and tie."

"Charcoal will look good on me," Lindy said smugly.

"I love that you're going to wear a suit. It's going to be amazing," Beth enthused. "How does Dean feel about it?"

"He smiled when I told him and didn't have much else to say about it. But he showed a little more enthusiasm for the dress we found for Maya online. It is adorable."

When the server approached with their drinks, they went ahead and ordered lunch before picking up where they'd left off. "We still need to find the dress," Libby said with a sigh. "But at least we've gotten the bridesmaid dresses done."

"Are you sure it's a good idea to get those first?" Rachel asked again. She'd pointed out more than once that Libby might want to plan the bridesmaid dresses around her own.

"No, I'm sure. I love them. But I hope we can find something. I know it's the first day looking, but we don't really have that long."

"It's more important to find the right one than to find it fast," Keely reminded her. "We have a few more places to look when we leave. What else has been decided, and what's left to decide?"

"The florist found me the perfect arrangement with sunflowers. They're my favorite! But we decided on lavender instead of rose petals for the flower girls." Libby nodded to Rachel whose daughters were both going to be flower girls in the wedding. "The farmhouse is putting together a brunch. I'm meeting them next week to go over the menu, but I'm thinking of having a coffee bar and a mimosa bar."

"That sounds spectacular," Beth told her. "I can't wait to see it." She noticed her phone buzzing, more than once, and checked the messages. Jamie had texted a handful of times. She looked through the messages and then told Libby. "Hey, we need to make a quick stop on the way to the next shop." When the table looked at her quizzically, she just shrugged. "Just trust me on this."

"Let me check with Rose and see if she can meet us there," Libby suggested.

***

"This is nowhere near on the way," Lindy complained as they made their way out of Athens and into the outskirts of Watkinsville. She was anxious to see Maya. She'd left plenty of breast milk in the fridge, and Dean seemed happy enough to have a whole day at home with the baby. Lindy just missed her. She missed Dean, too. She was ready to get back home and could hear the edge in her own voice. She took a deep breath. One day, they'd be shopping for her dress, and she needed to summon a little more patience for the process.

"Just trust me," Beth said cryptically, as the GPS directed them to a large plantation-style house in the woods. As they pulled up, Jamie came out of the house with Ansley and waved. Rose was already parked and sitting on the hood of her car looking perplexed.

"I thought we were looking at dresses?"

"What in the world?" Keely asked, looking up at the house in confusion.

"Dillon would have been welcome to come, too," Libby told Rose as they walked toward the house.

"I know, and she appreciates it. She had to go back to court after lunch," Rose told her, referring to her girlfriend. They walked over to meet Jamie and Ansley while the rest of the group followed.

"I'm so glad Beth convinced you to come. She didn't tell you anything, did she?" Ansley asked.

"We don't even know why we're here," Rachel spoke up.

"Come on in. I'm Ansley, but you can wait to tell me who you are once you see why you're here." She headed into the house, and they all followed behind looking bemused.

Jamie caught up to Beth at the back of the group. "What did you think?"

"If you hadn't sent pictures, I wouldn't have believed it."

"Well, the timing was perfect. When I saw it, I mentioned to Ansley you were out shopping with Libby for dresses today, and she insisted that I text you first," Jamie explained. We were just doing inventory for the estate sale when we got to this room. It's incredible."

Ansley was waiting at the door of a room, and with a flourish, she opened it. Beth nudged Libby to go first, and then they all followed in behind her. There was a collective gasp and then hushed silence.

Lindy spoke up to break it. "What is all this?"

The room was filled with dresses, shoes, and accessories. It looked like a little boutique had spilled over. There were racks of wedding dresses, ball gowns, and even prom dresses lined up around the room.

"The owner used to have a dress shop in Atlanta. She retired a couple of years back, and her daughter convinced her to try to sell the stock online. She just never got around to doing it, and after she passed, her daughter decided to sell the house. She asked me to hold an estate sale, but I thought you might want to have first look. They're all new gowns, and she'd be reasonable about an offer," Ansley explained.

"We're going to leave you to it and go do some inventory," Jamie told them. "Just let us know if you find anything you're interested in."

"Thank you so much," Libby breathed out. "It's like a dream in here."

"He sent me pictures. I wouldn't have believed it if he hadn't. Isn't it amazing?" Beth smiled at Jamie and headed to check out a stack of shoe boxes.

"There are some vintage pieces in the mix, too," Jamie told her. "I think they're in that back closet, if you can get around those racks. Just call if you need me to move anything."

"This is the sweetest thing, Jamie," Keely told him. "And thank you, Ansley, for thinking of us," she told the girl who smiled shyly from the doorway.

"We'll let you look through them, and don't feel you need to rush. We've got the rest of the upstairs and a couple of outbuildings to inventory still," she told them warmly, as they walked out.

"I can't believe this," Libby told them, walking around the room. "They're gorgeous."

"This is incredible," Rose agreed, looking through the dresses. "They're even sorted by size."

"Here's what we'll do," Lindy said firmly. "Everyone pick out a dress or two we love, and Libby can start trying them on. While you're doing that, I'll sort through the shoes."

"Of course you will. I'll help." Rachel and Lindy looked gleeful as they headed toward the racks and boxes of shoes.

"Hey, grab the dresses first," Beth reminded them.

"I'll look through the jewelry while you try them on," Keely offered with a smile. She'd already spotted a couple of things she wouldn't mind buying.

"I'll keep the dresses coming and help you get in and out of them," Rose suggested.

"I'll go through the vintage items in the back. You never know what we might find there," Beth said with a shrug.

"Okay, let's get started," Libby said.

When Jamie and Ansley headed back downstairs a couple of hours later, the women were all filing out of the room with boxes of dresses, shoes, and jewelry in bags. "We might have found a few things," Libby said with a smile.

"Let's go down to the dining room and take a look. I'll take pictures and send them over and see what kind of prices she'll take for the lot of them," Ansley suggested. "Did you find a dress?"

"I found the most perfect dress. Let me show you," Libby told her, removing the garment bag from the one she had selected. "It's not what I expected, but it's absolutely perfect. Thank you so much for this."

"Don't thank me yet," she warned. "Let me make sure I can get you a good price for it."

Ansley and Jamie cataloged everything the group had found and started sending over pictures after a quick call to explain what was going on. They made a few notes about each item, and then they all watched as Ansley and the owner went back and forth over a price. When she hung up the phone and told them what they'd agreed on, Libby let out a happy sigh. "I can't believe we're getting it all for that."

"She wants it gone. She's just happy to get so much for it. It's become more of a nuisance for her lately. Hopefully, we'll do as well with the rest at auction," Jamie told them.

"If not, maybe she could try a pop up shop in town," Keely suggested. "You let her know we could arrange it if she'd like. We could advertise between the tea room and antique store and maybe get a social media campaign out. She might bring in a little more money that way."

"I'll suggest it," Ansley beamed.

"You have to come to our wedding," Libby said impulsively, laying a hand on Ansley's arm. "I wouldn't have found the perfect dress without you."

"Thank you," Ansley told her warmly. Jamie shot a quick look over at Beth who was looking at Libby with an inscrutable expression on her face. Jamie and Beth had planned to go to Seth and Libby's wedding together. Beth finally looked his way and shrugged. Clearly, if Ansley was going, he would have a date.

"Is that okay?" he asked her, as they were heading out to the cars parked outside.

"It's fine," Beth said shortly. "It's just been a long day. Movie night later?"

"Well, I ... um ..." he shot a look at Ansley who stood in the doorway of the house still chatting with Keely.

"You have a date. Right," Beth said flatly. "That's good. I'm really exhausted. I think I'm going to call it an early night," she told him and got in the car. He closed the door and hesitated before heading back to the porch.

"Is that going to be a problem?" Lindy asked from the front seat.

"What?" Beth asked her.

"Libby inviting her to the wedding. I thought you were going with Jamie."

"Well, of course he needs to take his girlfriend. I don't have a problem going by myself anyway," she said with a one-shoulder shrug, looking out the window. She'd been looking forward to having a date for the wedding. She wouldn't have to worry about sitting out any dances or being seated at the singles' table. Now she tried to readjust her expectations.

"Just checking," Lindy told her, turning back to the front. She suspected it was a problem, but it wasn't her business anyway. She just wanted to get home to Dean and Maya. "Dean's friend Lucas is currently single if you need a date to this thing. I know you don't care to go alone, but he'd be a good wedding date if you'd rather have company. He's entertaining at any rate."

"Maybe," Beth replied noncommittally. "We'll see. The dress was perfect."

"It was amazing," Keely agreed, as she slid into the driver's seat while Libby got into the back with Beth. Rachel was already heading home to pick up her kids and waved as she pulled away. Rose was standing by her car showing Ansley a pair of shoes and getting ready to head out herself. "Did you see the earrings I found? Just gorgeous!"

"I may have gotten a little bit of a haul from the closet, too," Beth said happily.

"It was a good day," Libby told them with a smile. "I'm so glad we did this. How do you know Ansley anyway?" she asked Beth.

"She's dating Jamie."

"Wait ... she's ... " Libby stopped, her brows drawing together. "Why didn't you say something?"

"How did you miss that?" Lindy asked with a laugh. "Wasn't it obvious?"

"I kind of got tunnel visioned looking for a dress," she admitted sheepishly. "Oh, and I invited her to the wedding! I'm sorry, Beth," she said sincerely, feeling dismayed. She'd hoped the wedding might provide a little bit of the romance necessary to push Jamie and Beth together. Of course, she thought, Seth already told her she was wasting her time, but now she'd gone and ruined her own plan.

"Why? They're dating. He was bound to invite her anyway. It's not a big deal." Lindy and Libby exchanged a look, and Keely deftly changed the subject.

"We need to talk about cake," she began, as they pulled out of the drive and headed back to town.

Chapter 12

Beth took Mr. Darcy for a longer walk than usual. The temperature was still a bit too hot for her taste, but they had plans to join Libby and Lindy at the lake later. She wanted to walk and think. Of course, mostly she was walking and talking. She'd already filled Mr. Darcy in on the best parts of her week at work, and she flushed pink from embarrassment rather than heat when she noticed Presley sitting on a bench on the path leading back to the park.

"Hey. What are you doing here?" She knew Presley lived in Athens and rarely just hung around downtown Madison. "Is Layla here, too?"

"I'm meeting Dad and Keely for lunch in a bit. Layla's working," Presley explained, looking amused. "So Libby found a dress, did she?"

"Oh, you overheard that? I was just catching Mr. Darcy up. He's not big on weddings since he mostly can't attend, but he likes to be included."

"I'm sure he does," Presley said with a wide smile. She was well aware of what most would consider Beth's eccentricities. She found them charming. She leaned over to pet Mr. Darcy, and Beth watched her say hello. Presley was wearing white shorts and a paisley top with a single shoulder strap. Her black hair was pulled in a matching paisley headband, and she wore sneakers to complete the ensemble in solid white. She rarely seemed to wear makeup, but she did have a bright pink lipstick on today. Beth looked down at her own dress and was pleased she'd managed to snag it from the raid on the vintage closet at the estate sale. It was very 50s housewife, but she'd paired it with sneakers of her own for the walk.

"How's Layla doing?" She didn't know either sister well, but they'd spent a few holidays together. Beth had gravitated toward Presley. Layla could be a bit more prickly than her older sister. Still, she liked them both and worried about Layla as much as she did about Naomi.

"She's good. She's working today. I'm taking a break."

"It must be hard to live with family. Although I always wanted a sibling."

"Want mine? It's mostly been fine. Just a little weird."

"I'm sure. Has she heard from Noah at all?"

"Not lately. Thankfully," Presley said, her expression darkening. "Anyway, he stopped by once, and I sent him packing. He knows we'll file a restraining order if he comes around again. Anyway ... I'm hoping that's the last of it."

"Are you bringing a date to the wedding?"

"Probably. I haven't decided who though. Are you going with Jamie?"

"No, he's got a girlfriend he'll bring. You'll like her," Beth explained, leaning down to pat Mr. Darcy who was following the conversation with the apparent eagerness of a tennis fan at a match.

"Oh. I sort of thought the two of you were dating."

"Oh. No, we're not. We're just friends."

"Why?" Presley asked bluntly. Although she was the more friendly of the sisters, she did have a certain directness that could be intimidating. Beth thought wistfully of Layla's reticence with fondness. She might be prickly, but she mostly minded her own business.

"Why are we friends?"

"No, why only friends? You don't think he's attractive?"

"No. I mean, yes, of course I do."

"Who wouldn't?" Presley asked rhetorically. "Broad shoulders, muscles for days, and I think the tattoos are kind of hot. Plus, those full lips? You can't tell me you haven't noticed."

"Of course I've noticed. That's not the point," Beth said, blushing.

"Is he not smart enough for you?"

"What? He's very smart! He's a very intelligent man," Beth insisted indignantly.

"But can't carry on a conversation?" Presley assumed with an air of sympathy.

"Not at all. He's a very interesting person. We have tons of great conversations," Beth insisted.

"Okay. So you admit he's hot, interesting, and intelligent." She waited a beat. "But you're just friends. Why, again?"

"It's just ... it's um ... he's not interested in me like that."

"Oh," Presley said, drawing out the *o*.

"What's that supposed to mean?"

"You're interested in him, but you think he's not interested in you," Presley summarized.

"No, that's not it?" Beth asked, a question in her own voice, as she tried to sort it out.

"Maybe you should find out. I'm off to lunch. I'll see you later."

"Well, I'll be damned," Beth said, sinking down on to the bench. "Maybe I am." She looked at Mr. Darcy who was too distracted by a chipmunk to pay her any mind.

***

Jamie showed up just after seven and waited at the door. He was glad that Ansley had told him that she was going out with friends so he could say that he was doing the same. Of course, he'd told her about the regular movie nights with Beth. There was no deception involved. It had just been the first time in a long time that he had what was shaping up to be a real relationship while he was spending time with Beth. It felt strangely disloyal.

"I wasn't sure if you'd make it," Beth told him without preamble when she opened the door. "I'll call in the order now," she told him, tossing him the menu to the local Chinese restaurant.

"Why wouldn't I be here?" he asked quizzically, as he bent down to scoop up Mr. Darcy.

"You know, girlfriend stuff," Beth said with a shrug and roll of her eyes that was softened by her smile.

"She's hanging out with her friends. Why shouldn't I hang out with mine?" he asked with a shrug, tapping the menu. "I want that. Want to split it?"

"Of course. They always bring so much." She walked around the room as she placed her order, Jamie and Mr. Darcy following her frenetic movement with interest.

"What's your deal?" he asked her when she got off the phone. Jamie took a closer look at her. If he wasn't mistaken, she was wearing a little more makeup than usual, but it looked slightly off. She was wearing a black vintage jumpsuit with harem pants and a belted waist. It was pretty but a little more dressed up than usual. He guessed that she hadn't had time to change after work. He looked at her face again, closely. "I think you forgot to do one of your eyes."

"What?" she asked him, appalled. She rushed to the mirror and laughed at her own reflection. "BRB," she told him, rushing for the master bedroom.

"What?"

"Be right back."

"It would have been quicker just to say that," he told Mr. Darcy with a look of exasperation.

In the bathroom, Beth looked at her face in the mirror in annoyance. Yep. She'd forgotten mascara on one side. She remembered that Mr. Darcy had distracted her midway through her routine, and she'd clearly forgotten. She hadn't as much as looked at a mirror since. She contemplated taking her makeup off entirely. She was being silly, she told herself. She added a layer of mascara to her lashes and stood back to look at herself. She looked a little nicer than usual, for a movie night. Since her conversation with Presley, she'd been overthinking everything. "Stop that," she told herself firmly.

"Did you say something?"

"I was just saying I'll be right out." She shook her head and headed back into the living room.

"Tough day at work?" he asked her, as she collapsed onto the couch with a sigh and reached for her favorite pillow.

"No. Just a long one."

Jamie sat down on the couch next to her. Beth shifted in her seat, angling toward him. "I like this," he told her, tapping her knee to indicate the jumpsuit.

"I found it in that treasure trove that you and Ansley found. One of many outfits I couldn't resist."

"It suits you."

When the doorbell rang, he motioned for her to stay seated while he went to get the order. She'd bought dinner this time so he gave the delivery woman a generous tip and then started dividing the food up on plates while Beth watched him from the couch.

Jamie was easy in her kitchen, Beth thought. She looked at him in the pale blue T-shirt and faded jeans. Another man might have looked sloppy in an outfit so casual, but the shirt molded to his body, and even Beth had to admit those jeans were something else. She looked down and blushed. That was not a helpful direction for her thoughts, she told herself. "Need any help?"

"No, I've got it. Want wine?"

"I'll just go with a soda." After all, she told herself, she needed to keep a clear head. Although, she reasoned, a glass of wine might help her relax. "Never mind. I'll take the wine."

Jamie rolled his eyes to the ceiling, putting the glass bottle of Pepsi back in the fridge and reaching for the wine glass. "Why are you being so weird?"

"I'm not. I just changed my mind. Woman's prerogative."

"I can't argue with that."

"How's Ansley doing?" Beth asked, after Jamie handed her the wine. She took a slightly larger sip than she might have otherwise. There. She'd asked the question. Even if it did stick in her throat a little.

"She's good. It's a busy time of year. Of course, it never really slows down. Not with the market the way it is right now." He brought over their plates and his bottle of beer and settled himself beside her.

"That's a good thing. We're getting more business at the bookstore, too." They were both silent for a minute when they remembered those years where business wasn't at a peak, and home prices fell dramatically. Jamie had been laid off from his corporate job and left with his part-time income at Lost Horizon. Seth had offered him a full-time position, but it had still been a cut in pay from what he'd been used to. Beth, meanwhile, had kept the bookstore afloat but couldn't afford to hire any help. Long days were made all the longer for it. They were both glad that the recession had ended. The recent boost in the economy was helping them both.

"I guess Naomi's working out?"

"She's great. I'm not sure what I did without her. So, what movies are we watching?"

"I picked out a few," he said, reaching into the messenger bag he'd brought with him. "Here." He spread them out on the table.

She looked at the titles and back at him. Then, she carefully looked again. *When Harry Met Sally. My Best Friend's Wedding. Clueless. 13 Going on 30. Easy A. The Jane Austen Book Club.* "What's happening here?" she asked him, waving a hand at the movies.

"I picked out a few I think we'd both like. What?"

She looked at them again and wondered if he didn't realize that they all had a best friend love story. Then she realized that she was probably just overthinking everything. Again. After all, *When Harry Met Sally* was one of their favorites. She'd loved *My Best Friend's Wedding* and *Clueless* in high school, a fact that Jamie knew about her. They both enjoyed any movie that paid homage to the 80s. She sighed. They were good choices, and she was just being crazy.

"We can pick something else."

"No. This is perfect. Double feature?"

"Of course. What'd you have in mind?"

"*Clueless* and *The Jane Austen Book Club*."

"I figured you'd pick a Jane Austen night. Which one is *Clueless* based on?" he asked, knowing the answer already but knowing that Beth enjoyed telling it.

"*Emma*. It's a great remake, much better than some of the others that tried to pull that off." Beth went to put in the movie, and they settled back onto the couch with their plates. Mr. Darcy jumped on to the other chair and watched them mournfully. He knew that they wouldn't feed him people food, but if he could bide his time, there was likely to be a treat in it for him.

During the movie, Beth felt uncomfortable a few times as she watched the plots play out. Feelings for Jamie, she wondered. How had that happened? But she drank the wine and started to relax. It was just another movie night, and he was her best friend. Nothing had to change. He didn't even have to know. After all, she assured herself, the feelings would probably pass. She leaned her head on his shoulder when she'd finished eating, and Mr. Darcy jumped up to settle down on his lap.

Jamie smiled over her hair. Beth had been keyed up when he got here, but she seemed to have settled down. He wondered what it was that was making her so jumpy but then decided that the situation with Ansley probably put them both a little ill at ease simply because it was new. They would adjust. He'd probably be coming over for movie nights a little less than usual, but there was no reason they couldn't stay friends. He adjusted his arm around her and rubbed Mr. Darcy's head. There was no reason any of it had to change.

When Jamie dropped his arm around her, Beth nearly gasped aloud. She managed to turn it into a cough and settle back down, but she immediately felt the heat in her body radiating outward. She could see now how it could be if they were together. Just like this, but more.

She knew then that she'd have to see him less. After all, he has a girlfriend, she thought. She wasn't going to be one of those women who tried to undermine the relationship to get what she wanted. She couldn't do that to another woman. No, she'd have to accept her own feelings and either own up to them or make excuses not to be around him. Not while he was in a relationship. It was just too confusing.

Besides, he didn't see her that way. Likely wouldn't ever see her that way since he hadn't already, she thought with a sigh. She snuggled in a little closer and realized that this would have to be the last movie night for a while. She wanted to feel sad but decided that she'd do that later. Right now, she just wanted to remember what this felt like for all the times she wouldn't have his shoulder there to lean on.

After it ended, Jamie held out the movies, "Want to borrow any of these?"

She looked at them, sorely tempted. "No, I'm good," she told him, reminding herself that she was going to have to avoid movie night as long as her feelings and his relationship were in direct conflict.

"Well, let me know if you change your mind."

"I will," she told him, more earnestly than she'd intended.

"I should go," he told her, glancing at the time.

"Okay." He gave her a strange look and then came over to hug her. They did this. Hugging. She hugged him back and tried not to hold on. After all, she reminded herself, she'd still see him around.

She just needed to take a step back and give them both some space. She watched him leave, standing in the doorway a little while after his car had driven off. Then she turned back to Mr. Darcy. "We'll just have to adjust," she told him, going inside to get ready for bed.

Chapter 13

Libby sat down on the bench with a happy sigh. Seth sat down beside her, taking her hand. They looked at each other for a minute. "This is my favorite spot in town," Seth told her with a smile.

"Mine, too," she said, leaning into him. "I wonder sometimes what my life would look like if you hadn't stopped me that day."

They were quiet for a minute, thinking of the time when they'd broken up. Months had passed before Seth had bought coffee and waited on this very bench to catch Libby on her run. He'd wanted another chance and had gambled on her crossing his path that morning. When he'd proposed at the same spot, it had been like coming full circle.

"I don't," Seth said quietly. "I don't even want to imagine it." Libby laid her head on his shoulder. He leaned over and kissed her on the top of the head. "Are you ready for tomorrow?"

"As ready as I'll ever be," Libby said calmly. She'd been training for a half marathon, but she had a 10K to run in the morning before the Fall Festival in town.

"Dean's been complaining about it, but watch him place first in his age group." The run was to raise money for the local firefighters, and Dean always participated. The previous year, he'd been the one to run in full fire gear, though this year, he'd joked, someone else had drawn the short straw on that.

The Firefighter 5K and 10K was a tradition in town. It was always followed by a fall festival and chili cook-off. Keely had entered the tea room's chili in the competition and would be there all day, with Beth helping out. Libby was entering her sweet cornbread recipe for the non-traditional cornbread category, after Keely had tried it a few months back and urged her to enter. She'd agreed, and then spent the last couple of months perfecting her recipe and training for the run. She was making good time so she wasn't worried about it.

Behind them, in the park, the city workers were already setting up the tents. The festival usually had a number of arts and crafts booths, as well as a few live musical performances throughout the day. Lindy was setting up a booth for face painting and for a craft from her painting studio geared toward both kids and adults. She hadn't been back to work for long, and she had shortened her hours. She was over at the tents now talking to the city workers while wearing Maya in a sling. She waved when she saw them and started over.

"Are you running tomorrow?" Libby asked her.

"Ha! Not me. Dean keeps reminding me that I could run with the jogging stroller, but I would much rather watch. We'll be your cheering section."

"I'll be right there with you," Seth said with a smile. He was planning to run the half marathon with Libby, but he'd opted out of the 10K since he would be helping his mom set up her booth right after the race. They looked up when they heard a familiar voice coming around the corner. Sure enough, Mr. Darcy trotted ahead before Beth who was laughing at her own joke.

"One of these days, someone is going to think you're crazy," Lindy told her.

"They probably already do, but we don't care, do we, Mr. Darcy?" Beth asked the dog. "At least I think I'm funny. Is this a family meeting? What's up?"

"We're just out for a walk," Seth told her. "This one is setting up her booth." He nodded toward Lindy.

"The tent, anyway," Lindy said with a shrug. "We'll have to be out early tomorrow between the race and the festival. Mom's going to watch Maya while I set up, and then we'll trade off while she sets up."

"You know I'll be here to help out, too," Beth reminded her. "We'll take it in turns." She leaned forward to peek at Maya who was sound asleep. "I like the wrap."

"I do, too, now that it's cooling off a little out here," Lindy agreed. "You'd put Mr. Darcy in one of these if you could."

"It'd be tempting. But he likes a good walk."

"Is Jamie running tomorrow?" Libby asked.

"I'm not really sure. I haven't talked to him that much lately," Beth admitted. She'd been able to make excuses to cancel movie night over the last month. After all, she really did have to help prepare for the festival, and they had been a little busier planning for an upcoming author event at the store. She certainly wasn't going to tell him about these pesky feelings she was having. She was sure they would pass if she just gave them some time. Lindy and Libby exchanged a look over her head while she poured a bottle of water from her running pack into a travel dish for Mr. Darcy. "Are you all ready for the wedding?" she asked Libby and Seth, changing the subject.

They looked at each other and smiled. "We're all set," Seth said with a smile.

"Don't forget that the bachelor and bachelorette parties are next weekend," Libby reminded her. "And the wedding is the following week."

"Don't you usually do those sort of things the night before?" Beth asked quizzically.

"Not if we don't want to be hung over going into the big day," Seth said with a grin. "Besides, this worked better for everyone's schedules."

"Well, I'm in," Beth said agreeably.

"I'm in if there are strippers," Lindy told them while Seth rolled his eyes.

"I don't want to know about it if there are," he told them.

"You're not worried," Libby told him with a smile.

"Not even a little," he agreed. "We're not having strippers, in case you were wondering."

"You know I don't care," she said with a smile, leaning her head back on his shoulder.

"Aren't they the cutest?" Beth asked Lindy.

"Something like that. Are you bringing a date to the wedding or not?" Lindy asked Beth.

"I don't mind going by myself."

"You know Lucas would probably go with you. Let Dean set it up."

"I don't need to be set up!"

"It wouldn't have to be like a date-date. Just think of it as having someone to dance with."

"Fine! Fine," Beth said, throwing up the hand that wasn't holding Mr. Darcy's leash and waving it at Lindy. "You're going to do it anyway."

"He said he can pick you up on the way," Lindy said with a mischievous grin. "I figured you'd relent."

Beth laughed. "Just as long as he realizes it's not an actual date, I'm fine. Can you add it to the seating chart or will it mix things up?"

"I kind of already had you sitting by him," Libby admitted sheepishly. When Lindy barked out a laugh, she continued. "I just didn't want you sitting alone, and I wasn't going to insult you by putting you at the kids' table with my nieces and nephews. Besides," she added with a smile, "Lucas is kind of hot."

"Is he?" Seth asked, curiously. He wouldn't have thought so, but what did he know about it?

"Not for me. For Beth."

"Beth doesn't need to be set up," Beth objected loudly.

"She does if she keeps referring to herself in the third person," Lindy insisted with a wide smile.

"I'm just saying. Happily single here."

"And there's nothing wrong with that. Faith is single and loves it," Libby said, referring to her sister. "She dates around when she feels like it, but she's determined to stay single all her days."

"Will she make it to the wedding?" Beth asked curiously. Faith worked on a cruise ship and couldn't always get the time off for holidays.

"Yes. She's got a couple of weeks off this month. She'll come to the bachelorette party and the wedding, and then she's back on a ship that next week."

"Where are you at on numbers? Is everyone coming?" Lindy asked. She'd gotten distracted with festival planning and hadn't been as involved in the wedding planning lately as she'd have liked, she thought guiltily.

"We have your mom and Theodore," Libby told her. "And my parents. Rachel and her family. Faith. My grandmother might make it. Jenna from work and her husband Finn. My boss Gloria and her partner. Then, there's your family," she explained, nodding to Lindy.

"So, me and Dean and Maya here." She leaned down to kiss Maya's head where she was still sound asleep. "Beth and Lucas, Jamie and Ansley. Who am I missing?" She asked, trying to get a head count.

"Marnie and Patrick are coming in," Seth spoke up. "Chase and Farrah are covering the store and can't make it. I thought about closing for the day, but we're trying to keep the numbers down."

"Otherwise, we were afraid we'd have to invite half the town," Libby admitted. "We really want to keep it small."

"My dad is coming," Beth reminded them. Her parents divorce had taken her by surprise, although it shouldn't have. She should have seen it coming a mile away. They seemed happier apart, and Beth wasn't as bothered as she thought she would be. "He said he probably won't stay long." She shrugged. Her dad wasn't big on family events, and her mother was happy to no longer have to come with him, not that she'd done so often in the first place.

"Layla and Presley will be there, too," Lindy reminded them. "At least that's what Mom said."

"Of course. I told them they could bring dates, but they opted not to," Libby explained.

"I can't imagine Layla wants to date again any time soon," Beth said knowingly.

"That sort of thing is bound to linger," Lindy agreed, thinking of how they'd all misjudged Layla's ex-boyfriend so badly. He'd been so clean cut and *nice*. Even she had been hoodwinked, and she was normally more suspicious than that.

"I'm surprised you didn't set one of them up with Lucas," Beth told her.

"I might have thought about it. But they don't know him, and you've met him at least. I thought it would be more comfortable."

"We'll have just under thirty people there. Not counting the two of us, of course," Libby explained. "We wanted to keep it small."

"It'll be perfect," Lindy assured her. "Anyway, I'm going to do a last check over there and then head to the studio to make sure everything's ready to go." She turned back into Town Park where the workers were just finishing with the tents.

"See you in the morning," Beth told her. "I better get Mr. Darcy home. We're got book club soon."

"Oh, I hate to miss it," Libby said regretfully. "I'm making one more batch of cornbread tonight. But you catch me up tomorrow if you get a chance."

"I will. See you later," Beth told them, folding up Mr. Darcy collapsible dog bowl and heading home.

***

At the bookstore, Jillian shifted uncomfortably in her seat.

"What is your deal?" Rebecca demanded.

"Maybe this isn't such a good idea," she said, toying with her phone.

"Yes, it is. If you stay home alone, you're just going to text him, and that's against the rules," Rebecca reminded her. "At least if we do this book club thing, you won't be tempted."

"I know," Jill said with a sigh. She and her boyfriend had broken up a couple of months before. Their relationship had always been intense, but the last several months had been on again, off again. After she found out that he'd run up a credit card in her name, she'd had enough. It was bad enough that she'd been paying almost all of the bills, but now she had several thousand in credit card debt that she couldn't afford and hadn't been able to dispute since she'd let him use it a couple of times.

Of course, Mark had promised to pay it all back, but so far, she'd only gotten a couple of payments. Her interest rate was so high, she'd had to pick up extra shifts at work to try to pay it down. *And* had a yard sale. *And* donated plasma once a week for the last month. She shifted again in her seat. She loved him. She really did. But enough was enough.

"Did you block him on Facebook yet?" Rebecca asked, pushing her curly blond hair over one shoulder. She kept thinking about cutting it, but she knew she'd regret it if she did. She looked over at Jill and, as always, admired her style. She'd dyed her hair pink a couple of years back and kept it pixie short, but after the last breakup, she'd gone silver, boy short, and changed out the diamond stud in her nose for a little silver nose ring.

Rebecca wouldn't have gone silver, but it looked amazing on her friend who was always on top of the latest trends. She was trying to talk her into a tattoo, which was Rebecca's personal weakness. None of hers were visible, her job at the library wouldn't have allowed it, but she liked having a few sexy secrets up her sleeve. She limited it to lingerie and tattoos but admired Jill's style.

"I'm going to."

"Give me that," Rebecca said, taking Jill's phone. They'd been friends and roommates through college. Jill handed over the phone with a sigh. She put in the code to unlock the screen, opened it, and had him blocked in a couple of minutes. "There. He's blocked across the board. Instagram, Facebook, Snapchat, all of it."

"But he can still text me."

"Block him there, too."

"This sounds intense," Naomi said as she walked over to add one more book to the display. There, she thought, that looks more even.

"Ex-boyfriend drama," Rebecca explained.

"Ah. I know all about that," she said with a roll of her eyes.

"We just blocked him on everything," Jill said.

"Yeah, my ex was bothering me, too," Naomi said, sitting down beside them. "I had to do the same."

"It's me actually," Jill admitted.

"Not just you," Rebecca pointed out. "They tend to cyberstalk each other," she explained to Naomi.

"We just keep pulling each other back in."

"And you can't work it out?" Naomi asked curiously.

"No," Jill said, as Rebecca said, "Absolutely not."

"Then it's best to block him," Naomi agreed. "I'm Naomi. Is this your first meeting?"

"I'm Rebecca, and this is Jill. I've been here once before, but it's been a while. It's Jill's first meeting though."

"I could use the distraction," she admitted with a smile. "But I haven't read the book."

"That's okay," Naomi told her. "But after tonight, you'll probably want to read it."

"We can keep it spoiler-free," Beth offered, joining in on the conversation, as the group started filling in and taking their seats.

The refreshment table had a line, but some of the group had already grabbed a pastry and headed to a seat.

"I don't mind spoilers," Jill said with a shrug.

"This one had a pretty big plot twist," Beth told her.

"Good guy turned out to be an asshole," Rebecca said, biting into a pastry.

"I know how that is," Naomi said with a laugh.

"Yeah," Jill said with a sigh. "I wish I didn't."

"This is why I'm single," Beth declared.

"Huh. Are you?" Rebecca asked. "Good. You can come with us then."

"Come with you to what?" Beth asked. She'd met Rebecca once before and had been introduced to Jill when she'd come in.

"Speed dating," Jill said with a shake of her head. "She's making me," she said shooting a dark look at Rebecca.

"It's fun." When Rebecca snorted, she continued. "Well, it's entertaining anyway," she admitted. "Come with us. Both of you."

"Not me," Naomi insisted. Then, she added, softly. "I'm not really ready yet." Rebecca looked at her curiously, sensing something in the quietly delivered statement.

"You then," she said to Beth. "We'll grab dinner first. They're having it at a bar in Athens, and I promise we'll have a good time."

"Maybe I will," Beth said. "When is it?"

"Next week," Rebecca told her. "Friday."

"Oh, good. That works out then. I have a bachelorette thing on Saturday," she told them. "I guess it's worth a try. Have you ever met anyone that way?"

"Oh, hell no," Rebecca said with a laugh. "But it's fun anyway. And I did make a friend that way once. But we were not compatible to date at all."

"We're about to get started. Let's exchange numbers afterwards," Beth suggested and then called the meeting to order.

Chapter 14

Jamie sat down in the recliner and picked up the book he'd been reading. He was catching up on the book club pick. He could have gone to the meeting, even without finishing it, but things had been weird with Beth lately. She hadn't wanted to get together as much, and when they talked, she seemed distracted. He missed her. It was weird to go this long without hanging out, but he suspected she was trying to give him some space since he and Ansley were dating.

He'd tried to explain that he didn't need space. Ansley understood that they were friends and didn't expect them to stop hanging out. Beth had brushed it off and said that she was just busy with work and the upcoming festival. He wondered if that were true. Something had seemed off lately, and he wondered if he'd done something to upset her.

He'd suspected that taking Ansley to the wedding might have been a problem. After all, Beth loved weddings, but she didn't enjoy going solo. There was always someone who would interrogate her about why she hadn't brought a date. She enjoyed being single, but she didn't enjoy having to explain it. He sighed. Had Libby not issued the invitation to Ansley directly, he would have explained to her that he and Beth had already made plans to attend together. After all, she would understand. But what's done is done, he thought with a shrug.

He tried to focus on the book. He'd started to suspect that one character wasn't what he seemed, and the book had been a solid page turner. But he kept losing focus. He put it down with a sigh and texted Ansley to make sure she got home safe. They'd had dinner, but she'd called it an early night since she had to meet a client before the festival in the morning. Besides, he was running the 5K and planned to get to bed a little earlier than usual. He looked at the time and thought about texting Beth. She'd still be in the meeting though.

Jamie gave up on the book and turned on the TV instead. He flipped through the guide and ended up putting it, briefly, on a Hallmark movie he'd watched with Beth. When he'd first met her, he'd scoffed at her penchant for watching anything with a romantic plot, but he had to admit that he usually enjoyed the ones he watched with her. He turned off the television with a sigh. Things were changing between them, and he wasn't sure why. He was determined to corner her before the 5K and find out.

***

It was overcast the next morning as Jamie walked into town. He'd run the 5K, shower at home, and then meet Ansley at the festival. It was early still, but he wanted time to find Beth. If she wasn't setting up for the race, she'd be at Town Park setting up with Keely. He went by the park first and didn't see her so he kept walking. Sure enough, he found her sitting on a curb holding Maya while Dean picked up his registration packet and Lindy chatted with Libby.

"Hey," she said, looking up at him as he came by.

"Hey," he replied, lowering himself down beside her.

"Where's Ansley?" Beth asked, her eyes on Maya.

"She had to meet a client. She'll be here later for the festival."

"Is it her first festival?"

"Yeah," he paused, wondering why she wasn't even looking at him. "Are you going to tell me what I did wrong?"

"What do you mean?" she asked warily, looking up to meet his eyes.

"It's been over a month since we hung out. You don't ever call me anymore. When I text you, I get the replies you usually reserve for the assholes that hassle you. What's up? If I did something, you know I'm sorry for it. I just want to know what it was I did."

"You haven't done anything. I'm not mad at you."

"I know it's not just about you being busy. You're always busy."

"I was just giving you a little space," Beth said with a shrug, turning her attention back to Maya.

"Did I ask for space?"

"No. But I figured you'd need it anyway."

"Ansley doesn't care if we hang out. I'm allowed to have friends." When she didn't respond, he asked, "Do you just not like her? Is that what this is about?"

"What? No. She seems perfectly nice."

"Hmm," Jamie replied. She'd said it calmly enough, but he sensed subtext.

"What?"

"Is *perfectly nice* some kind of insult women use? Like when you say *bless your heart*?"

"No. She seems nice. I'm not mad at you. I don't know what else you want to hear."

"How about, *we're still best friends, Jamie*?" he asked with a smile.

"We're still best friends, Jamie," she replied with a small smile.

"Then why don't I feel like we are?" he asked her, nudging her shoulder with his own.

"It's nothing. I was just giving you some space."

"We've already clarified that I haven't asked for any."

"Well, *I* needed the space," Beth said defensively. She rubbed her forehead with her free hand and sighed. "Don't worry about it. I've just been busy. I'm sure we'll get together again soon." "Why won't you tell me what's wrong?"

"Because nothing is."

"So … movie night? Maybe Friday before the big bachelor and bachelorette nights?"

"I can't Friday night."

"Why not? Hot date?" Jamie joked.

"Well, more of a speed dating thing," she said uncomfortably.

"Wait—what?" Jamie asked, flummoxed. "I thought you weren't dating."

"I promised Rebecca and Jill I'd go with them

"Who are Rebecca and Jill?"

"Some new friends," Beth explained. Jamie just looked at her. She had friends he didn't know about, was going out on some kind of date night, and didn't want to spend time with him. He wasn't sure what was up, but he didn't like it.

"Okay. Another night then?"

"Sure." She looked down to readjust Maya, and Jamie just looked at her. He had a feeling that *sure* didn't mean sure at all.

"I'm going to go register," he said, standing. "I guess I'll catch you later." He walked away slowly to the registration table, and Beth watched him go.

"Want to explain that?" Dean asked, plopping down beside her.

"Were you eavesdropping?" Beth accused.

"Absolutely not. I was just waiting to reclaim my daughter and just so happened to be standing close enough to hear it all."

"*I* was eavesdropping," Lindy said, sitting down on the other side of her. "Why are you being so mean to Jamie?"

"I wasn't being mean."

"What'd he do?" Dean asked.

"What do you mean? He didn't do anything."

"But you're avoiding him and clearly blew him off," Lindy pointed out.

"And he knows it, too," Dean told her, nodding over to where Jamie was sitting on the curb by himself waiting for the races to start.

Beth looked over at him uncomfortably. She hated to see him hurting, but she just couldn't spend time with him right now with all of these *feelings*, she thought. It was just too painful. "It's nothing. I'm just in a mood."

"Well, I can't watch the man suffer. If you won't hang out with him, I will," Dean said, standing up and heading toward Jamie.

"So what's the real story?" Lindy asked after he left.

"There's no story."

"Girl, there's always a story. Isn't that what you always say?"

"He has a girlfriend. I just thought they'd be more comfortable if I gave them some space."

"Well, you're kind of being a shitty friend."

"I can't do it, Lindy. I feel bad about it, but I don't feel right hanging out with him while he's dating her."

"Why?" Lindy started to ask, and then cut herself off. She looked closely at Beth, who was still looking down at Maya and avoiding eye contact. "Oh," she said, finally catching on. "We wondered when you'd realize it," she told Beth frankly who looked up in confusion. "You and Jamie."

"Who's *we*?"

"All of us. I mean, you're perfect for each other. Seth didn't see it, but the rest of us agree."

"Well, Jamie's not interested in me like that. I'm just going to give him space until it goes away."

"Well, don't wait too long." When Beth just looked at her, she explained. "I know you need the space, but he doesn't know why you're acting like this. If you're not honest with him, you may just end up burning that bridge."

"I can't tell him. It's too embarrassing."

"You don't think he might feel the same?"

"I'm sure he doesn't."

"Well, just be careful. That's all I'm saying," Lindy told her, opening her arms to take Maya back.

"I'm not trying to hurt him," Beth said honestly, looking over at Jamie and Dean stretching out for the race. "I just need a little more time."

"Are you so sure you'll get over it?"

"I have to," Beth said firmly, still watching Jamie.

***

After the race, they all headed off to shower and change for the festival. Beth and Lindy went directly over to the park to get set up for the cook-off and craft fair. Keely was already at the tent, organizing her booth. "Well, how did it go?"

"Dean beat his best time. Jamie placed second in his age group, and Libby was first in hers," Lindy told her. "I'm going to get set up, but Libby said she'd be over to help you out in a bit," she explained. "Remember what I said," she told Beth cryptically as she walked off.

"What was that about?"

"Nothing really," Beth said with a shrug. "How can I help?"

"I've really got everything in hand. Why don't you take a turn enjoying the festival when it starts, and we can switch off every half hour or so?"

"That sounds like a plan. Want anything before I go?"

"Snag me a Coke?" Keely asked. "It's getting warmer, and I'm all out."

"I'll grab you a Coke and a few waters, too, in case you want them. Just give me a few minutes."

Beth headed into the festival to grab the drinks and nearly ran into Ansley as she turned the corner. "Hey, sorry," Ansley said with a laugh.

"It's okay. I wasn't looking where I was going," Beth said with a small smile.

"Have you seen Jamie?"

"He went home to shower and change after the race, but I haven't seen him since."

"Okay. Need some help with the drinks?"

"Sure. Thank you," Beth told her, looking at her curiously. Ansley was wearing a sundress in a soft pink that Beth knew she could never really pull off. Only Molly Ringwald could really get away with red hair and a pink dress, Beth thought. Her hair was clipped back, and she was wearing open toed sandals that Beth admired, and told her so.

"Thanks. We haven't seen much of you lately. I know you're Jamie's best friend so I don't want you to think you guys can't hang out because of me."

"I don't think that. I've just been so busy with work lately."

Ansley glanced over at her and wondered. Beth was wearing a retro style housedress in a forest green. It had cap sleeves and flared out at the waist with a white, wide belt. She wore matching earrings that Ansley was sure were vintage clip ons. Her red hair was pulled up in a high pony tail that Ansley was sure she herself could never pull off. "Well, maybe we can get together for dinner or something once things slow down."

"That would be nice," Beth lied. They dropped the drinks off with Keely and then headed back toward the tents lining the park.

"Well, if you see Jamie before I do, can you tell him I'm looking for him?"

"Of course," Beth replied with a smile. As Ansley walked away, she strengthened her resolve. She was nice. Like really nice. They would have been friends if things were different. Beth knew she couldn't hang around Jamie without betraying her feelings, and she couldn't do that when he was dating Ansley. It wouldn't be fair, and it would just make everyone feel awkward. No, it was better that she just keep to herself until she could look at him only as a friend.

Chapter 15

Libby kissed Seth, slow and deeply, winding her fingers through his hair and holding it tight. He moved his mouth slightly away from hers and said, "Keep that up, and we're not going anywhere tonight."

She smiled, her lips against his already. "It's tempting," she murmured.

"Well, we can't exactly miss our own parties." Seth was getting ready to go out for his stag party. He was leaving a little later and had just gotten out of the shower when Libby had stopped him with that steamy kiss. She was dressed and about to head out. He looked at the form-fitting blue dress and high heels and considered. "On the other hand … "

She stood on her tiptoes to place a kiss on his nose. "Nope, we've got to go. I'll see you after though," she said with a smile. He watched her walk away and wrapped a towel around his waist. He headed over to the window and watched as the limo pulled up to the curb, right on time. A couple minutes later, Libby came outside with her evening bag in her hand and a big smile as she approached the limousine. He'd ordered it for her but had only said that he'd have a car waiting. She looked up at the window and saw him and blew him a kiss before climbing in. He smiled and went back to getting ready.

Libby slid into the limousine and looked around, impressed. She'd ridden in a limo before, of course. She'd had the typical American prom experience. But that had been ages ago, and they'd fit as many couples as they could in the limo to save money. She'd been wedged tightly between her date and her best friend Rose. She smiled when Rose was the first one to be picked up. Her friend slid in with a wide smile.

"This brings back memories," Rose said with a laugh. "Although

I don't remember champagne the first time around."

"Your parents would have killed us," Libby said, referring to Rose's staunchly conservative parents. They had been teetotalers from way back and had spent much of Rose's childhood and adolescence preaching the danger of doing anything that might resemble fun. Of course, Rose had gotten very good at living two lives—the goody two shoes at home and the wild one everywhere else. Dillon slid in after her.

"Her parents are something else," she said with a shake of her head.

"I guess they still haven't adjusted?" Libby asked. Rose and Dillon had only recently been public about their relationship, to Rose's parents' consternation. Of course, Rose had always been bisexual, but her parents had been the last to know.

"Nope. Firmly in denial," Rose replied, opening the champagne with a pop. "I expected that though."

"We've decided it's easier just to accept them for who they are, even if they can't do the same for us. My parents have been cool about it though," Dillon told her.

"They would adopt me if they could," Rose said with a smile. She'd worn a short black dress and had braided her red and blonde hair into an updo that seemed to set off her smokey eyes, heavy with eye liner for an evening out. Dillon sat beside her in a red dress with only a strap at one shoulder. It set off her olive skin and dark hair, which she had braided to one side. They were both wearing killer shoes that Libby took a few minutes to admire.

"How are your parents with Seth?" Dillon asked when Libby finally took a break from her exclamations over the shoes.

"Oh, they like him okay. That's the best I'll get," she said with a laugh. "They're fairly disinterested in everything but travel at the moment."

"That must hurt," Dillon said, reaching out to pat Libby's hand.

"Well, I'm used to it," Libby said with a shrug.

"But Keely's a peach," Rose pointed out, as the limo pulled up to pick up Lindy and Beth where they were waiting at Lindy's house. Keely was on the porch holding Maya and waved as they drove off. She'd insisted on staying behind to babysit.

"She really is," Libby said with a smile as the women piled in.

"Is Rachel coming?" Beth asked.

"We're getting Rachel and Faith on the way after we pick up Jenna and Presley. Gloria couldn't make it. Layla's working," Libby explained.

"So … what are we doing anyway?" Lindy asked. "And will there be strippers?"

"We've got dinner and dancing tonight. If you really want to hit a strip club, I don't care," Libby said with a laugh. "But we're checking in at the hotel first."

"I'm good with just dancing. What do you have planned tomorrow?"

"Well, there might be itineraries. You'll see."

When they got to the upscale Atlanta hotel, they all separated to check into their rooms. They'd gotten adjoining rooms on the same floor, two women to each. Rose and Dillon, naturally, were sharing a room with Jenna and Presley in an adjoining room. Libby and Rachel were sharing an adjoining room with Beth and Faith. Lindy would share with her mother when she arrived. They each went into their room and then met up in Libby's suite where she was handing out goody bags and itineraries.

"Did my mom help with this?" Lindy demanded.

"Of course," Libby said. "I made her one, too. We're sending a car to pick up her and Maya and bring them here for the night, too, so you don't have to go home. Besides, we don't want your mom to miss out on the fun tomorrow," she said as she waved the itinerary in front of her.

"Oh my God," Beth said with a gasp. "Brunch? Spa treatments? Sounds like heaven," she said, flopping back to lay on Libby's bed. "Best weekend ever!"

"I know Keely is missing out tonight so we're covering room service for her dinner, and I have the spa appointments staggered so she can have one, too.

"She's going to love it," Lindy told her.

"We're all going to love it," Rachel said with a happy sigh.

"What are Seth and the guys doing?" Jenna asked curiously.

"They're staying here, too, but they're coming a little later. Dinner and drinks at a club, I think, and then they're making a day of it tomorrow, too."

"And we can pick our spa treatment?" Presley asked curiously.

"You can pick your massage type, but we're all getting massages, facials, and a mani/pedi combo. Of course, you can switch the massage out for a body wrap, if you prefer it."

"Layla will hate to have missed it," Presley told her.

"I'm sending a voucher for her. We didn't want anyone to miss out."

"That's the sweetest," Beth said with a sigh.

"We just want everyone to have a good time."

"Is Theodore going to the stag party?" Lindy asked.

"Oh yeah," Presley said with a laugh. "I think he was just excited to be invited."

"They're sweet together," Beth commented.

"If everyone is ready, we can head out to dinner," Libby told them. They made a few last minute makeup touch-ups and set off— just as the limo was pulling up to pick up Seth.

***

"Nice ride," Dean commented as he slid in.

"It's not bad. Just give me a sec." He hopped out with a large gift bag and headed up to his mom on the porch. He gave her the gift bag and some instructions that made her grin before getting back in.

"What was that about?"

"We're sending a car to pick her and Maya up. They'll stay with Lindy at the hotel so she can get the full spa treatment tomorrow."

"Where's my goody bag?" Dean demanded.

"Never mind that," Seth said with a laugh. "Let's pick up the rest of the guys and go. Libby left about an hour ago, and we need to check into the hotel before we go out."

"You getting cold feet yet?"

"Not even a little. I'd marry her right now."

"Can't say I blame you," Dean commented. He'd liked Libby from the start. He might have thought about hitting on her, but Seth had started dating her first. "Good thing you called dibs."

Seth rolled his eyes. "When are you marrying my sister again?"

"Whenever she'll have me. Which I'm hoping will be sooner rather than later, but you know Lindy."

"Yeah, I do. Good luck with that."

"Hey, she asked me to marry her so it's not like she's going to change her mind."

"So what's the hold up?"

"Beats me. But I wish she'd hurry it up."

***

Libby was the last one to be dropped back home, her limo pulling up as Seth's left. She got out with a sigh and thanked the driver. Seth was sitting on the porch waiting, two cups of coffee sitting beside him. She sank down next to him with a sigh and rested her head on his shoulder. He passed a cup of coffee over to her, which she accepted gratefully.

"How long have you been back?"

"Just in time to make coffee," he said into her hair.

"How did it go?"

"It was good. Missed you," he murmured. "How was yours?"

"Blissful," she sighed. "But I missed you, too. So, who all is still hung over?"

"Lucas, a little. But we warned him. And Theodore." Libby sat up and looked at him in surprise. "But he said it was worth it."

"Well, that's good. Keely was so pleased we included her. I can't believe she thought we'd just leave her out and let her babysit," Libby said with a roll of her eyes.

"I'm glad you like my mom."

"I don't like her," Libby corrected him. "I *love* her. She's just the best."

"In a week, we'll be married."

"I know," she said, putting her coffee down and leaning in to kiss him. He smoothed a hand down her hair and then threaded his fingers through it.

"Come inside."

"Coffee will get cold," she murmured.

"I'll make us more," he promised.

"Okay," she agreed, letting him lead her inside.

When the door closed behind them, he spun her around and against the door, fusing his mouth to hers. She let out a sigh and sank into him, wrapping her arms around him and holding on. "Miss me?" she asked when her mouth was free.

"Were you this sure before?" Seth asked. "With Collin?" He hadn't wanted to ask. Hadn't wanted to invoke her ex-husband's name now or at any other time near the wedding. He knew she had feelings for him and probably always would. Once, he'd almost let it destroy them. He *had* let it destroy them before he'd come to his senses.

"No," Libby told him honestly. "I've never been this sure of anything."

She drew his mouth back to hers and tried to show him. She knew Collin was a sore spot for him. Collin had come back while she and Seth were dating, hoping that they could fix their broken marriage. She'd turned him down, but Seth couldn't get past the fact that she still had feelings for him. They'd been apart for months when he'd finally come back to her, something she had never imagined would happen. She drew the kiss out, letting it deepen. He lifted her up in his arms smoothly, and she gasped.

"Nice move."

"Thanks. In a week, I can carry you over the threshold."

"When we get back from the honeymoon anyway." They were scheduled to spend ten days in Italy. She'd already started packing.

"I'd marry you right now."

"You'll marry me Saturday," she reminded him and laughed, drawing his mouth back to hers.

***

Beth let herself in with a sigh. Jill and Rebecca had agreed to watch Mr. Darcy in her absence. They were bringing him over later and then staying for a movie night. She'd gone to their speed dating event, and it had certainly been interesting, to say the least. She hadn't met anyone, but Rebecca had. She'd ended up with the phone number of the event organizer, and Jill had chatted up their Uber driver, to some success. Beth hadn't been impressed with the choices, but it had still been fun. She'd gotten to have dinner with her friends and had a few interesting, albeit awkward, conversations.

She'd decided over the weekend that she'd try dating again. After all, she hadn't dated anyone in a while. She still liked to occasionally date, even if she wasn't looking for a relationship. Plus, she thought it might be a good time to get under to get over, as Rebecca told her.

She'd spilled out the whole sorry tale about how she and Jamie had always been friends and how she was ruining it with *feelings*.

They'd sympathized. She'd shown them pictures of Jamie and of Ansley and explained how much she actually *liked* Ansley, which made it harder. They'd understood and offered her support. Jill thought it was great that she was willing to give them space so she wouldn't interfere. Rebecca suggested she find a nice, handsome distraction to help her get over it.

Beth didn't think it was a bad idea. In fact, during their movie night, they were going to help her set up a dating profile. Rebecca was a self-proclaimed expert, and Jill was ready to update her own profile as well, now that she'd been successful at ignoring Mark for the last couple of weeks.

Well, at least she already had a date to the wedding on Saturday, she thought. That would be one event she wouldn't have to get through alone. Besides, Lucas was attractive, and nice enough. But if she was going to get over Jamie, she'd have to make a real effort. Online dating it is, she thought with a shake of her head. She'd have to explain it all to Mr. Darcy when he got home.

Chapter 16

Seth took a deep breath. This was it. They had stayed the night at the farmhouse the night before. He had stayed on one side of the inn, and Libby had stayed on the other. Their out of town family members had booked rooms there, too, and the others were all coming in the morning. Seth had already done a walk-through to see how it was all coming along. They were getting married under a large oak tree on the property. The chairs were already set up and ready to go by the time he'd finished his coffee and a small breakfast in his room. He'd already walked into the garden to see how the reception was shaping up. They were having a mimosa bar and brunch after the ceremony.

He was already dressed in his charcoal suit with the dark plum tie and wondered what Libby was doing. He was tempted to find Lindy and get her to find out, but she insisted on hanging out with the best men since she was technically one of them. She'd found a charcoal suit with a skirt and had on a matching plum tie. He thought it suited her. She looked a little fierce, but then she always had. Of course, he'd had to tell Dean to keep his hands off his sister so they could get to the ceremony on time. They'd laughed, but he'd been afraid they were going to be late.

Of course, they were early. He was waiting, ready to walk out as soon as all the guests had taken their seats. He'd never been ready for anything more in his life. He had screwed it all up once before. He wasn't going to make that mistake ever again.

***

Libby looked in the mirror and took a deep breath.

"You look beautiful, dear," her mother said, patting her arm and then moving off to help Faith with her zipper. Keely sidled up beside her.

"You really do look lovely," she told Libby warmly. She met her eyes in the mirror. "Nerves?"

"A little. I've done this before."

"I know you have." She held her hand. "You know I did, too, before Theodore." Libby remembered that Keely had been married once before. Seth's father had left when they were so small they couldn't remember him. He was living on the West Coast now, and they still had no contact with him. Keely had only remarried recently. "It's different when it's the right one."

"I know. I know Seth is the right one. I'm ready now."

She turned and took another look in the mirror at the deep plum dress with its sweetheart neckline and open back. She looked down, sure that this was the dress and knowing, in her heart, that Seth was the man for her. She looked back up at the flowers in her hair with its soft waves pulled to the side over her shoulder. She'd chosen not to have a veil and not to walk down the aisle escorted by her father. She wouldn't be given away. She was choosing this freely. She would walk toward Seth and their future together on her own.

The music started, and the horse and carriage pulled up where she was waiting. It would take her down to where they were waiting. Nat King Cole's voice crooning *Unforgettable* floated out to her on the short drive, and soon she was disembarking and heading down the aisle toward Seth whose eyes were locked on hers. His eyes stayed on hers, and hers on his, and every last thought of Collin and the last wedding were banished.

There was only Seth.

And her.

And their future together.

She passed her bouquet of sunflowers to Rose who stood beside her and stood in front of Seth as the last words floated away. They faced each other until the last note and then turned toward the minister. She smiled as they faced her and began the service. They'd chosen slightly nontraditional vows and said them softly to each other.

I take you to be my best friend, my faithful partner, and my one true love. I promise to encourage you and inspire you and to love you truly through good times and bad. I will forever be there to laugh with you, to lift you up when you are down, and to love you unconditionally through all of our adventures in life together.

They repeated the words, their eyes leaving each others only long enough to retrieve the rings and put them on. The wedding set was inscribed with the words *Ever thine, ever mine, ever ours*—a snippet from a letter from Beethoven to his "immortal beloved." Seth showed her the inscription and then slid the ring on her finger.

Keely reached over and took Theodore's hand in hers, holding it tightly as tears sprang to her eyes. She thought about holding Seth for the first time. The first time he took steps on his own. His belly laugh as a toddler playing on the floor with his sister. His first day of school. All those big moments leading up to this.

Lindy stood beside her fiance and watched her brother get married. This was right. Libby was perfect for him. She reached over and took Dean's hand. She wasn't ready yet, but soon. Soon, it would be them. He squeezed her hand as they watched Seth slide the ring onto Libby's finger.

Beth sighed happily as she stood beside Rachel and watched the exchange of vows and rings. She was a sucker for a happy ending. She'd come with Lucas who was waiting for her in his seat. She glanced his way and caught his eye.

Lucas watched her and thought that bringing a date to a wedding could be tricky. He didn't want her to get the wrong idea. On the other hand, he might get points for romance if he played his cards right. He smiled at her, and she smiled back, wondering what he was thinking before redirecting her attention to the bride and groom.

Jamie didn't realize that Beth was coming with Lucas. It was strange to think of her dating since she'd been so resolute not to date the entire time he'd known her. He looked over to find Ansley in the seats just behind Lucas and couldn't help but notice his eyes on Beth the whole time. What was that about anyway, he thought, as he refocused in on Seth and Libby. He could see Beth just on the other side. He met her eyes, briefly, but she glanced away. He wondered why she was being so weird around him these days. She'd been his best friend. Until lately, anyway, he thought.

Rose liked weddings but wasn't sure she'd have one of her own. She just wasn't that traditional. She and Rachel stood together and remembered Libby's first wedding, to Collin. Rachel hadn't had any doubts, but Rose had wondered a little. It had been such an intense, whirlwind romance. Still, neither had doubts this time.

The only thing that Rachel doubted was if her own marriage would last another year. After all, even now Alec was in his seat checking his watch. She wondered, not for the first time, if it was work, a game, or even somebody else that was waiting for him after the ceremony.

The vows and rings were exchanged and after a brief blessing on the couple and a long kiss, *Unforgettable* started to play again as they walked back toward the waiting horse and carriage. Beth understood that Seth and Libby would have photographs first, but she had her eye on the mimosa bar. She waited for her turn to walk down the aisle behind the happy couple. Dean escorted Rose, followed by Lindy and Rachel, and then Jamie met Beth to escort her down the aisle. She placed her arm through his and tried to squash the feelings rising. She looked up at him and then away. *This felt right, and it was wrong so it couldn't be right, right?* she thought to herself in confusion. The guests followed behind, walking over the aisle covered in lavender to the garden reception.

When they made it to the other end of the aisle, Beth slipped her arm out of Jamie's.

"I'll see you at the reception," she said with a brief smile before walking over to meet up with Lucas. Jamie was flummoxed that she hadn't even wanted to walk as far as the reception with him, but he shrugged it off and went to find Ansley instead. Dean and Lindy were walking up just ahead of them, and Rose and Dillon were following just behind, their heads close together as they discussed the wedding.

"That was beautiful," Ansley said with a smile. "I love her dress. I would have expected her to go with traditional white, but it was perfect."

"It worked," Jamie agreed. "I'm glad they didn't go with a traditional wedding song."

"What they chose seemed to suit them. Have they been together long?"

"Not as long as you'd think," he said with a smile. He'd told her that they'd broken up at one point and later got back together, but he didn't elaborate.

"Beth looked beautiful. I love the bridesmaid dresses."

"Lindy liked them, too, but she decided to go with the tux."

"It suited her. She looked very impressive." Lindy intimidated her, just a little. She'd launched into an interrogation every time she saw her. After seeing her interact with the others, she decided it was just a personality quirk and nothing personal, but sometimes she wondered.

***

Seth and Libby finished with the last of the photographs and headed in to brunch. "I ate a little earlier, but I'm starving," Seth admitted, as they walked in to cheers.

"Me, too. What are the odds of getting a mimosa any time soon?"

"You distract them, and I'll grab drinks," he said, making a beeline for the table.

"You're married five minutes, and he leaves you on your own," Dean said with a shake of his head.

"I'm the distraction so he can get drinks."

"Well, you're a beautiful distraction. I'm happy to escort you to your seat, and then we can all eat before the dancing starts."

"Thank you, Dean." She made her rounds, speaking to each guest as she navigated her way through the room, her eyes tracking Seth who was doing the same with two champagne glasses filled nearly to the brim with mimosas.

"We made it," he said, when at last they sank down into their chairs. "A few speeches, and we can finally eat. I spied a waffle bar," he whispered in her ear. "And donuts. Oh my God, donuts," he breathed.

"That's not all," Libby said with a smile. "It's a pretty loaded brunch selection."

"I'm eating one of everything," he said ardently, as she laughed and leaned against his shoulder.

"Give that girl some space," Keely insisted, coming around to hug Libby. "Welcome, officially, to the family."

"That's so nice," Libby said, tearing up.

"No crying," Lindy said sharply. "You'll screw up your mascara."

"Waterproof," Libby offered with a smile.

"Smart girl," Dean said, as he plopped down in his seat with Maya.

"*My* girl," Seth insisted, taking her hand.

"Y'all are just the sweetest," Marnie told them, coming up to the table with a big smile and her handsome husband Patrick trailing behind. "Congratulations," she told Seth sincerely, hugging him and then turning to Libby. "I'm just so happy for you." She started to tear up.

"Sorry. Pregnancy hormones," Patrick explained. "She does this all the time. I'm trying not to take it personally that she's crying at her ex's wedding." They all laughed.

"Ancient history," Seth returned with a smile. "We're just glad you could make it."

"How far along are you?" Libby asked with interest.

"Six months. Just over now," Marnie returned brightly. "At least I'm finished with the morning sickness. But I'm as big as a house and going to get bigger with twins," she told them with a rueful smile.

"Twins? Oh my God," Libby breathed. "That's so exciting! You look lovely." She had once been intimidated by Marnie. After all, she'd been with Seth over six years. They were each other's first love. But then they'd met and had become friends of sorts. Lindy and Marnie were still close, and they all hung out when Marnie came to town.

"Thank you," Marnie said, flushing and glancing down at her growing belly. "I don't feel it, but I appreciate it."

"She's perfect," Patrick said warmly, putting an arm around her. "We're going to grab some juice and something to eat, but you save me a dance."

The dancing began after brunch, and they'd chosen an Ed Sheeran song for the first dance. Seth and Libby had taken ballroom dance lessons, and Beth watched with a sigh. It was all so perfect. She was perfectly happy being single, she thought to herself, but every now and then she missed romance like this and wondered what it would be like to marry someone you knew was right for you. Her eyes drifted over and caught Jamie's, and she quickly looked away.

"I'm going to find a restroom. I'll be back in a minute," she told Lucas, heading out, as the bride and groom finished up the first dance.

She took a few minutes and came back to find Jamie waiting by the entrance. "Dance with me?"

"Won't Ansley mind? You're supposed to dance with your date."

"I told her I had to dance with you first," Jamie explained.

"Lindy isn't dancing with Rachel."

"That's because Rachel is dancing with her husband, Lindy is dancing with Dean, and Rose is dancing with Dillon," Jamie said patiently.

"Then I should dance with Lucas, and you should dance with Ansley," Beth told him, starting to brush passed him.

He took her arm and leaned in before she could walk by. "Do you have some kind of problem with me?" he asked, anger flaring in his eyes.

"No," she said belligerently, stepping away.

"Then prove it." He held out a hand. She took it, but only because the challenge was out there, and her blood was boiling. She shouldn't have to prove a damn thing she thought angrily.

They stepped out on to the dance floor, and she felt his hand around her waist as he pulled her closer than she thought was strictly necessary. She looked around for Lucas, hoping she might signal him to cut in, but he was talking to Faith over at the mimosa bar. She wasn't jealous, but she was annoyed. *What was the point of bringing a date if he wasn't going to be on hand for a rescue*, she thought in frustration. She looked around for Ansley, too, and noticed that she was having a drink and chatting with Libby's parents. Dammit!

"Are you going to tell me what your problem is or just stew about it?" Jamie asked her, accurately guessing that she was trying to figure out an exit strategy.

"I don't have a problem. You're the one with the problem," Beth insisted, angrily, looking up at him. "You don't have to be so damn *bossy*," she hissed. "You could dance with your date, and I could dance with mine."

"You and Lucas have some kind of thing going?"

"What? No! That's not the point!"

"Then what is your point?" he asked, leaning down to ask her quietly.

"There's no need for all … this," she said, gesturing to them dancing.

"Beth," he said quietly. "I know you. You love romance and dancing and weddings. You're my best friend, and I want to dance with you. Why does that make you so angry?"

"I'm not angry," she countered in frustration.

"Really? Because you just stomped on my foot for the fifth time."

"Well, dammit, I'm sorry," she told him. "I just … I need … air."

"We're in a garden, Beth," he deadpanned, gesturing around.

She looked at him in disgust and began walking toward the parking lot before the song even ended. He shot a glance over toward Ansley, who was turned away talking to Libby's parents, and followed Beth.

"Are you okay? What's going on?"

"I said I need *space*," she told him angrily. She'd walked to the far edge of the parking lot, where he'd followed.

"I know something's wrong. I don't understand why you won't talk to me!"

"Just let me *be*," she insisted, putting a hand up to her temple where a tension headache was brewing.

"Fine," Jamie hissed, stepping as close to her as he could manage. "You want to be left alone, I'll go. But dammit, Beth, you ought to trust me enough to tell me what the hell is up with you," he said, his face as close to hers as he could get.

She stood there, trembling, and understood, all of a sudden, exactly how all those characters in all those movies could go from an argument to sex. The tension vibrated unseen between them like a taut wire, and the heat rose to her skin, spreading like wildfire. She inhaled sharply, and he shook his head in frustration.

"I'm going," he insisted. "I'm done with this." She watched him go and leaned on the nearest parked car, Lindy's beat up old Jeep she'd named Francis. She took a deep breath and then another, steadying herself.

"Hey, I've been looking for you everywhere," Lucas said from a few feet away. "Everything okay?"

"Yeah, it's fine. Everything is fine. I just needed a minute."

"Want to dance?" he asked, admiring the flush in her cheek and wondering if he could talk her into leaving a little early.

"Of course," she said with an over-bright smile.

Chapter 17

Beth woke up and nearly groaned aloud. Mr. Darcy was standing on the bed beside her growling at Lucas, who was fast asleep on the other side of the bed. She rolled over with a sigh. It had seemed like a good idea at the time with Jamie dancing with Ansley. They'd left early, and she had assumed, wrongly, that Jamie hadn't noticed them going.

They'd had a few drinks when they'd gotten back to her house and then had found themselves in bed where Lucas had thought he'd expertly steered her, but she'd been planning all along. After all, she'd known the moment he smiled at her during the wedding what direction his thoughts had headed. She wasn't going to sleep with him. Absolutely not. But then she'd had that argument with Jamie, and Lucas had swooped in right after while she was still frustrated and aroused.

God, she thought. She'd just used Lucas because she was turned on by Jamie. If that wasn't messed up, she wasn't sure what was. Of course, it's not like Lucas had minded, she thought watching him sleep.

"I know," she told Mr. Darcy. "Let's go out." She slipped into her clothes and took Mr. Darcy outside where he glared at her every time he peed on a bush. "Hey, I got back as early as I could. You could have used your doggy door, you know," she told him, gesturing to the house where Lucas was standing in a pair of jeans only.

"Oh, hey."

"Were you talking to the dog?"

"Who else would I be talking to out here?"

"I don't know anyone else who has conversations with dogs," he told her with a smile, walking out to her where she stood in the leggings and tunic top she'd thrown on to come outside. It wasn't her usual sort of outfit, and he looked at her, wondering what she'd be like if she wore clothes like this all the time rather than what he considered thrift-store-chic. He sauntered to her and pulled her in for another kiss.

She didn't resist, but her response was less enthusiastic than it had been on mimosas followed by white wine before noon. It was getting later in the afternoon, and she was trying to think of a way to get rid of him before nightfall. The sex had been good, but there were hours until dark, and she thought of the hours of conversation that would have to fill the time between now and morning.

"You know, I was thinking I could cook us something to eat or maybe we could order something in."

"Sure. We could do that," she agreed, resigning herself to an evening of awkward conversation.

"You know, we don't have to talk," he told her, pulling her in. "How about we grab something to eat and then go back to bed?" She remembered then that the sex was maybe a little better than just *good*.

"Okay," she agreed, meeting his lips for a kiss that was warmer than the last. "If you insist. But maybe we could go back to bed first, then eat."

"I like the way you think," he said, pulling her inside. Mr. Darcy watched them go with disapproval and headed over to Pemberley with a sniff.

***

Jamie had watched Beth and Lucas leave. He wasn't sure what she was so damn mad about, but he knew exactly what was going on there. Well, fine, he thought. If she wanted to sleep with Lucas, it wasn't his business. But damn, he thought, his expression darkening, she could at least have talked to him.

"Are you okay?" Ansley asked him. Jamie didn't seem aware of it, but she'd watched him dance with Beth and then follow her outside. He'd come back in positively glowering, and she could tell he was still stewing about it long after Beth had left with Lucas. "Want to talk about it?"

"Talk about what?"

"Beth, of course," she said, kindly.

"What about Beth?" he asked, dumbstruck. She sighed.

"The fact that she's avoiding you. The fact that you had some kind of argument in the parking lot. The fact that she went home with Lucas. The fact that you're obviously hurt and angry about it all." She ticked them off, one by one.

He looked at her, impressed by how astute she was. She'd summarized it all breezily and then just watched him. "I just don't know what's wrong with her. She's been so angry with me when she's not avoiding me."

"Oh, Jamie," Ansley said with a sigh. "You don't know," she told him with a shake of her head, as if he was hopelessly clueless.

"Know what?"

"She has feelings for you."

"Wait—she has what?" Jamie asked. "That's not what's going on."

"Really? She stops spending time with you when we start dating. She watches you when you're not looking. She is angry when you confront her about her behavior. Can you seriously not see it?" She watched it dawn on him and then saw a curious expression cross his face, fleetingly.

"Oh," she continued. "Oh, well, I didn't see that coming. I mean, I should have. Obviously," she said with a little laugh.

"See what?"

"I'm the one that's been clueless. You have feelings for her. And didn't know she felt the same. Well ... " She cleared her throat. "I knew we weren't a serious thing. I mean, I like you, but I didn't think you were it for me. But she's definitely it for you," she said calmly, with only a little sadness in her voice.

"It's not like that," Jamie said, objecting and trying to find a way to put the conversation back on solid ground.

"Isn't it? I'm not mad. Not really. I can see you didn't even realize it. Well, now you do. I wish you'd have realized it sooner, but you didn't. Anyway, you should probably go over there and tell her."

"Maybe I should. I'm sorry, Ansley. Really."

"I know," she told him, wondering how she always ended up with the most emotionally unavailable men.

"Do you think we could at least stay friends?"

"Don't push it," she told him with a small smile. "I don't know if I'm that okay with it. And don't you dare apologize again," she warned, as she saw him open his mouth. He closed it sheepishly and started to walk away. She sighed. She looked around the wedding and tried to figure out how to make a graceful exit, all things considered.

***

When the knock sounded at the door, Beth rolled out of bed with a happy sigh. Okay, the sex was impressive. She had to admit it. Lucas had left about an hour ago, and she'd stayed in bed relaxing. When she heard the knock, she wondered if Lucas had left something behind. She grabbed an over-sized button up shirt and put it on in a hurry and headed to the door. She opened it, realizing only at the last minute that if it had been Lucas, Mr. Darcy would have been barking at the door.

Jamie stood there and took in her messy hair and large shirt. She shifted awkwardly, realizing for the first time that she hadn't even slid back into her underwear in her hurry to get to the door. Of course, the shirt came down to her knees, but that didn't cover up the fact that she was bra-less with sex hair. She tried to act normal but knew she failed miserably.

"Hey. What's going on?" she asked him, leaning on the door, while Mr. Darcy trotted out happily to sit beside him.

"Nothing," he said shortly, taking in the situation. "I just wanted to make sure you were okay. You seemed upset when you left." He waited a beat. "You seem fine now." With that, he turned around and headed for his truck.

"Jamie, wait ..."

"You might want to grab some pants if you're coming outside," he told her and waved to her neighbor who was out watering her garden and watching it all with a look of interest on his face.

"Dammit," she muttered. Of course, by the time she'd run in and thrown on pants, he had driven off. She tried calling, but he didn't answer. She texted him and then waited for him to respond. He could at least say *something*, she thought in frustration.

***

"Oh. My. God. Just tell us one more time. What were you wearing when you opened the door?" Jill asked with a laugh, refilling her wine glass.

"It's not funny," Beth said, a smile tugging up the corner of her mouth.

"Well, it kind of is. The sex had to be pretty good then?" Rebecca asked, needing confirmation. "Like how good? On a scale of *ohmygod* to *meh*."

"Whatever happened to 1-10?" Beth asked.

"That's boring," Rebecca said with a grin. "So?"

"It was more like *ohmygodohmygodohmygod*. But then Jamie showed up and ugh!"

"Yeah, you don't have to explain *ugh*," Jill told her sympathetically, refilling her glass as well. "What did he say?"

"He all but said he knew I had just had sex and then left," Beth said with a helpless shrug.

"Meanwhile your neighbor is watering the flowers and enjoying the show," Rebecca said with a laugh. "Oh, I'd have paid to see it."

"Thanks for your support," Beth said with a roll of her eyes.

"Well, it wasn't your bright and shining moment, but still. Great sex. That has to count for something," Rebecca said philosophically. "You going to see him again?"

"Lucas? I don't know. Maybe." When Rebecca looked at her blankly, she went on to say, "We don't have anything in common. There's literally nothing to talk about."

"Then don't talk. Or, you know, dirty talk. I bet he can do that."

"Oh yeah. Still."

"I get it," Jill said. "You want connection. I've missed that, since Mark."

"Ugh," Rebecca groaned. "Not Mark," she objected. "He was such a tool!"

"He had his moments. But in the bedroom ..."

"Yeah, he just used a different tool there," Rebecca reminded her. "But still—a tool."

"I'm just saying that a connection, not just a sexual one, can be nice."

"It's true," Beth agreed. "Not that I've had that in ages."

"Have you been celibate?" Rebecca asked curiously.

"God, no. I just haven't had anyone regular in a minute. Lucas might be good for a booty call, but it'd be nice if we could talk in between. Even his pillow talk is sorely lacking."

"And now there's the Jamie complication," Jill pointed out.

"Yeah. I'd hoped that it would all go unnoticed. Not that he can complain, since he has a girlfriend and all."

"True. Men and their double standards," Rebecca said in disgust.

"Haven't you ever had that? The connection?" Beth asked her.

Rebecca and Jill exchanged a look. "Well, there was Ian."

"Another rat," Jill explained.

"A real silver fox. He was dreamy though. We had sex in the library—I mean, fantasy level."

"So what was the problem?"

"Oh, selfish. You know, the usual. And married," Rebecca admitted.

"Married? You never said he was married?" Jill said, aghast.

"That's because I didn't know. At first, at any rate. Then, I did, and I couldn't un-know it. So I'd try to get out of it, and he'd reel me back in. It went on longer after I found out than I'm proud of. Anyway, I felt like such a fool. Of course, he was married. It explained so much, once I found out," Rebecca said, reaching for the bottle of wine. "But there was a connection." She shrugged. "Men can manufacture that. I'm sure he had a connection with his wife, too."

Beth reached out and patted her hand. "So, no one else?"

"Not really. Not for a long time. Anyway, I'd rather have excellent sex than a half-assed relationship."

"Here, here," Jill called out with a laugh, raising her glass and clinking them with the others. "To mind-blowing, phenomenal sex," she intoned solemnly.

"To multiple orgasms," Rebecca said with a laugh.

"Oh, I'll drink to that," Beth told them, holding up her glass. "Cheers!"

Chapter 18

Keely sat down to a cup of tea in the kitchen with a sigh. The afternoon had wound down efficiently enough. One baby shower had run longer than expected, but she never minded that. She'd booked the terrace for them for the full afternoon so they wouldn't feel rushed, a fact that resulted in a sizeable tip for the servers. Naomi had helped out, but she hadn't bothered to ask Beth who'd been frazzled all week.

Of course, she'd noticed some of the drama at the wedding. Theodore had caught part of it and filled her in, and then she'd watched the rest. Then she'd heard some of it from Lindy who had heard bits and pieces of it from Dean. She got the general idea of what had happened. Beth hadn't said anything, of course. She was nonchalant about the whole thing, willing only to talk about what a beautiful wedding it had been. Keely kept her peace, knowing that Beth would talk about it only if and when she wanted to.

Seth and Libby were almost back from their honeymoon. They were flying in on the thirtieth so that they could be there for Maya's first official Halloween. She'd be nearly four months old and would be the cutest Ruth Bader Ginsberg ever! Keely had laughed when Lindy had told her what costume they'd chosen. Apparently, it was between that and Sophia from the *Golden Girls*. Her daughter never had picked out the typical costumes. There was the year that she was the Paper Bag Princess. Of course, that was *last year*, she thought ruefully. It was always something interesting. And empowering, of course. But she'd wanted to raise strong children, and she had.

They had planned a welcome home celebration at the farm. Once she finished her cup of tea, she had to head home and get started. She could usually count on Beth to help out, but she was far too scattered these days. Presley and Lindy had been quick to lend a hand, and Rose and Dillon offered to come by early to help set up. They already had a large outdoor farm table and chairs, but if the weather didn't cooperate, they'd simply move the party inside. She sighed and noticed Lindy watching her from the doorway.

"Everything okay?"

"Good as gold. I'm ready to hear all about their trip to Italy, just as soon as they're safely home."

"Libby's already uploaded about a thousand pictures."

"It's not the same. Besides, I miss them," Keely admitted.

"Yeah, I do, too. I think this is the longest Dean and Seth have been apart ever. Dean's been driving me crazy. Soon as Seth gets back, they need to work out a play date and get out of my hair."

"I heard that," Dean said from the doorway. "I thought we were getting ready for a party." "It's not until tomorrow. Just come on over in the morning," Keely told him.

"Your daughter doesn't really do mornings. Nor does her daughter," Dean reminded her, indicating Maya who was asleep in her carrier. "She'll have us up all night."

"Fine," Keely said with a laugh. "Let's see what we can get done tonight. You'll stay for dinner, too. Theodore is cooking, and his girls are coming over. There's always plenty."

"I was hoping you'd say that."

"I know you were," Keely said as Lindy mouthed "So obvious" in his direction.

"I saw that," Keely said with a laugh as she walked out.

"You see everything," Lindy said with a roll of her eyes, as she followed. Dean lifted the carrier easily and trailed behind.

"Want us to bring anything?"

"Just yourselves," Keely said. "And maybe see if Beth wants to come. That girl is driving me crazy."

***

Lindy strode into the bookstore with determination. "Hey," she told Beth. "Stop annoying your aunt and come to dinner. Hey, Naomi."

"Hey, Lindy," Naomi said, rolling her eyes toward Beth.

"I'm just going to go home."

"What's your problem?" Lindy asked. "Why are you annoying people?"

"Like who?"

"My mother, for one. Your staff, I'm guessing, by the way Naomi is staying out of the way."

"You said it, not me," Naomi called out from the shelves where she was ostensibly stocking books but actually waiting for Beth to clear out.

"See? What happened with you and Lucas? Did he upset you?"

"No! Of course not."

"But you slept with him, right? Was it awful?"

"Apparently, it was really great sex," Naomi offered.

"Hey, you! Stock shelves."

"Right, boss," Naomi said with a laugh she tried to disguise as a cough.

"Who gets grouchy about great sex?" Lindy demanded.

"Not me," Dean said from the doorway, as Beth groaned.

"Go away."

"Who'd you have great sex with?"

"Lucas," Lindy told him helpfully, as Beth rolled her eyes.

"Oh, good," Dean said. "I'll tell him he gets good reviews. Hey, Naomi," he said, over his shoulder, where Naomi was trying to quietly move to the stock room. They hadn't seen each other much since they'd stopped dating some time ago.

"Hey, Dean," Naomi said with a smile. She'd been initially pissed that he'd broken things off. Then she'd been determined to get him back. When he started dating Lindy, she'd been angry and then heartbroken. But she'd recovered. They were all friendly enough now, although it was a little awkward sometimes when she and Lindy were there together.

"So, great sex. Why are you annoying people? Shouldn't you be happy about it?" he asked Beth. "Is that a female thing?"

"Not in my experience," Naomi offered, as she edged out of the room.

"Or mine," Lindy said, as the women exchanged a bright smile that they shot toward Dean.

"Thanks. I like a good review myself," he said with a wink.

"He's incorrigible," Lindy told Naomi with a roll of her eyes as she laughed and scooted out of the room.

"It's not about the sex. Which I don't want to talk about."

"I wasn't going to ask for details," Dean pointed out.

"I was." When Beth barked out a laugh, Lindy continued, "Later. Anyway, what's your problem?"

"Jamie came over after."

"Oh my God, did he walk in on the two of you ..."

"No. God, no. Nothing as bad as that. Just, you know, after."

"How long after?" Dean asked curious.

"You know, no pants. Sex hair," Beth said with a shrug.

"Oh my God. Well, he could not have taken that well," Lindy agreed.

"Nope."

"And you haven't talked to him ..." Lindy began.

"Nope."

"Want me to talk to him for you?" Dean offered.

"Nope," Beth and Lindy said at the same time.

"Thanks for the dinner invitation, but really I just want to go home. I'll be at the party tomorrow and will try not to annoy anyone."

"You better not," Lindy warned. "Hey, are you still coming trick or treating with us?"

"Of course. We're going as a ringmaster and a lion," Beth said.

"Cute! Well, we'll have little Chief Justice Ginsberg with us. I'm not sure what the rest of the crew is doing yet, and we're still in discussions."

"Discussions on discussions," Dean said with a laugh. "She won't do sexy cop or sexy maid or any of that. You could wear a paper bag, and you'd still be sexy."

"You said that last year," Lindy said, rolling her eyes.

"And I meant it," Dean said, crossing his heart.

"Okay, we're going now. But we did ask. Can I tell my mom the reign of terror is at an end?" she asked Beth.

"Yeah, I'll get it together. Sorry."

"No problem. I'll call later. About those details."

"Fine. Whatever. Get out," Beth said, laughing.

***

Beth stood on the outskirts of the garden and took a deep breath. The long farm table with benches was already set up with floral centerpieces. Fairy lights were strung up through the trees in the event that the party ran into the evening. Everyone was already milling about the back garden with its pumpkin and roses themed décor. Everyone, Beth thought, included Jamie. She looked around and wondered why he hadn't brought Ansley but then assumed she must be working. Well, she thought, squaring her shoulders, she had promised Lindy and Dean that she would adjust her attitude. After another deep, cleansing breath, she shook off her mood and made a beeline for Libby.

"I'm so glad you're back," Beth told her warmly.

"It's nice to be home," Libby said with a smile, pulling Beth in for a hug. "We had ten days of bliss, but when we came down Main Street, it was like everything just settled in here," she said, tapping her chest over her heart. "Home."

"Have you been home yet?"

"We dropped off our luggage and showered first, but that's about it. We were there long enough to see that Keely had brought by fresh flowers and champagne and had stocked the fridge," Libby told her. "I love her."

"She's good people."

"So ... what did I miss? Catch me up."

"What? Oh, nothing. Everything is pretty much the same as always."

"I've been home all of five minutes, and that's not what I hear."

"What have you heard?"

"Well, I heard about Jamie and Ansley. And I have eyes so I know about you and Lucas. Tell me everything. Spare no detail!"

"You've been talking to Lindy, haven't you?" Beth asked darkly, glaring over at Lindy as she passed, who smiled cheekily back.

"Well, Dean was filling Seth in on a few details. But I saw you leave with Lucas. Is that a thing now?"

"No, it is not. Just the one time. Anyway," she said, waving her hand in dismissal. "What about Jamie and Ansley?"

"Oh, they broke up at the wedding. I thought you'd know that," Libby said, watching Beth carefully. She'd known for a fact that Beth had not known but wanted to gauge her reaction.

"No," Beth said, looking over at Jamie. He was talking to Seth and Dean, a Coke in his hand. He didn't look upset. He just looked—normal. Like Jamie. "We haven't talked much lately."

"Well, anyway, ten days can be a long time around here."

"I guess so," Beth told her absently, wondering how she felt now that Jamie and Ansley weren't together. It didn't really change anything, she thought. She still had feelings, and she was sure he didn't feel the same way. Until they passed, it was probably best that she kept her distance, she thought uncomfortably, missing him with a sharpness that surprised her.

"Everything okay?" Libby asked, reaching out to touch her arm.

"I'm just going to go get a drink," Beth told her, heading inside.

"Well?" Lindy asked when Beth had gone in.

"She knows now. My work here is done."

"How'd she take it?"

"She looked a little sad actually. But she's been watching him—and avoiding him—since she got here."

"Huh," Lindy thought about it. "Keep her inside for a minute. I'll fix that," she said, turning away and taking long strides toward Dean.

Libby headed in, shaking her head. Lindy had some kind of plan in mind. She just hoped it wouldn't backfire. She walked in and saw Beth pouring a tall glass of lemonade. She seemed lost in thought so Libby didn't see the need to engage her in chit chat. Instead, she decided to position herself near the door. She could distract her if she tried to leave, until whatever events Lindy set into motion would begin.

***

Lindy walked over to Dean, scooping up Maya from her carrier on the way. Dean was sitting down on the picnic table by Seth with Jamie standing in front of them. They stopped talking when she walked up and took a minute to admire the baby.

"I'm glad it's going to be a little warmer than we thought. You never can tell this time of year," she said without preamble. Dean automatically reached out for Maya.

"Get your own," she said, swatting his hand away and shifting Maya to her other side.

"That one is mine, if you'll remember."

"She needs to eat soon, and you can't feed her."

"I could if you'd use the pump."

"You use that instrument of torture if you want to, but I'm going to pass," she told him, rolling her eyes and nudging him to move over. She sat down with a sigh. "Jamie, could you go inside and get me a lemonade? I'm parched."

"I can go get it," Dean began, and then caught the look Lindy shot him. "But I'll just go get the diaper bag in case you need anything," he said instead, looking at Seth with his eyebrows raised.

"Thanks," Lindy told him. "Jamie?"

"Sure," Jamie said, wondering what all those looks had been about. He shook his head and walked toward the kitchen as Seth scooted closer to Lindy, ostensibly to look at Maya.

"So what's going on?"

"Nothing," Lindy said smugly.

"Did you send Jamie in there because Beth is inside?" Seth asked. When Lindy just gave him a wide smile, he continued, "I saw you and Libby with your heads together and figured you were plotting something."

"Well, you're smarter than you look."

"Ha. Thanks," Seth said. "And you're nicer than you look," he said, nudging his shoulder into hers. "Now pass the baby. She's not hungry. She's sleeping, which Jamie would have noticed if he hadn't already been looking for an excuse to go inside."

"Can I come back now?" Dean demanded, holding the diaper bag up. "What was that?"

"A push," Lindy said smugly.

"You're crafty," he said, leaning over to kiss her.

"Why aren't you keeping Beth occupied?" Lindy demanded, as Libby walked over to sit down beside Seth.

"Don't need to. I came out as Jamie came in."

"Good," Lindy said with a nod. "Now when are we eating?"

Chapter 19

In the kitchen, the silence stretched out until it seemed to hum in the air between them. Jamie had nodded when he'd come in, and Beth had returned it coolly. Then she'd attempted to scoot out of his way so that he could pour a glass of lemonade, but she'd managed to get stuck between Jamie, the open fridge door, and the counter. Well, stuck, she thought, as in there was no way to get past him without brushing up against him. She stood there, awkwardly, waiting.

"Oh, sorry," Jamie said, looking over at her. He shut the fridge door and carefully stepped to the other side of the kitchen island, giving her a wide berth.

Beth made to leave the room and then remembered her lemonade. She turned around and saw that he was offering it to her already. She started at that, how he always seemed to anticipate her. She'd forgotten that. It had been so long since they'd spent any real time together that she'd forgotten the ease they had. Or had, until she screwed everything up. Her fingers brushed his as she took the glass, and she trembled just enough to slosh lemonade over the side of the glass.

"Sorry," she said automatically. "My fault." She reached over to get a paper towel to clean up the mess, and he just watched her with an inscrutable expression. She almost left the room the second the floor was dry, but then paused. "I heard about you and Ansley. I'm sorry," she offered awkwardly.

"Well, you know. Just one of those things," Jamie returned with a shrug.

"It seemed like it was going so well."

"Yeah, it did," he returned shortly. He watched her, trying to see if what Ansley had said could be true. She didn't seem like she was interested in him. She seemed pained by even a brief conversation with him. "How's Lucas?"

"Oh," Beth said, looking up to meet his eyes. "I wouldn't know. Fine, I guess. You could ask Dean."

"I just thought …" Jamie started and then shook his head. "None of my business," he said turning away to pour the glass of lemonade.

"It was just a …" Beth shrugged her shoulders in dismissal. "Anyway, I haven't talked to him."

"Sorry about the other day," Jamie offered, realizing that his reaction at her home might have been over the top for a friend.

"It's fine," Beth said shortly, awkwardly shifting her weight to the other foot, as she waited for the conversation to be over. She missed the ease they had always had, how she could lean her head against his shoulder or tell him about her week. She sighed, and he looked over at her sharply, as if seeing her for the first time.

"Where's Mr. Darcy?" he asked. Beth looked tired, he thought, and a little sad around the eyes. He wanted to ask her what was wrong but knew she'd be unlikely to tell him.

"The groomer's," she explained, briefly. "I have to go pick him up in a little while." She'd timed the appointment to offer an early escape, in case she needed one.

"I'm going to—"

"Do you want to have a movie night sometime?"

"Oh," Beth said, taking a deep breath. "I don't know that it's a good idea."

"Okay," Jamie said shortly, and she looked up and met his eyes. He looked angry and hurt. "So it was never about me and Ansley then. Just me," he summarized, searing her with his eyes. "Well, that's clear enough," he said, striding out the door and letting it slam shut behind him. Ansley was wrong, he thought. She was just wrong.

Beth looked at the lemonade glass sitting on the counter, full nearly to the brim where he'd over-poured it. She stood and took a few deep breaths, willing the tears back. In the past, she'd have taken the glass out to him, teasing him for being so forgetful. Now she just left it sitting there on the counter and walked away. She went outside and found a place to sit in the sun. She sank into the old porch swing in a corner of the garden and pushed it back and forth.

She thought it should be easier to be friends with Jamie now. She wouldn't have to worry about Ansley. It's just, she thought, that she didn't trust herself. She couldn't tell him the truth. How could they ever come back from it? No, she decided, it would just embarrass him and humiliate her. It was better to just let it all pass and then reach back out. She looked over at him where he was looking anywhere but her direction and realized then that she'd never be able to reach out, not after this. The tears fell then, and she wiped them away quickly.

"Why," Keely asked Jamie quietly, "is Beth crying?"

Jamie was standing by the grill where Keely was talking to Theodore. He'd offered to help and then stood around talking about the farm and the bees they kept. Keely had been quiet until something behind him had gotten her attention. He glanced behind him when she asked and saw Beth sitting by herself on the porch swing, looking down at her feet. He turned resolutely back. "She looks fine to me," he said dismissively.

"Does she?" Keely countered, walking away toward Beth.

"Was she—" Jamie started to ask Theodore.

"She sure was. Brushed the tears off quick enough, but she looks upset. You say something to her?"

"No. Yeah. I don't know," Jamie admitted in frustration. "We had a bit of an argument."

"Well, better go apologize," Theodore suggested.

"It's not like that. It's just one of those things."

Theodore looked at Jamie for a minute and then shook his own head. "Well, it's hard to watch a pretty girl like that sit by herself and cry, whatever the reason." He watched Keely head over. "At least she's not alone now," he said pointedly, as Jamie shifted uncomfortably to his other foot.

"I don't know what's going on with her."

"Did you ask her?"

"Of course. She won't say."

"Well, then. Shouldn't that tell you something?" Theodore asked politely, wondering how such a smart man could be so slow.

"I'm giving her space, if that's what she wants."

"Did she ask for space?"

"Now, this sounds just like a conversation I had with her," Jamie said with a small smile.

"Well, if she didn't ask for space, maybe that's not what she needs," Theodore said pointedly, aiming a significant look at Jamie. When Jamie failed to pick up on it, Theodore shook his head and turned back to the grill.

***

Layla and Presley sat side by side in lounge chairs and watched their dad at the grill with Jamie. Presley had just come off a night shift and was exhausted. She was ready to switch back to days, but she was stuck on this shift until one of the other midwives returned from maternity leave. She took a long drink of coffee from the over-sized travel mug she carried and wondered how long she could be reasonably expected to stay before she could go home and sleep.

Layla sat beside her bouncing her feet, contrasting with Presley's lethargic slump in the adjoining chair. She had to work later, and the family scene wasn't usually her favorite. She always felt like a bit of an outsider. She glanced over at her sister quickly. Presley was drinking coffee, still in scrubs with her hair pulled up in a ponytail and a little eye liner smudged around her eyes. Layla, on the other hand, had paired a button up shirt and heels with a pencil skirt. She realized, now, how impractical her outfit was, since they were eating outside. She'd already watched, helplessly, as her heels sank into the grass in the yard. Well, there was nothing she could do about it now, she thought, wishing she could just fit in for once.

She thought about going over to talk to Jamie. They knew each other from CPA classes in town. But he was talking to her father and seemed to be glowering a little so she knew to steer clear. In fact, she'd gotten a little too good at sensing emotions. Her therapist said she was being hyper vigilant, and she guessed that was true enough. After all, she'd had to be, living with Noah. She rolled her shoulders and tried to shake off the thought.

"Has he been bothering you lately?" Presley asked. Layla didn't have to ask who she meant. They weren't twins, but they used to be close enough to finish each other's sentences, back before their mother had died. They still had that sense of each other sometimes.

"No. Not in months."

"Good."

He'd come around the apartment once after Layla had moved in. She hadn't told her sister. Presley had sent him packing with a few choice words, all of her anger coalescing the moment she saw him waiting at their door. She hadn't held back, and the neighbors had opened their doors for the show. He hadn't said much, but the look on his face had been downright scary, if she was honest. She'd known he was an abuser, but that look had been something else. Evil, she thought. She'd worried that she had made things worse for her sister, but Layla hadn't had any contact.

"Has Naomi?" she asked, knowing the two of them were friends now. She wanted to make sure there would be no backlash from the incident with him.

"No. I mean, yeah, at first. But not for a long time," Presley closed her eyes at Layla's answer and hoped that her conversation with him, if one could call that encounter a conversation, would be the end of it.

"If he bothers you, we'll get a restraining order."

"I know. I don't really want to talk about him. I appreciate the concern, but I don't want to feel like a victim."

"Yeah, okay. Think there's any more coffee?"

"I'll go check. You should get a little sleep before lunch is ready." They weren't close, at least not like they had been as kids. But they were trying. That ought to count for something, Layla thought, as she headed inside.

***

Seth carried Libby over the threshold of the house for the second time that day. He'd done it the first time when they'd gotten home from the airport. He did it again when they finally made it home from the party, much later that night. They came inside and looked around with pleasure.

"I love Italy so much. But I am so glad to be home."

"Me, too," Seth said, heading into the kitchen. "Want some wine?"

"I'd love some. Then a long bath. That sounds divine."

"Why don't you run the water, and I'll bring up the wine?"

"I would love that."

"I love you, Mrs. Carver," Seth said, leaning over to kiss her forehead before she headed upstairs to the bath.

"I love you back, Mr. Carver," she said with a pleased smile. She hadn't gotten used to the name change. Of course, she'd still use Reynolds as her byline for work, but she liked sharing his name, no matter how much Lindy scoffed. Lindy, of course, was advocating strongly for Walker-Carver, and Dean said he'd hyphenate either way if she'd just marry him already. They'd been arguing about it when they left the party the earlier.

She walked up the stairs slowly, more tired than she expected. Jet lag, probably, she thought. She came into the room and stopped in her tracks. There were candles lit and more sunflowers around the room in vases. She walked into the bathroom and saw more candles and more flowers. She started the bath, pouring in the scented bubbles she enjoyed, and admired the ambiance. She selected a playlist, a little French gypsy jazz she'd had the pleasure of hearing at a concert in town over the summer, and slowly undressed to get into the bath.

When Seth came in with a glass of white wine, he looked around. "The candles are a nice touch."

"It wasn't me. Who left before us who could have done this?"

"If I had to guess, I'd say Beth. She left to get the dog from the groomer's, but that could have been a cover story."

"No, it was definitely her. Look."

She pointed to the corner where Mr. Darcy had left the chewed up teddy bear he sometimes carried around. "We'll have to call and thank her."

"Tomorrow," Seth suggested, leaning down to pass her the wine.

"Want in?" Libby asked, gesturing to the large claw foot tub with plenty of room for two.

"Well, I was hoping you'd say that," he said, leaving the room and returning with a glass of wine of his own, which he set beside hers.

"Did your plot work out?" he asked, as he settled into the bath with her.

"What plot?" she asked, sipping the wine and relaxing.

"Whatever you and Lindy cooked up with Jamie."

"No. I think it backfired," she admitted, wincing. "I think I'm going to stay out of it from now on."

"Probably best. Lindy might keep pushing though."

"Not if she saw the look on Beth's face. It was tough, actually. I wish I hadn't stirred it up."

"Well, that's all been stirring up for a while. They'll work it out."

"You think so?"

"We're here, married," Seth pointed out. "After I acted like such an ass, did you ever think that would happen?"

"No," Libby said with a laugh. "But I'm glad it did." she told him, reaching out for him and drawing him closer. "You really were an ass."

"Now look at me. Luckiest guy around."

"About to get luckier."

"Really?" he said, quirking his eyebrows. "I can live with that."

Chapter 20

Dean pushed the stroller with a proud smile. They'd dressed it up like a bench, and Chief Justice Ginsberg sat regally upon it with a dissent collar and a big baby grin. "How's my baby?" Lindy demanded, coming out to get another look. "Okay, that's just the cutest."

"At least we finally agreed on something." Dean's blond hair had been darkened temporarily and slicked back. He wore thick black glasses, and his button up shirt was open to reveal a Superman costume underneath it. Lindy had finally agreed on Clark Kent and Lois Lane, stating that really Lois was a bad ass journalist in her own right and not just "the girlfriend."

"We could have at least tried to come up with a costume to match Maya's," Lindy complained.

"Well, we're kind of our very own Justice League. Superman, Lois out exposing truth, and the Notorious RBG fighting for our rights."

"You have a point," Lindy said, feeling a little more satisfied.

"Plus, you make a sexy Lois Lane," Dean said, leering at her.

"Try to remember you're the wholesome, upstanding Clark Kent."

"I'll try," Dean offered and leaned over to adjust Maya's dissent collar where it was listing to one side. "Are you sure this is safe?"

"I'll keep an eye on her. If she starts chewing it, I'll take it off."

"Well, aren't you three just the cutest?" Beth said, as she walked up.

"Look who's talking," Lindy returned.

"Why, thank you," Beth simpered. Even Mr. Darcy seemed to strut over. Beth had gone with a bold ringmaster costume, and Mr.

Darcy was currently being a lion, although he'd tried and failed already to remove the mane around his face. He'd finally resigned himself to the indignity of the costume.

"It's pretty cute," Dean admitted. "Are Seth and Libby coming?"

"No, but I promised we'd make their house the first stop," Lindy told him. "Then we've got to hit up the trick or treat neighborhood."

"Is Aunt Keely coming with us?" Beth wondered.

"No, she stopped by earlier to take pictures. They're going to a party with some of Theodore's friends. It's literature themed," Lindy explained.

"What'd they dress up as?" Beth asked.

"They've got the roaring 20s, Gatsby theme down."

"Very Mad Men," Dean offered.

"Or that," Lindy agreed. "It was pretty great. I'll show you the pictures in a minute," she told her, looking through the diaper bag. "Okay, we're all set."

***

Beth was glad she'd decided to come out. She'd spent the previous evening decorating Seth and Libby's home and had almost been caught. She'd gotten out of there minutes before they walked in. She'd seen them pull into the driveway as she walked home. Afterwards, she could admit that she'd spent the evening sulking. The conversation with Jamie hadn't gone well at all. She wished she could reach out to him and figure out how to be friends again, but now when he was around she was hyper-aware of all those things that she loved about him.

She cringed, as she thought about that word. Liked, she corrected herself. She really liked that he got her, really got her. He understood all of her quirks and was just so easy with her. Or had been, she thought, before she'd started acting like a spazz. She'd been tempted to sit out the Halloween festivities, especially since she and

Jamie normally had a classic horror movie marathon and handed out treats to the kids each year. She couldn't bear staying home and doing all that alone this year.

Of course, Mr. Darcy was appreciating the walk. Nearly every child, and most adults in town, had stopped to say hello and pat his head. He had even scored a couple of dog treats. She'd had to steer him away from candy that had been carelessly dropped on the ground. In fact, she'd been picking up the litter and placing it in a bag to throw away later. She stopped for a minute when she noticed someone else doing the same thing. She looked at him, trying to figure out how she knew him.

"Hey, Beth," he said when he looked up and saw her.

"Oh my God! Jonah!" she said with a laugh. "What are you doing?"

"Apparently, the same as you," he said, showing his bag of litter. "I'm trick or treating with my daughter and picking up litter along the way. You?"

"Oh, Lindy had a baby. I'm hanging out with them for the inaugural Halloween festivities. And this is Mr. Darcy."

"This is Emma," Jonah told her, as a little girl approached.

"Hi. How old are you?"

"Four," she said proudly, holding up three fingers. Jonah bent down to help her hold up one more. "Four," she said again, holding up the right number of fingers.

"I like your costume."

"I'm Merida," Emma told her.

"I can see that," Beth told her, taking in the red curly-haired wig and archery set she was carrying around. "It's very pretty."

"She's very *brave*," Emma corrected, and then added, "I like your hair."

"Thank you."

"Can I touch it?"

"Emma ..." Jonah began in exasperation, but Beth waved him away.

"Sure," she said, gamely, bending low enough for Emma to touch her hair.

"It's real?"

"Sure is. I like your curls though," she told her, noticing the mop of curly blond hair peeking out from underneath the curly red wig.

"Thank you," Emma preened.

"I didn't realize you had kids."

"Just the one. Her mom and I divorced a year ago, but we split the holidays. I'm on first shift, and she's taking over in another hour. Feel like grabbing coffee after or a drink? It'd be good to catch up."

"Dressed like this?"

"I've got these," he said, pointing to the bear ears he'd worn on his head.

"That's hardly a costume," Beth pointed out, gesturing to her own flamboyant ringmaster outfit.

"That's what Emma said," he told her with a charming smile. She looked at him and could still see that little boy in the grown man. His hair was darker, and he'd gone through a significant growth spurt. He'd filled out well, but he still had that same reckless grin she couldn't resist with the one slightly chipped tooth that she'd given him herself with an unexpected fly ball. "I think we'll probably blend in tonight," he assured her, gesturing around at all the adults in costume.

"Sure. Maybe an hour and a half? Want to meet at Brews and Blues?"

"Works for me. Okay, Emma, I'm coming," he said, as his daughter tugged his hand in the direction of the next house. He gave her an apologetic smile and waved as he walked off.

"Who's that?" Lindy asked with interest.

"Jonah," Beth told her. "He's an old friend from school."

"Was he the boy whose tree house you booby trapped?" Dean asked curiously.

"That's the one."

"Brave man," Dean commented.

"Shut up," Beth said with a laugh, glancing back toward the house where Jonah was waiting patiently with Emma for more candy.

"Divorced means single," Lindy pointed out helpfully.

"I know what it means," Beth said rolling her eyes.

"You know if you can't get over—"

"Okay, I'm going to go now," Beth said loudly, interrupting her. "I'll see you guys later," she said with a laugh, spotting Rebecca and Jill down the street. "Bye, Maya!" she said, with a kiss to the baby and a wave at Dean and Lindy.

"I didn't know you were going to be here!" Beth exclaimed as she approached.

"Party down the street," Rebecca said. "Then we stole a kid as a beard."

"Any kid I know?"

"Our friend Lynn has a ten-year-old she asked us to keep an eye on. The pirate," she said, nodding to a kid, jockeying for a place in line to get candy. "We're supposed to take him to the end of the street and back and deliver him to his mom. Want to go out after?"

"Can't. Meeting someone for coffee. I like this costume by the way," Beth told Rebecca, admiring the sexy steam punk look she was working.

"It's the one time of year I can be my true self," she returned with a sigh. "Coffee sounds like a date."

"Who's the date?" Jill asked.

"Not a date. Meeting up with an old friend. Amelia Earhart?" she asked Jill.

"Of course. It's comfortable and cute. So ... attractive old friend?"

"Maybe," Beth said with a laugh.

"Hey, if you're not interested, be a pal," Rebecca suggested.

"We'll see. I'll tell you all about it tomorrow."

"I still want Lucas's number," Jill reminded her. "You said you'd ask."

"Girl, he's trouble. And I think you've had enough of that."

"But if he's the right kind of trouble ..." Jill wheedled.

Rebecca and Beth laughed.

"Fine." she said with a sigh. "I hate being single!" she declared dramatically.

"Not me," Rebecca said, appreciatively, looking around. "How many hot dads have we counted tonight?"

"How many are married?" Jill countered, crossing her arms and leveling a glance at Rebecca.

"Not all of them, I'm sure. There are more hot men getting divorced every day," she enthused.

"That's sort of a depressing thought," Beth said with a dry laugh. "But I guess you're right."

"You could always date women," Jill suggested helpfully.

"Not really my thing," Beth said with a smile.

"I do, sometimes," Rebecca admitted.

"You do now," Jill pointed out.

"What? Who?" Beth asked.

"Oh, it's not like that. I'm doing a triad sort of thing," she told Beth in a lowered voice, glancing around them.

"What do you mean?"

"You know, seeing a married couple," Jill explained.

"You do like them married," Beth said with a roll of her eyes.

"This isn't cheating though," Rebecca protested.

"How do you even get into that? How does that even work?" she asked. "Wait—I've only got forty-five minutes before I've got to meet Jonah. We don't have time enough for this conversation.

Besides, you're losing your pirate," she pointed out, gesturing to a pirate moving about three houses down from them.

"Well, fuck," Rebecca breathed out.

"*Shhh*," Jill shushed her, laughing.

"Sorry," Rebecca said sheepishly.

"You should have come as a sailor yourself. I want details. Breakfast tomorrow?"

"Let's say brunch," Jill told her. "In case you get lucky."

"It's not like that," Beth said with a laugh, walking in the opposite direction as her friends tried to keep their pirate charge in sight.

"You don't know it's not like that," Rebecca said with a grin.

***

When Beth took her seat across from Jonah at Brews, Jamie was just cutting off *The Shining*. Beth hated that one. She couldn't get past the creepy twins. She'd have preferred the camp of *House on Haunted Hill* or the artistry of a Hitchcock film like *Notorious*. Of course, *Notorious* had sort of stressed him out. The characters kept misunderstanding each other when it was obvious to anyone that they were really in love. He sighed. He was sure people weren't that stupid in real life.

Of course, Ansley had thought that he'd been clueless about Beth being in love with him, but it turned out she was wrong, he thought to himself. He thought about calling Ansley and telling her that, but she was out on a date. They'd managed to transition to friends, and she'd been open about the fact that she was still dating. He took it in stride. He'd liked her, of course, but he hadn't been serious about her. Still, he'd almost thought for a minute that she was right. About Beth. Talking to Beth, of course, had convinced him otherwise.

He put in another movie. Not *Notorious* but another Hitchcock film. *Dial M for Murder* had been a mutual favorite, and Jamie saw no reason not to continue the tradition, with or without Beth. He got up to pop some more popcorn and grab another beer. He noted the wine on the shelf in the fridge. He still kept Beth's favorite brand on hand. He hadn't been with Ansley long enough to do that, but he knew Beth's preferences. They'd been friends long enough.

He sat down and stretched out. He was approaching his last semester of school. The classes were more challenging in some ways, but also more practical. He'd been helping out more at the antique store, but he was thinking about taking on a few private clients, too, maybe even helping out some of the other businesses in town. He knew that Layla was looking at interning in a private firm and going into accounting full-time, but he wanted to stay where he was. He didn't make a lot of money, but he was comfortable enough. He was going to enjoy the evening and relax. He'd have class tomorrow night and a busy weekend of estate sales ahead. He missed having Beth around to keep him company on Halloween, but that was on her. He was still her friend, whether or not she chose to be his, he thought with a shrug.

***

"It's weird, isn't it?" Jonah asked, tilting his head at Beth. "I mean, we've known each other forever but don't really know each other at all."

"It's been a long time," Beth agreed with a smile. "So give me the basics," she suggested, leaning back in her chair and taking in the ambiance of the room. Jonah had left on the bear ears when they'd gotten to Brews and Blues, in deference to Beth's costume. The room was filled with costumed adults and kids, having a drink and relaxing. He'd been right; she did fit right in, she thought.

"Well, you've met Emma. She's my world. Her mom and I have been divorced for …" he thought about it. "A year now, just over. I've got custody. Her mom has some—issues," he finished, shrugging. "Anyway, I prefer it this way."

"What are you doing for work these days? You know I'm managing the bookstore in town?"

"I heard. I'm in insurance, and the less said about that, the better. It's not very interesting. And I promise I'm not going to try to sell you a policy."

"Do people expect you to?"

"You'd be surprised. I've had dates hit the door the moment I mentioned my work. Either out of boredom or out of fear that a hard sales pitch would follow, I don't know."

"Maybe it was just you," Beth offered innocently, concealing a grin behind her drink.

"I forgot how mean you were," Jonah accused with a laugh. "I shouldn't have, after the tree house incident."

"Oh my God! I'll never live that down."

"Nope. Not ever. It was pretty great, until I broke my arm. Thanks for that."

"Guess I'm buying the next round," Beth said with a laugh.

"Fair enough. So, are you seeing anyone?"

"Other than you, right now, and all these other people?" she asked him playfully.

"You know what I mean," Jonah said, rolling his eyes.

"No."

"But there is someone." It was a statement, and Beth just shrugged.

"The kind of someone who doesn't feel the same way."

"Huh. Yeah, I can relate," Jonah said. "But there's nothing wrong with making new friends. Even from old ones. Especially hot ones."

"You're alright, I guess."

"I meant you," Jonah said, laughing. "But yeah."

"So I could cry on your shoulder, and you could cry on mine?" Beth asked, leaning forward.

"Something like that," Jonah held her eyes and let the moment stretch out.

"How about we have that next drink at my place. When do you have to pick up Emma?"

"In the morning," Jonah said with a wide smile. "Plenty of time."

Chapter 21

Beth walked Mr. Darcy around the neighborhood. She never really got tired of the scenery, even if it had been almost the same her whole life. Madison was something else, she thought. The antebellum homes were one thing, but all the lawns were so neat. The entire downtown was also picture-perfect with its barrels of flowers and neat storefront windows. She'd finish the walk downtown so that Mr. Darcy could score a dog treat by the visitors' center and a bowl of water by Brews & Blues. She sighed happily as she walked.

Halloween hadn't been what she'd been used to. After all, she hadn't seen Jamie at all, and while she missed their classic horror film festival, she'd enjoyed going out with Dean, Lindy, and Maya. Meeting Jonah had been unexpected, she thought. Nice, but unexpected. She smiled to herself. The night had taken a turn she hadn't anticipated, but she thought having a friend with benefits was pretty nice now that she'd considered it. She'd spilled out the whole story about Jamie, and he'd talked about his complicated relationship with his ex. There had been no judgment, just understanding.

She talked to Mr. Darcy about it as they walked, tactfully leaving out the more adult content in her story, and wasn't really paying attention to much else as they rounded the corner to head downtown. Never running out of things to say, Beth reminded Mr. Darcy of all the cute costumes they'd seen and how everyone had absolutely loved Maya's, even if they hadn't all been sure who she was.

"Can you imagine?" Beth asked Mr. Darcy with a roll of her eyes.

"Sounds like a fun night," Jamie said shortly. He was standing by the crosswalk, about to head across the street when she approached.

She stopped abruptly and looked up at him. She hadn't been aware of him until he spoke, and her conversation with the dog stumbled to a halt. Of course, Mr. Darcy trotted on ahead, happily greeting Jamie and nudging him with his nose.

"It's good to see you, too," Jamie told him with a smile. He looked up at Beth, and his expression was inscrutable, the smile falling away. "So you went trick or treating with Maya?"

"Yeah," she said, shifting uncomfortably. "She was—"

"RBG. Yeah, I heard," Jamie said, patting Mr. Darcy again. He turned back toward the crosswalk, lifting one of the pedestrian flags to take across. Beth hesitated for only a second, before she asked.

"What did you do?"

"The usual," he said with a shrug. "Couple of movies and handed out candy."

"Oh," Beth said quietly. She wondered if he had been alone and suspected that he had. She wanted to reach out a hand and just touch his arm, a comforting touch that she used to take for granted and felt she desperately needed herself at that moment. But by the time she thought to lift her hand, he'd started walking across the street.

"See you around," he said shortly. She watched him walk across the street and then around the corner to the gym. It was weird, she thought, how many times she'd seen him go and had never felt so sad. She wondered if Lindy was right. Maybe she should just tell him, she thought. She wanted to ask Mr. Darcy but felt sure he was far too biased when it came to Jamie.

***

Libby stepped out of the shower. She'd managed an early run, and she was heading into work in the next hour. She had come in just as Seth was getting up, and she was sure that he'd make coffee before she came downstairs. It was strange, she thought, to be married again. She'd lived with Seth a while beforehand so she was used to living with him. It was just the fact of the marriage that seemed to sit with her. She'd had such a honeymoon period with Collin, and then it had all changed. She rubbed lotion into her skin and reminded herself that Seth wasn't Collin anyway.

"You look lost in thought," Seth commented, standing in the doorway with a large mug of coffee. He'd even added whipped cream and a sprinkle of cinnamon. She looked over at him and the mug and couldn't decide which looked more delicious at the moment. He smiled at her.

"I know you want the coffee first," he said with a laugh. He set it down on the counter. "Want to tell me what you were thinking about?"

"No," she said with a laugh. "Just us, I guess. The marriage thing." She started to get dressed.

"Can I talk to you about something I've been thinking about?" Seth asked, watching her put clothes on with a small feeling of regret. He'd been enjoying the view. Still, she looked so pretty in the pale blue shift dress she was sliding into.

"Sure. What's up?" she asked, heading to the mirror to put on her makeup.

Her assorted makeup products were spread across the counter in a chaos that made him shake his head. Sometimes, he would carefully organize it, and it would stay that way for a couple of days before returning to chaos. He didn't mind, really. Libby's head was a wondrous place, but often chaotic. She'd fiddled, in Italy, with a couple of short stories, and he'd read some of her poetry over her shoulder on the plane. He thought she might be interested in going from blogs and work at the newspaper to something else entirely. She had a knack for it.

"I was thinking ..." he began carefully, "about babies."

She paused, looking down at the mascara wand in her hand and then slowly brushed it on her lashes, leaning close to the mirror as she applied it. "Oh?"

"I want a family with you," he told her frankly. "You know that."

"You know I might not be able to ... " Libby began. Seth waved it away. "I'm serious," she told him, turning to look at him before applying mascara to the second set of lashes.

"I know. But you said that you were open to adoption," Seth told her. "What if we tried both?"

"How do you mean?" she asked him, turning to face him and leaning on the counter.

"What if we both went to the fertility clinic and started with that and started on the adoption process at the same time?"

"And see which one works first?"

"No. I mean, do both," he told her. "If they both were to work out, we'd have two. And if one fell through, we'd still have one."

"How big of a family are you wanting, exactly?" Libby asked with a quirk of one eyebrow.

"I wouldn't mind a big one," he answered honestly. "I just want a family with you, Libby."

"And if we can't do a big family? Adoption is expensive. The fertility clinic might be, too."

"Take the money out of it. What would you want if you could have anything?"

"A big family. With you."

"Then can we start?"

"Well, we haven't exactly been using protection lately. I'm not on birth control."

"I thought we could start looking into both processes and make some appointments."

"Okay," Libby said, turning back to the mirror to finish applying her makeup.

"That's it?" Seth asked. "Okay?"

"Okay," Libby said with a happy laugh, turning to kiss him. She pressed her cheek to his and said softly, "I love you."

"I love you back," he told her happily. "My wife."

"My husband," she replied with a sigh, winding her arms around his neck and tangling in his hair.

"You could come back to bed now. Really get started," he murmured in her hair.

"I've got to get ready for work. Want me to make breakfast?"

"I'll do the cooking. What do you want?"

"I'd take some French toast, if you don't mind. And bacon," she told him with a smile.

She loved that he cooked. It was more his thing than hers, although she wasn't bad at it. She just didn't have quite his flair. She watched him head downstairs and thought how lucky she was. Not because he cooked, although there was that, she considered. He knew she wanted a family, had wanted one for years. And he'd give it to her, in whatever form it came in. He wouldn't care about age or race or any of that when it came to adopting. He just wanted a family with her. She took a deep breath and took out the hair dryer to get her hair in some semblance of order before work.

***

Lindy headed toward work with Maya in the wrap. One benefit of owning her own studio was that she could take Maya in with her. For a while, at any rate. They would have to think about a daycare or nanny later, she realized uncomfortably. Of course, she mostly called her own hours so she could balance it for a bit. Dean was happy to take care of Maya on his own in the evenings if she had an evening class. That usually only took a few hours. Her mom was happy to take a turn in the mornings before the tea shop opened. She could even take evenings, when they weren't catering an event or hosting a shower. Libby and Beth had both offered to take the baby for a few hours when Lindy needed to work or simply wanted a break.

Everyone had been great.

Her path overlapped with Naomi's as she headed over to the studio. The tea room, and bookstore where Naomi worked, was just up the street from the canvas painting studio, Tipsy Canvas, that she owned. She hadn't often been alone with Naomi. They hadn't gotten along back when Naomi and Dean had been a thing and then shortly after. Of course, Lindy reflected, it hadn't been a jealousy thing. She had just hated to see Naomi become yet another woman chasing down a player. And Dean, Lindy admitted, had been exactly that before their relationship. Still, they'd seemed to bury the hatchet after everything with Noah came out. There were more important things to worry about.

"Hey," Lindy greeted her.

"Hey," Naomi replied, peering at Maya.

"Want to hold her?"

"Can I?" Lindy started to take Maya out of the wrap.

"Sure. I can see you want to." She passed the baby over and watched Naomi carefully hold her close, breathing in that baby smell.

"Careful," she cautioned, as Naomi glanced up at her. "First, you smell them. Then you want one."

"Not any time soon," Naomi said with a smile. It was sort of weird to be holding Dean's baby. She'd once entertained a fantasy that she'd have a baby of his. Of course, it had been a blurry fantasy, too far in the distant future to even consider. But even she could admit that Lindy and Dean worked. They were easy together in a way she and Dean had never been. He'd been trying too hard to get her, and she'd been trying too hard to keep him. Then he'd been trying to get away, and she'd been trying to keep him interested. It had, she thought, been exhausting. She smiled at Lindy. "She's perfect."

"I know."

"Is that my baby?" Keely asked.

"It's your baby's baby," Naomi confirmed, passing Maya over to

Keely. "I'm going to head in. Thanks, Lindy."

"No problem," Lindy said, watching her go. She turned to look at her mom who was showering Maya with kisses and making her laugh. "Is she doing okay?"

"Naomi? She's good. He hasn't been bothering her again, if that's what you mean," she replied, knowing full well that they had all been concerned that Noah wasn't done with Layla or Naomi.

He had been so quiet after the relationship ended that they had all worried. It had felt eerie and unfinished. Then the calls started and the messages, the hacking into social media, and the visit to Presley's place. Yes, Keely knew about that, she thought, although she hadn't told anyone else. Presley wanted someone to know, just in case. But she hadn't wanted to worry Theodore or Layla. Sometimes Keely wondered, uncomfortably, if she shouldn't have kept the secret. But whatever Presley had said seemed to have worked. Noah hadn't bothered anyone since, and that had been months before.

"Just checking. Hopefully, that's all over now."

"That's what we hope, too."

"How's Theodore?"

"Busy writing the next book and caring for the bees. He's hired out most of the farm work for now. He just can't handle it and work on the book."

"Why doesn't he hire someone for the bees, too?"

"Too few people are trained for that, and they're his babies. Besides, this book is going to be a sequel to the last, and working with the bees helps him focus on the plot. I can't wait to read it."

"He won't let you read it now?"

"Oh, I get the occasional part read out loud. But, no. He wants at least the first draft, and maybe a second, finished first. But it'll be worth it. And we'll have the launch party at the tea room when it's done."

"I'm going to head in. Gimme," Lindy said, reaching out her

arms for Maya as Keely planted one more kiss on top of her head.

"Come over at lunch."

"Planning on it," Lindy said with a laugh as she headed into the studio.

Chapter 22

Lindy felt Dean shift away from her, and she snuggled closer to Maya. "I know everyone says we shouldn't co-sleep, but I can't help it," she told him sleepily, as she looked up to where he was sitting on his side of the bed preemptively turning off his alarm before it went off. She glanced at the clock and noted that it was just shy of 6:00 a.m. She'd been up feeding Maya not long before, and she was exhausted.

Every day had been a long day lately. They were heading into the week of Thanksgiving, which for most people, meant a week of feasting or travel. With her mom's restaurant and bookstore and her own studio, it meant the fervor of Black Friday preparations. They had less than a week to go, and she'd been busy promoting and preparing. They had classes scheduled all day on Black Friday and then discounts going live online for Cyber Monday the following week. Plus, she knew that the Shop Local initiative on Saturday would drive a crowd into the tea room, bookstore, and studio. She'd been helping her mom out every day before and after work when she could manage it, although they'd brought in some temporary staff for the week.

"I've got to work my forty-eight, and then I promise you can sleep all day when I'm done," Dean explained, standing up to get dressed quickly.

"I've got breakfast with Mom and Theodore in a few hours," Lindy murmured, reminding him. "If I'm lucky, they'll watch Maya long enough for me to take a nap if I need one."

"That's not a bad idea," Dean told her, leaning down to kiss Maya and then Lindy. He got dressed quickly.

"You are so noisy," Lindy growled into her pillow. "Can you do that in the other room?"

"I'll put my shoes on downstairs, grouchy. Love you," he called back.

Lindy was already asleep before he left the room and didn't answer. Dean shook his head as he walked downstairs. At least he lived right downtown. He could be at the station in five minutes at a jog. Today, he'd drive in though. He sat on the stairs and laced up his shoes. He looked up at the darkened hallway. Maybe if Lindy had a good enough nap, she'd stop by with leftovers from her big breakfast. He brightened at the thought and then grabbed his keys and headed out.

***

Lindy could hear a noise somewhere far away. She tried to figure out what could be making that sound. It took her a minute to realize that there was a steady knock at the door. Then, her mom was shaking her.

"Lindy, you've got to get up," Keely was saying. Lindy was so disoriented that for a minute she was transported back into high school when she'd sleep until the very last minute.

"What's going on?" she asked, sitting up slowly. She'd had breakfast with her Mom and Theodore downstairs, and then they'd agreed to sit with Maya for a couple of hours to give her a chance to rest. The last few nights had been grueling, and the dark circles under her eyes were only getting larger. "What time is it?"

"Lindy, you need to come downstairs," Keely said again.

"Do you need to go home?" Lindy sat up groggily, feeling like she'd been asleep for only minutes. "Did I oversleep?" she asked in confusion. "I'm sorry."

"Jimmy is here." Lindy sat up and rubbed her eyes, the words sinking in now. Jimmy Shannon was the fire chief at Dean's precinct. She felt her heart jump into her throat. "Jim," Lindy breathed. "Dean

...." She got out of bed so quickly the blood rushed to her head, and she swayed. Keely grabbed her arm.

"Breathe now. He's okay, but there's been an accident. They won't tell me anything. They're waiting for you."

Lindy hurried downstairs, her mother a step behind her. She could see another officer waiting with Jimmy in the living room. She couldn't think of his name, although she knew him. She knew them all, had met them all at events around town. She'd laughed with him, she thought, at the 5K. He was the one who had run in full gear, but his name fluttered on the edge of her consciousness. "Is he ..." she began, unable to finish.

"He's alive. There was an accident, but he's alive," Jimmy said, reaching out to steady her where she leaned against the doorframe. Lindy felt her face go white. Jimmy had watched her grow up, had even nursed a crush on her mother for some years. She tried to focus on what he was saying. "Lightning struck a house in town, and Dean was the first in. We were venting the place when the floor gave out. He was on the second floor when it gave out." He broke off at the cry of the baby from the kitchen.

"Theodore's feeding her. Don't worry," Keely said, stroking a hand down Lindy's arm and holding her against herself. "How bad is it?"

"We're going to take you to the hospital, and our liaison is going to go over everything with you. We came as soon as we cleared the house. He's alive, but we don't know the extent of the injuries yet," Jimmy said, more to Keely than Lindy.

"Dean had you listed as next of kin. Is there anyone else we should call?" The other officer asked her. The name hit her then. Craig. The other man was named Craig.

"Seth," she breathed, looking at her mom.

"I'll call him," Keely said, leaving the room.

"I need to check on the baby," Lindy said abruptly, heading toward the kitchen.

Lindy hated the thought of Seth taking that call on his own, wishing it was earlier so he'd have been home with Lindy rather than at work in his office. She couldn't even remember who else was working at the shop today. Dean was his best friend, Lindy thought. He'd likely beat her to the hospital. She stopped to drop a kiss on Maya's head, wondering if she'd even get the chance to know her father. She looked at Theodore, "It's Dean. I need to go to the hospital. Can you bring Maya?"

"We'll get her things together and meet you there," Keely said, coming into the room. Don't worry about it. Just go."

"Was anyone else hurt?" Theodore asked.

"I didn't even think to ask," Lindy said, still thinking only of Dean.

"Couple other guys have minor injuries," Jimmy told her from the doorway where he stood awkwardly. "We really want to get back to check on them. We'll take you when you're ready."

"Seth is already on his way," Keely told them.

"I'll go change," Lindy told them. She looked at Jimmy. "And Dean? How badly was he hurt? Did you see him?" She could barely form the words, she'd started shaking so hard.

"He wasn't conscious, but he's alive. I don't know much more than you do right now. You go on up and change. We'll wait. We're going to take you to the hospital, and you can see what the doctors have to say. We'll wait," Jimmy reminded her, standing by the door. She nodded and ran up the stairs. Keely started to follow her, but then they heard heard footsteps and turned as the door opened without preamble.

Libby was in yoga pants and a sweater, struggling into her coat. "Seth called. He's headed to the hospital, but I'm going to ride with Lindy. I was working from home and came straight over."

"She went upstairs to get dressed," Keely explained. Libby headed upstairs immediately while Keely began packing the diaper bag.

Libby jogged up the stairs toward Lindy and found her leaning over the toilet in the bathroom, throwing up.

"How can I help?" Libby asked, going to help Lindy up off the floor.

"I don't even know what to pack."

"Don't worry about this. Go to the hospital, and I'll come back with your mom later to grab a few things," Libby told her, bringing her in for a fierce hug.

Lindy discarded her pajamas and threw on leggings and a tunic style sweater, grabbing thick sweater socks from a chair in the room where she'd tossed them earlier. The temperature had dropped in the last few days, and she thought only fleetingly of how much work they still had to do to this week. She shook off the thought and went to the door where Libby was waiting patiently.

"How's Seth doing?"

"He's worried. I don't think either of us expected ..."

"Me either. I should have, of course." She frowned, wondering why she'd never thought Dean's career was even remotely dangerous. They hurried down the stairs where Lindy made a beeline for Maya, dropping a kiss on her head and heading out. Libby followed her quickly, grabbing her coat on the way and pushing it at her as they headed to the car.

***

At the hospital, Lindy tried to swallow the panic rising in her chest. It hadn't taken long to get to Morgan Memorial. She was thankful that they were headed there and not to the old hospital. The old location would have been closer, but she wouldn't have felt confident in their ability to handle any injuries. The new hospital was certainly more extensive, with new equipment and new staff ready to handle any local emergency. They'd even built a pediatric emergency wing, which had given Lindy a sense of comfort. She tried not to think in worst case scenarios as she waited for the hospital liaison, but she couldn't seem to help it. Tears fell unchecked down her cheeks.

She'd never worried about Dean's job before. Fire fighting didn't seem dangerous in Madison. His work seemed more routine, small house fires and school visits and the occasional birthday party appearance. She'd never thought about the danger that went hand-in-hand with the uniform or considered that anything like this could happen. She sat in the waiting room with her arms crossed around her.

"Can I get you anything? Coffee?" Craig asked solicitously. Libby had gone to the restroom, but Lindy suspected that she'd really gone to look for Seth who had arrived at least fifteen minutes earlier.

"No. Thank you," she added. She looked at him. He was young, one of the newest on the crew. This was probably the first visit he'd had to make, and it couldn't be easy. "Were you there—when it happened?"

He nodded.

"What was it like?" She thought for a minute he wasn't going to answer.

"It happened so fast. He couldn't have seen it coming at all. I heard it before I saw it. One minute everything was fine, and the next we just saw it all collapse. I was just coming in the door and made it back out but Dean and another guy were inside." He broke off, thankful he'd been one of the last to go in. He felt guilty for thinking it, but if he'd been a little faster, it could have been him. "Anyway, we got them out, and then the ambulance came while we got the fire under control," he told her with a pale, pinched look on his face. Lindy looked up as Jimmy came out; she stood and went straight to hug him.

When she broke off the hug, Jimmy patted her shoulder and then indicated the woman beside him. "Lindy Carver, this is Dr. Rita Moss. Do you two know each other?"

"I think we know of each other," Rita said warmly. She'd seen Lindy at a number of events around town. In addition to being the hospital administrator and liaison for the fire department, she served on the board of the local conservatory and did the occasional docent duty for the historic society. "It's nice to meet you, although not under these circumstances," she said kindly, taking Lindy's hand in her own.

Of course, Lindy had seen Rita before. The town was small enough that nearly everyone was familiar or a tourist. She stood just barely over five feet with carefully coiffed blonde hair. She looked like she was about sixty or thereabouts, although with the careful application of makeup and stylish clothes, Lindy couldn't be sure. She appreciated the kindness but thought brusquely that what she needed was information.

"Let me brief you first, and then we'll see if he's ready for visitors," Rita began knowingly. She hated this part of the job, but she was good at it. She knew how to deliver the information with efficiency and warmth and then step aside to allow the family to process what was going on. The hospital staff would make sure that all of their needs were met, and she would brief the next family as they arrived.

"The doctors are with him now, and I can give you a little more information about the extent of his injuries," she told Lindy as they took a seat in her office.

Seth walked in and greeted Rita by name. "I called his family. His dad and Danielle ought to be here later today, and his mom is driving up now. She's likely to hit rush hour traffic in Atlanta, but she'll still get here in a few hours." He sat down beside Lindy, his shoulder against hers in solidarity.

"I was just about to tell Lindy what to expect when you see him. The doctors have been with him since he came in. He did regain consciousness, but he's heavily medicated at the moment so it's not been for long." Lindy breathed a sigh of relief. It was a good sign. Rita continued. "We can confirm the left leg is broken. He has a compound fracture in his lower leg, with the tibia and fibula both broken," Rita said with a nod. "He also broke a couple of ribs. We expect him to make a full recovery, with rehabilitation. He's in surgery for the leg now. He didn't seem to sustain any burns. You can expect him to be here for a week or more and home recovering for at least six months. He has some cuts and abrasions, and he sustained a concussion in the fall."

"Can we see him soon?" Seth asked. "When will he be out of surgery?"

"The doctors are still with him, but it shouldn't be too long. He went straight in when he got here. I'll take you over to the waiting room," Rita offered.

When they made it to the waiting room, Keely and Libby were already there with Maya, and Theodore was just coming in with the bags they'd packed.

"Concussion, broken leg, and broken ribs. Some cuts from the fall. No burns that they know of yet. He'll live," Lindy told them shortly, reaching for Maya and holding her tightly. Seth went straight to his mother and wrapped her in a hug. When he broke off to go to Libby, Keely put her arms around Lindy. Theodore started placing coffee mugs and muffins on the table, giving them their space.

"Thanks for that," Seth told him, as he and Libby took a seat. He reached gratefully for a travel mug and sipped it while Libby doctored her own with the cream and sugar the hospital kept by their own coffee service. It was bold and strong, just what he needed to get through this night.

"It'd be a damn shame if he messed up his pretty face," Seth commented wryly, trying to lighten the mood. Lindy choked out a laugh and sat down on the other side of him, reaching for a coffee.

Lindy looked over at him. "He's never even had as much as a sprain."

"Well, he said he had one in training," Seth said with a shrug. "Jumped and landed wrong. Anyway, he wasn't down for long."

"Why didn't I know that?"

"You were seeing what's-his-face then. You weren't around much"

"Right. Tyler."

"Dean *hated* Tyler."

"Yeah, he made that clear."

"I can't say I cared for him much either," Keely admitted. "What?" She asked Lindy who shot her a look. "He was always so superior."

"Well. You're not wrong. He was kind of an ass."

"Poser, I think, was the word that Dean used," Seth pointed out.

"That, too," Lindy said with a small smile. That sounded like Dean. He'd needled Tyler every time he saw him. The dislike had been mutual. It was no wonder she hadn't known Dean had been injured back then. She'd done her level best to keep the two men apart to keep the bickering to a minimum.

"Has anyone called Dean's family?" Keely asked, changing the subject.

"Seth did," Libby answered for him. "But if you ask me, his family is already here," she told them, sitting down and sipping her coffee.

"Can we see him?" Keely asked Lindy.

"Soon," she told her, breathing in that baby scent as she held Maya. She could have lost everything, she thought. Their little family. But they hadn't, she reminded herself. He was going to be okay.

"Craig's here. He saw the whole thing and stayed with Dean until the ambulance got there."

"I'll just go say hello," Keely said after hugging Lindy hard. "Then I want that baby." Theodore walked with her, falling into step as they left the room.

Libby watched them go and leaned her head on Seth's shoulder, knowing it would comfort them both. She took his hand in both of hers and kissed it, watching Lindy shift Maya in her arms. "I brought the sling, if you need it. I grabbed it as we were heading out. It was hanging up by your coat."

"You're a gem." Lindy put it on gratefully and tucked Maya in.

"Well, enjoy while you can. His family will be here soon, and it'll be a game of pass the baby the rest of the day," Seth told her, with a roll of his eyes.

"As I recall, you always take a turn," Lindy returned.

"That's true. She's irresistible."

"Just like her daddy," Lindy said, and then broke off. She took a deep breath. She'd gone to sleep worried about the week of retail madness and woken up to this. How trivial it all seemed now, she thought.

Chapter 23

Beth was walking Mr. Darcy down the street just a little after 9:00 a.m. when she noticed Jamie round the corner abruptly and head to Lost Horizon. Curious, she headed his way. He normally didn't work this early. In fact, it looked like he was still in his gym clothes, although he had his gym bag slung casually over his shoulder as he hurried to unlock the front door.

"Did you forget to change clothes? What are you doing here so early?"

"Seth called and asked me to open the store. Dean was in an accident. He'd have called earlier, but he just forgot. I came straight from the gym."

"Wait—what? Is he okay?" she asked, the color draining from her face.

"There was a fire, and some floors collapsed with Dean inside. I don't have all the details, but Dean's in the hospital, and Lindy's there with him. Libby went with her, and Seth and Keely met them there. He said Dean's okay, but they're all waiting to see him," he explained, going inside and turning on the lights.

"Here's what we're going to do," Beth told him calmly. "You are going to go back to the gym and shower and change, so you don't scare away the customers. I am going to stay here until you get back."

"I can't do that," Jamie started to argue.

"Have I not worked in this store off and on since I was a teenager? I've got this. Mr. Darcy will sleep behind the front desk, and we'll be out of your hair as soon as you get back," Beth told him.

"I appreciate it. I'll be quick."

"We're not in a hurry. Just go. I've got this." He headed out in a rush, and Beth pulled out her phone. Mr. Darcy looked affronted that Jamie had walked out without as much as a pat on the head or scratch behind the ears so Beth found a dog bone from behind the counter and settled him down with it. Then she sent a text to Libby.

"Heard Dean's in the hospital. Everything okay?"

Her phone rang almost immediately, and she answered it when she saw Libby's number pop up. "I'm so sorry no one called you," Libby said without bothering with a greeting. "We're trying not to call everyone too early. Dean is hurt, but he's okay. Or will be okay. Lindy is going to go back and see him soon, and then the rest of us will check on him after that."

"What happened? Jamie said there was a fire? I'm at the store. I ran into him when I was walking Mr. Darcy. He's going back to the gym to shower while I hold down the fort. I thought I heard sirens this morning, but I didn't think anything about it."

"Lightning hit an old house downtown. They went in to clear it, and the second floor gave out." She'd stepped outside to make the call and paced just beyond the doors, the phone pressed tightly to her ear.

Beth shivered at the thought. "But he's okay?"

"He will be. We know his ribs are broken and the left leg. We're not sure what else he's dealing with yet. A concussion and some cuts from the fall." Her voice caught. "Anyway, it could have been so much worse." They were quiet for a minute.

"I'll come by after work. I'll go over early and get things ready, so tell Aunt Keely not to worry. We should have everything well in hand for the week. Jamie's got the store under control, and I'll get the tea room in hand. How about the studio?"

"I need to call her manager. They have a back up plan for when childcare falls through or Maya gets sick so we'll put that into place. Lindy thought of it earlier, but I told her to let me call a little later in the morning."

"Has Dean's family gotten there yet?"

"No, but they'll all be here soon. I've never met them."

"Well, they don't come around much. Anyway, Deanna, Dean's mom, doesn't much like Aunt Keely."

"Really? Why?" Libby asked, not understanding how anyone could develop a dislike of her.

"It was a sort of jealousy thing. Dean spent more time over at their house than his own. It used to make his mom mad. Jamie's heading back in. Can you call me later? Let me know when you know something? I'm going to take Mr. Darcy home and head to the shop."

"Of course. Tell Jamie we appreciate him," Libby said, as Jamie walked in, freshly showered and changed into his work clothes.

"Will do," Beth said. "That was Libby. Lindy's going to go in and see him soon. They said thanks for taking care of things here."

"Of course," he said shortly, not knowing what else to say. At times like this, he missed their friendship and that ease they'd had more than he could say. Beth must have felt the same because she stepped forward and put a hand on his arm.

"I appreciate it, too. The heads-up and everything else. Can we … Do you want to go with me to the hospital later?"

He recognized an olive branch when he heard one and accepted it gratefully. "Sure. Call me when you're done at the store, and I'll come by and pick you up."

"Okay. I'll call Jill and see if she can take Mr. Darcy for a couple of hours this afternoon so he's not on his own."

"I can stop by on lunch and take him out, too, since you'll probably have the lunch rush. Farrah will be coming in for her shift by then."

"Thank you. I appreciate that. I'm going to head out," she said, realizing her hand was still on his arm and withdrawing it shyly.

"Okay, I'll see you later," Jamie said with a small smile. "If you hear anything about Dean before I do, just give me a call."

"Yeah, same with you," Beth told him, as she headed out.

"Wait a second," Jamie said, halting her. "I forgot something." He walked over and bent down to pet Mr. Darcy. Then he took a treat out of his pocket and handed it to the dog. "Better," he said, as Beth smiled at him.

She knew everything wasn't fixed. After all, she still had too many confusing feelings she didn't much care for, but at least she'd made an effort. She felt bad it had taken something like this to make her realize how much she missed him. She heard her phone buzz and looked down to see a message from Jonah.

They'd been casually hanging out for the last couple of weeks. She liked him, just as she always had. He was funny and sweet, and she had to admit that he'd gone from a cute boy to an attractive man. Plus, it was a relief to be able to talk over the Jamie situation with a guy and get his read on it. He wasn't so sure Jamie was uninterested, but then he didn't know Jamie as well as she did. She answered the text, filling him in briefly on Dean, and declining an invitation to go see a movie later.

As she walked Mr. Darcy home, she called Jill and asked her if she could take him for a couple of hours later in the evening while she was at the hospital. She let herself into the house, depositing Mr. Darcy with a fresh bowl of water and food. She sent a couple of texts to the staff to ask them to be at work a few minutes early if they could manage it for a quick meeting. She imagined, in a town as small as Madison, that the word would be out by the time she got there anyway.

***

Dean was asleep when Lindy finally had a chance to see him. She walked in slowly, unsure of what to expect. When she saw he was sleeping, she just stood there and watched him for a minute before approaching the bed. She hesitated to touch him. She wasn't quite sure what might hurt. His face was cut up, and it looked like he had stitches in his forehead. She couldn't imagine the amount of pain he must be in.

She brushed his hair back. She'd never really told him, but she loved his hair. Not just the blonde, but how it always felt like silk. It was thick and soft, and no matter how often he cut it, it would grow out so fast. She thought it was sexy and endearing at the same time. She had to admit that running her fingers through it was satisfying, but yanking it during sex had become a favorite pastime, too. Her lips quirked in a small smile, and she bent over to kiss his forehead softly, avoiding the stitches carefully.

"You missed," he murmured. Lindy leaned back and looked at him. His eyes were still closed, and she ran a hand over the hair that she loved. She kept stroking his hair and leaned over to place a kiss on his lips.

"Better," he told her, reaching his hand for hers. She took it, noting the cuts on his hands and arms, too.

"You're supposed to be sleeping," Lindy told him softly.

"Maya?"

"Mom's with her. Everyone's here."

And it was true. Everyone who really mattered was there waiting. Dean's sister and father were on their way, and his mother was only a few minutes out. But everyone who Dean loved had gotten there shortly after they'd heard the news.

"Everybody else get out okay? Someone was behind me right before all hell broke loose ..." He trailed off, remembering that horrible feeling of the floor giving way. He'd lost all perspective then, as the world went black.

"Couple of injuries, but it looks like you got the worst of it. I'm going to yell at you later, when you're feeling better."

"I expected no less," Dean told her, peeking out at her and then closing his eyes. "You okay?"

"I'm fine. It's you we have to worry about," Lindy told him, dropping into the chair beside him, pulling it closer to the bed so she could lean her head against his own. He drifted back to sleep on the pain medication that kept him from feeling the worst of it.

She felt a hand on her shoulder after a few minutes and looked up. She hadn't even heard her mother come in. "His mother is here. She'd like to see him," Keely said softly. "Seth has Maya right now."

"I just need a minute," Lindy said, laying her head back down next to Dean's.

She wouldn't break. Not now. But she took a minute just to assure herself that he was okay. After a minute had passed, she sat up, her face pale and drawn, as the morning's events hit her with a shock. It could have been so much worse, she thought. If things had happened differently—she couldn't even finish the thought.

"I'm ready now." She leaned in to kiss Dean again. "I'll be right outside," she told him softly, knowing that he wouldn't hear her in his sleep, but needing to say it anyway.

Keely walked beside her down the long hall back to the waiting room. As they approached the room, Lindy stopped suddenly. "Can you watch Maya? Just for a few minutes? I need … I have to …" she started and stopped, unable to get the words out.

"Go. She'll be fine."

She watched Lindy head for the exit rather than the waiting room and hurt for her. Keely had wanted to cry for Dean herself, but she'd make time for that later. Now, her family needed her. She headed into the waiting room and moved to the blond, a few years younger than herself, who stood anxiously by the front desk.

"Deanna, I'm so glad you made it," she said, moving to speak to Dean's mother. They'd never been friends, but they'd been friendly enough over the years. She'd sensed Deanna's dislike but had understood it in a way. "Lindy just stepped outside, and Dean is sleeping. I'll take you to his room if you're ready."

"I always knew this would happen," Deanna said, as she fell into step beside Keely in the hall. She was several inches shorter than Keely's 5'8" and had put on a little weight over the last few years. Her hair was cut shorter than she'd had it in those years Dean had been small. "I told him it was a dangerous job, but he never listened," she complained. "Not to me, anyway."

Deanna looked over at Keely, the woman who had likely seen her son more than she had while he was growing up. She'd resented it some of the time, but mostly she'd been grateful, although she doubted that she'd ever showed it. Things with Nathan, Dean and Danielle's dad, had been rough all those years. She'd been glad when he'd had somewhere peaceful to go when the tension had been unbearable. She'd only wished she'd had an escape, too.

"He's so lucky it wasn't worse." Keely explained what had happened as they walked down the hall. She'd been lucky she was with Lindy when Jimmy had stopped by. She hated to think how her girl would have handled it alone. She was more than capable of handling anything, but that didn't mean she needed to do it all alone. She knew that Deanna was his mother, but Keely had looked at Dean as another son since he was a boy. She could understand both her fear and grief all too well.

"I just don't understand how this could have happened," Deanna exclaimed and kept up a litany of exclamatory remarks, her heels clicking along sharply as they headed down the long hallway with its bright fluorescent lights. Keely kept her own counsel, her heart with all of her babies—Dean included—as they walked toward the room.

***

Libby walked outside and spent a few minutes looking around near the entrance. She even went as far as walking over to the parking garage to see if Lindy had headed out to her car. She finally found her in the garden outside the cafeteria, deserted so early in the morning. Lindy sat with her head in her hands on a bench as far from the hospital as she could manage. Libby stopped, knowing how very private these moments of grief could be. She started to walk away, and then she decided instead to follow her instinct.

She walked over to Lindy and sat down beside her. She put an arm around her and pulled her in, saying nothing. Lindy didn't say anything, but she let herself lean. So Libby did what you do when your friend and soon to be sister-in-law was broken. She ran a hand over her hair and let her be. After a while, Lindy sat up slowly, taking the tissue Libby offered her without comment. They sat like that in silence for a few minutes, and then Lindy reached over and held Libby's hand.

"He's okay. I mean, he will be. He just looked ... it was so ..." She couldn't finish it, couldn't explain it, but Libby seemed to understand.

"What do you need?"

"Can we just sit here for a minute? I'm not up to seeing his mom yet." Lindy had never liked Deanna. She knew that the moment she saw her, Deanna would begin a litany of complaints- about Dean's job, about how little she saw Maya, about how hard her life had been. She looked up quickly. "Is Maya okay?"

"She's fine. Seth has her, unless Keely took over. You know they enjoy it." They sat their quietly for a few minutes before Lindy stood up slowly.

"I'm ready. Let's go."

Lindy sat in the waiting room, feeding Maya and watching people come and go. Libby went outside to call Beth and make arrangements at the studio, something she really should have thought of first. Seth and Libby left to pick up lunch for everyone, taking orders and writing them down. She made conversation with Deanna, although she couldn't remember what they spoke about other than the baby. She talked to Nathan and Danielle when they came in and watched how carefully Nathan and Deanna avoided each other while

Danielle went back and forth between the two of them anxiously. She never wondered why Dean would prefer their home to his own. That, she'd always understood. She watched everyone come and go and tried to project a semblance of calm. She thought she was successful until Seth sat down beside her.

"I know you too well to suggest that you go home and rest. But you need to eat," he said, pointing to the boxes of carry out food in the bags on the table. "We're heading down with this to the cafeteria. You should come, too."

"I'm fine," Lindy replied with a shrug. "I'm not hungry."

"Well, Maya is, and you're feeding her. Come on. We've got a little time while Nathan and Danielle are visiting with Dean, and I mentioned we would be in the cafeteria. They'll come straight there to get you when it's your turn with him. Theodore, Keely, and Libby were splitting up the bags, carrying them out to the elevator and down to the cafeteria.

Lindy got up reluctantly and walked with her brother. They shared the same strong facial features and coloring. Lindy favored her mother so much, except around her eyes. They headed down to the cafeteria, taking the elevator. Seth carried Maya in the baby carrier where she slept, and Lindy had the diaper bag slung over her shoulder. The elevator was empty and slowly descended.

"Why are you looking at me like that?"

"What's going on in your head?" Seth asked, knowing that her silence was more ominous than any other reaction she might have had.

"I never really thought of his work as dangerous," Lindy explained. "Not really."

"It can be. It's part of the work. I thought it was going to be so much worse, when Mom called me." He shook his head slowly. "I thought, for a second, it was the call I've always been afraid of."

"But that's just it. I never really have been afraid of it. I never even thought …" She paused. "We have a daughter now." She looked down at the ring on her finger. "Maya could have lost her father." She didn't even mention that she could have lost her fiancé. She didn't really need to.

"I know. He's my best friend, Lindy." She looked at him for a long moment and nodded.

"I know that. I just don't know if I can do this," she told him, as the elevator descended. "I don't know how to be with someone who can go out to work and not come back home." "Lindy, look at me. That's true of any of us. He'll still be Maya's father, regardless," he reminded her. "Do you want him to change jobs? Or stop driving? Stay inside the rest of his life? You can't keep him safe."

"I know that," Lindy said, sharply.

"But he is safe right now," Seth reminded her, following her thoughts. They'd been close for long enough that he could see the dark path they were heading down. "And he's happy now—happier than I've ever seen him. He's got you, and he's got Maya. Are you going to take that from him?"

"I'm not saying that," Lindy said with an anxious shrug. "I just need time to think." She rubbed her head.

"Migraine?" he asked with some concern. She'd been plagued by them for years before she'd gotten the daith piercing.

"I'll be fine, if I just get some food. Maya's going to be hungry soon."

"Let's sit down and eat. You'll feel better then," Seth told her, leaning his shoulder against hers as they stepped out of the elevator. "Then you can go back up and check on him."

Chapter 24

Dean sighed heavily. He was at least relieved to be home. His nearly week-long stay in the hospital had been an annoyance. He'd had plenty of company with family and friends on hand at every moment, but he wanted to be home. Of course, it wasn't an ideal situation. They had moved a bed, temporarily, into a downstairs room until he could handle the stairs without help. He had rehabilitation scheduled once a week. But mostly he was bored and hurting. He'd had headaches, nightmares, and a body that felt like—well, like he'd had a house practically fall in on him, he thought. Still, he'd been lucky.

He'd taken the ax in to vent the house. It was old and abandoned. The lightning strike had been called in quickly, and they'd gotten there in good time. He'd been halfway through the second floor when he heard the tell-tale rumble beneath him. He'd cursed and started to turn when the floor gave way. He'd seen another body in the building, but he couldn't remember who'd come in after him. He'd lost consciousness when he hit the floor beneath him, but he woke up as they were loading him into the ambulance, briefly. The pain had been blinding, and he had no other memories before he came to in the hospital.

He grimaced as he looked at his leg. He was nothing but trouble for Lindy now, he brooded. Couldn't get around easily or go pick up the baby. She'd moved them all into the downstairs room, an old rarely-used parlor that they'd converted into a family room. They were having Thanksgiving in there later that day, and Dean tried not to feel annoyed at the intrusion of more people. He loved them all, but he missed the time with just Lindy and Maya.

"You need anything?" Lindy asked, as she passed the doorway, heading toward the kitchen where she and the others were getting ready for the Thanksgiving meal.

"No. I'm good," Dean said shortly. She stopped, looking at him and the scowl on his face.

"Want the baby?"

"Is she awake?" he asked, brightening.

"Only just," Lindy told him. "Give me a second to get her."

She walked out of the room, and Dean tried to cool his jets. After all, Lindy hadn't complained at all about having to take care of him. He was going to be down for the count for at least a couple of months. But she was doing something else weird that Dean decided he didn't like at all. She was being so damn *nice* to him. He wished she'd stopped. It was creeping him out.

"Here you go," she said, settling Maya in his lap and brushing a hand over his head before leaning in to kiss his forehead. "Can I get you anything else?" she asked solicitously.

"Nope," he said, eyeing her with suspicion. "What's your deal?"

"Nothing. Just busy getting everything ready."

"Huh. I know for a fact that Keely and Seth are doing all the work, and you and Libby are probably just drinking wine and watching."

Lindy smiled at him but looked away absently. "Something like that."

"Well, do that in here."

"Fine." How did he, she thought in exasperation, expect her to be able to talk about him when he was sitting in the same damn room all the time? "Libby!" Lindy called down the hall. "Bring the wine. Dean wants us to hang out in here."

"You didn't have to yell for her," Dean said, rolling his eyes.

"It worked, didn't it?" Lindy said, politely.

Dean looked at her, missing her sarcasm as much as he missed the use of both legs. He looked at Maya who was grinning at him.

"Who's my best girl?" he asked her, covering her in kisses and trying to keep her from simultaneously kicking his ribs.

"I can take her back, if she's hurting you."

"I've got her," Dean said stubbornly. "Drink your wine."

Libby handed her the wine glass and set the bottle down on the table. "How are you feeling?"

"Fine," he said shortly. "I'm getting better," he told her, softening his reply. It wasn't Libby's fault Lindy was being so damn weird, he reminded himself.

"I'm glad. Seth said he'll be in with a beer for you as soon as he checks the turkey."

"How's he making it this year? Deep fried?" Dean asked, hopefully.

"No, he said with you down for the count, he's smoking it instead."

They had deep fried the turkey the year before, with Dean standing by with a fire extinguisher and plenty of commentary. It had been delicious, but they'd decided to do something with a little less risk this year, all things considered. Seth had started smoking the turkey in the early hours of the morning. It smelled wonderful. They were just waiting a couple more hours for it to finish and the rest of the family to arrive.

"Who's coming anyway?" Dean asked, perking up at the thought of smoked turkey.

"Beth is supposed to come by with Uncle Miles," Lindy told him. "And Theodore is bringing Layla and Presley over." She thought about it. "And I think that's it."

"No dates this year?" he asked, thinking of Noah the previous year.

"No. Though I think Beth has been seeing someone."

"Jonah," Libby offered.

"The Parent Trap one? Not Jamie?"

"That's about the size of it," Lindy agreed.

"But Jamie and Ansley broke up. I thought he'd ask Beth out. Aren't they hanging out again?" He'd seen them both at the hospital and assumed they were together.

"They're hanging out some. Not the same as before," Libby said. "Though I think they're both still hung up on each other. Jamie anyway."

"Beth, too," Lindy offered.

"Really? Are you sure?"

"She told me," Lindy admitted. "That's why she stopped hanging around him. She thinks it would embarrass him to find out."

"But he's interested," Dean said, confused.

"Yep," Lindy agreed.

"And she thinks he's not?" Dean asked. Lindy nodded. "Why don't you just tell her?"

"She doesn't believe me," Lindy said with a shrug. "She'll have to figure it out for herself."

"That's true enough," Libby said. "I hope she does it soon, though."

"And there he is," Seth announced as he walked into the room with his mother. "Surrounded by women, as always."

"Two of these are mine. But in an I-belong-to-them way and not a women-are-property way," he said shooting a cheeky smile at Lindy who rolled her eyes.

"He always was a charmer," Keely agreed, going over to make faces at Maya who chuckled and reached out her hands. She picked her up smoothly and ruffled a hand across Dean's hair.

"Why do women always play with my hair?" he asked, rolling his eyes.

"It's so soft and pretty." Keely said, patting it. "Just wait until Maya gets a handful."

"Oh, she already got a handful last week, nearly pulled it out by the roots," he said ruefully. "Like all women, pretty but dangerous."

They looked at Lindy, waiting for her to launch into a feminist defense of women or at least attack the patriarchy, but she just sat quietly watching with a neutral expression on her face, as if distracted.

"Well, I'm getting more wine," Libby announced. "Lindy's coming with me."

"I am?" she asked, surprised.

"You are," Libby agreed. "Beth will help," she added, as Beth walked in with an uncomfortable Miles.

"Okay," Beth said gamely, not sure what was going on but willing to play along.

"What's your deal?" Libby asked when they made it to the kitchen.

"How do you mean?" Lindy asked, pulling out another bottle of wine from the fridge where she'd stashed it earlier.

"You're being weird. Like nice-weird," she clarified. "No offense. You just missed an opportunity to educate the men about the patriarchy, and Dean was clearly baiting you."

"Oh, that. I just didn't feel like it. And it's not the job of women to educate men on the patriarchy."

"See? That's more like it!" Beth said with a smile. "There's the old Lindy!"

"I'm just trying to be nice."

"Are you okay? Really?" Libby asked.

"I'm fine," Lindy replied, rolling her shoulders. "It's just strange. I mean, having him underfoot all the time, having someone else manage the store."

"You know we're happy to help out if you need a break," Beth offered. "We could take it in shifts so you got out of the house more."

"It's not that. It's not even that I mind it all. It's just … different," she said, struggling to describe how her life had been perfect, and now she was worried every day about what it would mean when

Dean could walk again and go back to work, the fear that she would have to live with—or choose not to.

"Well, ask if you need help," Libby told her. "You know none of us mind. We love you both," she reminded Lindy, rubbing her arm in comfort.

"Why didn't you bring Jonah?" Lindy asked Beth curiously, changing the subject.

"Oh. That's not really a thing. Well, more of a friends with benefits thing, to be honest," Beth admitted. "But he had plans with his own family today."

"Huh. Well, you could have asked Jamie," Libby reminded her. "We always love having him around, and it seems like you two are friends again."

"You know Jamie," Beth reminded them. "He has a pretty big family."

"Still, he might have liked to be invited," Libby suggested, as Lindy elbowed her.

"Now you're being weird," Beth told Libby.

"Okay, let's bring the wine back before they send out a search party," Lindy suggested, nudging them toward the family room.

***

Theodore, Presley, and Layla came in shortly after the turkey came out of the smoker. It was clear that they had argued on the way over by Theodore's discomfort and how they scattered to opposite directions as soon as they walked in the door. Presley went straight to the wine, and Layla headed over to the distraction of the baby.

"What happened?" Keely asked Theodore quietly.

"They're finding the living situation—challenging."

"That's nothing new. Did something happen?"

"Just the usual sort of thing. They just rub each other wrong, and they bickered all the way here from the farm. You should have seen them when their mom was alive. Thick as thieves."

"Well, things like that are bound to change people," Keely said calmly, thinking of how she had changed after Zeke had left her. She'd been such a wallflower then, so eager to please. Well, she'd developed a spine of steel, that's for sure. And she'd learned she was far more capable than she had ever known. She hoped that the girls would learn that, too—although they were hardly girls. Women in their mid- and late-20s now. "How about I get you a drink?"

"I might just go pour myself a glass of tea actually."

Keely walked over to greet Presley as Theodore headed back to the kitchen. He could drink a little, even with the heart medication, but what he really wanted was a big glass of sweet tea. He'd spied a couple of gallons in the fridge when he'd come in. He came down the hall and entered the kitchen, where Lindy was standing leaning against the counter. He thought she was getting a drink herself until he saw her face and the way she was white knuckling the counter.

"What is it? Did something happen?"

"Um, floaters," she said, shakily.

"What?"

"I see auras before I get a migraine," she told him, her face growing increasingly pinched and pale. "Or at least I used to, when I'd get them all the time."

Theodore had heard about Lindy's migraines, how severe they had always been. "Where's your medicine?"

"I haven't had one in years so I didn't get it refilled," she said, trying not to panic.

"Stay here. Sit down," Theodore told her, hurrying out of the room. He walked straight over to Keely and Presley. "Migraine medicine. Do you have any?"

"Lindy?" Keely asked. When he nodded, she headed straight back to the kitchen.

Presley said, "I don't, but I think Layla might." She walked over to her sister, pulling her aside. "Do you still have migraine medicine? Lindy's having one."

"I might, in my purse," Layla said, digging around to see. "No, I'm sorry. It's at home. Should we go get it?" She knew how bad they could get.

"No, it'll be too late then," Presley said, heading toward the kitchen.

"Thanks for looking, sweetheart," Theodore told Layla, rubbing her arm and then following Presley into the kitchen.

"What was that all about?" Dean asked curiously, when she sat down beside him.

"Lindy's having a migraine. They thought I might have medicine for it," Layla explained. "I don't have any with me though."

Dean shot a look toward the kitchen and mentally cursed his broken leg for making him useless. He'd seen Lindy's migraines firsthand, how quickly they'd hit and how long they'd stay. They'd all worried about her for years. After trying biofeedback and acupuncture and nearly everything else, she'd gotten the daith piercing and had gotten a little relief. She hadn't had a truly significant migraine in years. She was having one now, and he couldn't even go to her, he thought in frustration.

In the kitchen, Lindy was leaning over with her head between her legs. Keely was rubbing her back, and Presley handed her a glass of water with four Ibuprofen. "You need to take this, drink all the water, and then go lie down. If we're lucky, you'll have caught it in time."

Lindy looked up, her face waxy. "I don't think we caught it in time," she told them, shakily. "It's coming." She started to shake and shut her eyes, taking the glass carefully and downing the pills obediently.

"Let's get you in to bed," Theodore told her, helping Keely lift her up.

"I've got her," Seth said, as he came in. He picked up his sister, who laid her head limply on his shoulder, and carried her upstairs to the bedroom. Keely walked to the blackout curtains and pulled them closed while Beth ran into the bathroom to get a garbage can to place beside the bed. Presley stood back and watched, knowing they'd all been through this before. Theodore stood beside her, feeling helpless.

"Do you have any milk pumped in the fridge?" Keely asked Lindy quietly.

"A little," she whispered.

"That's plenty," Keely told her, kissing her forehead and pulling up the covers. "I'll stay with her."

"Let me," Presley offered. "You go downstairs and check on everyone. I'll stay until the worst has passed, and I'll come get you if she needs you," she told them. "I am the medical professional here," she said with a roll of her eyes.

Keely relented, hugging Presley. "Call me if she gets worse," she said as she left the room.

***

Beth sat with Dean while the others set the table and tried to distract themselves. He was scowling, but she noticed that he kept glancing up the stairs with an expression that looked far more worried than angry. She scooted closer to him and asked him quietly,

"Are you okay?"

"I hate this." Dean said softly. "I can't even go up there to be with her, and I'm not sure she'd want me to anyway."

"Why do you think that?" Beth asked, genuinely astonished. "Lindy loves you!"

"Then why is she avoiding me? She's doing great at the whole nurse bit, but you saw her. She's being so damn nice all the time, when she's not avoiding me altogether. She makes sure I have everything I need, but keeps her distance. When we talk, it's like she's not even hearing me," Dean said with a sigh.

"Have you asked her what's up?" Beth asked, her brow furrowing. This was sounding uncomfortably familiar, as she thought about how she'd been treating Jamie lately.

"Yeah. She says everything's fine. But clearly, it's not fine," Dean said flatly, watching the stairs. "She's going to leave me."

"You don't know that," Beth pointed out. "Lindy wouldn't do that."

"Are you so sure?" Dean asked her, his eyes never leaving the stairs.

Beth watched him reach over to grab the monitor from the end table and adjust the settings. Beth leaned over to look curiously. They couldn't see Lindy completely with the angle of the camera, but he could see enough. He turned off the volume as they heard the sound of retching come over the speakers. He kept watching it, only breathing a long sigh when she finally laid down to sleep. Beth looked at Dean's fingers, gripping so tightly to the monitor that they'd turned white. She watched the expressions playing over his face and wondered for the first time what it must be like for Jamie since she'd started acting so strange. She'd never considered it from that angle, and she shifted uncomfortably in her seat as she watched Dean watch Lindy with an intensity that spoke volumes about both his love and his pain.

***

Presley sat down in a chair after the door closed and breathed a sigh of relief. She hadn't felt like socializing, and this afforded her the perfect opportunity for some peace and quiet. She turned the sound off on her phone and watched the expressions pass across Lindy's face. No, they hadn't gotten her the medicine in time. Her face looked increasingly pinched, and Presley instinctively got up and grabbed the garbage can in time for Lindy to sit up and start vomiting into it. She rubbed her back and kept the hair out of her face as she threw up. Even when Lindy flopped back against the pillows with a moan, Presley stayed and waited. Sure enough, it all started again a few minutes later.

When the worst was past, Lindy finally fell asleep, her face still pale and pinched. It wasn't gone quite yet, but the worst was over. Presley cleaned up the mess and then crept downstairs where they were all still waiting in the family room, hoping Lindy would be able to join them for the meal. Dean was anxiously looking up at the staircase when she came down.

"She's asleep," Presley told them. "She should be through the worst of it, but I'll go back up and check in a bit."

"No need," Dean said, flatly, holding up the video monitor where he and Beth had seen what had happened. He had watched Lindy anxiously and had seen the way Presley had taken care of her each time she'd gotten sick and then cleaned up when she finally fell asleep. He'd known she was coming downstairs and had held the monitor tightly in his hands in case Lindy got worse again. Of course, he thought, he couldn't do anything even if she needed him. Not with all those stairs and his busted leg, he thought angrily.

"She'll be okay now," Presley assured him. "But she probably won't wake up for a few hours. The sleep will help."

"We should eat," Seth said.

"I'll make her a plate for when she wakes up," Libby said, heading to the kitchen to do just that.

"Thanks for that," Dean told Presley quietly.

"No problem. Does she get them often?"

"She used to. Not in years."

"Could be stress-related. Or an allergy."

Dean thought about all the stress he'd put her through lately. If it was stress-related, this was his fault, he thought. He looked down at the monitor where her face had finally started to relax and wished he didn't feel so damn helpless.

"You should eat. She'll be fine."

He nodded and then gratefully accepted a plate when Beth brought him one. He gave her a small smile and tried to show his appreciation by eating it. Still, his eyes kept traveling back to the monitor to watch Lindy sleep.

When Lindy woke up later, Dean was the first to notice and alerted Keely who had been up several times to check on her. They'd already fed Maya once in the four hours Lindy had been asleep using one of the frozen bags of breast milk they'd put aside for emergencies. Theodore had left already to take Presley and Layla back to their cars, and Miles had gone hours before, just as soon as they'd finished the meal. Beth had stayed a couple of hours longer, but then went home to check on Mr. Darcy, asking that they let her know when Lindy was up. Seth and Libby had stayed with Keely to keep Seth company and watch the baby. Seth had helped Dean get around the house, and they'd already set the table for an early dinner when Dean noticed that Lindy was waking up.

She came down a few minutes later, taking the stairs slowly. "Sorry about that," she told them, her voice rough from the sleep and the horrors of the migraine.

"Don't apologize," Dean said sharply, his fear coming out as anger.

She took one look at him and understood. Of course, she understood, she thought, when she'd felt that fear herself when he'd been hurt. She looked at his leg, broken and in a cast and realized what it must have been like to know that she was hurt and not be able to help. She saw the monitor clutched in his hand and realized that he'd been with her all the time, in the only way he could be. She wanted to walk over to him and put her arms around him, pressing her cheek to his. She wanted that so much it hurt. But she didn't.

Instead, she stood in the doorway, just looking at him.

"I'm going to get some water. Do you want anything?" she asked him softly.

"No," Dean returned, holding her stare, trying to figure out what she could be thinking, his anger burning away into hurt alone.

"I'll get the water. You sit down," Keely told them. Quietly, she headed to the kitchen, and Seth and Libby excused themselves and followed. They started getting the food back out, warming it up and taking it into the dining room where the table was set for dinner. When Lindy came in later with Dean leaning on her, Libby offered to light candles in case the light was still bothering Lindy.

"No, I'm better now. It's over. I just wasn't expecting it. But I'm starving now. Have the others gone home?"

"Just a while ago," Keely told her. "Beth asked that we call her when you're better, and Presley wanted us to remind you to get that refill."

"I'll call the doctor tomorrow," she told them, loading up her plate.

"I sent him a text earlier," Dean said and then shrugged when everyone looked at him. "I know it's a holiday, but we've known him forever. He said he'd call something in in the morning," Lindy shot him a grateful look and then started shoveling food into her mouth. She was starving, but she also knew her stomach was a little raw so she tried, and failed, to take it slow.

"You're a good man, Dean Walton," Keely told him.

"He's okay. But can he smoke a turkey?" Seth asked with a laugh, glad that Lindy was feeling better and Dean had stopped looking so upset.

"I'm deep frying that sucker next year," Dean warned him. "You can hold the extinguisher." All of the others laughed except Lindy, and Dean watched her quietly, wishing he could get inside her head and figure out what was wrong.

Chapter 25

Beth sat in a corner of the studio, holding Maya and watching Lindy with interest. She had a day off from work, and Lindy had a couple of hours to get the studio transformed from Thanksgiving to Christmas. She watched her go through the totes she kept in the back with interest.

"You know, you actually have staff for this," Beth pointed out, making faces at Maya and grinning when it made the baby give a deep belly laugh.

"I like doing it myself," Lindy said shortly, pushing her hair out of her face in frustration.

"You don't really seem like you like doing it yourself."

"It's just been a long week."

"How's Dean?"

"He's okay. I mean, he's cranky and frustrated most of the time, but I would be, too."

Beth watched the flicker of emotion cross Lindy's face and then disappear again. Lindy bent back over the boxes, pulling out décor and sorting it on the floor beside her. "Who's with him now?"

"Seth. He brought movies so that ought to give me a few hours to get this sorted," she said, waving a hand at the mess.

"Well, I'll help however I can."

"Watching Maya is helping. Besides, I work faster on my own."

"Okay," Beth said, letting it go. Besides, she thought, she was more than happy to spend a couple of hours playing with the baby. "How are you and Dean doing?"

"How do you mean? We're fine."

"Are you? You don't seem fine."

"It's complicated."

"Want to talk about it?"

"No," Lindy said shortly, and then sighed. "I'm just trying to work some things out."

"Well, when you do, maybe give Dean a heads up."

"Are you going to take your own advice?" Lindy asked her pointedly, as they watched Jamie approach the store.

"I might," Beth said quietly, as Jamie came in.

"Hey, Lindy, is this the box you needed?" Jamie asked from the door, hefting in a large tote he'd picked up from the storage room at the antique store. The store had more storage than the studio so Lindy had convinced Seth to let her put a couple of holiday boxes in the back. Jamie brought in the enormous box and put it down on the floor of the studio, hoping it was the right one so he wouldn't have to reverse and then repeat the process. "Hey, Beth," he said, noticing her in a glider in the corner.

"Hey," she returned with a smile. It had been good, she thought, to get back to being friends, even if it wasn't the same as before. They'd even managed a less-than-awkward movie night.

"Yeah, that's it. I appreciate you."

"Need any help?"

"Can you put the box over here so I can go through it?" Lindy asked, gesturing to a space nearer the table where she was working.

"Sure thing."

"How come he gets to help?" Beth asked, affronted.

"Because he can lift more than you can."

"Hey, I'm stronger than I look!"

"'And though she be but little, she is fierce,'" Jamie quoted with a grin as Beth smiled and Lindy rolled her eyes.

"Why don't you two go grab me some coffee and get out of my hair?"

"Can I take the stroller?"

"Or the wrap. Your choice."

"The stroller is easy enough," Beth said with a smile, going to unfold it from the corner where it rested. "What do you want?"

"Grab me the biggest espresso they have and maybe a muffin or scone. I don't know. Something to snack on," Lindy said with a shrug. "I'll have this more in hand when I have space to think."

"Message received," Jamie said with a smile. "We'll take our time."

"Do," Lindy said shortly, a smile quirking up the corners of her mouth. "Coffee on me," she said, as she flicked her card in their direction and laughed as Jamie caught it mid-air.

"It's nice to see Lindy getting back to her old self," Beth told Jamie as she pushed the stroller toward Brews & Blues.

"When wasn't she herself?"

"She was odd, after the fire. Like really, really nice. To Dean, especially."

"That's natural, I would think."

"Yeah, but still. Weird."

"Must be going around."

Beth stopped for a second and looked at him and then began walking again. "Oh, that," she said, uncomfortably. "I guess I *was* acting weird."

"Want to tell me what that was all about?"

"I probably should," Beth replied slowly. "It's just sort of ... embarrassing."

"Like women stuff?"

"No, you know that kind of thing doesn't embarrass me," Beth said with a shrug of one shoulder. "It wasn't anything like that— exactly." She paused, collecting her thoughts. She weighed the utter humiliation of telling him with the discomfort of continuing to pretend that everything was the way it had always been.

Jamie waited patiently, watching her. Maya, in the stroller, watched the town pass by with interest. Beth seemed to be experiencing an internal struggle and kept silent for the next block. It was a beautiful day, Jamie noted. It was crisp and cool with the autumn color still on the trees even this late in the year. In anywhere else but the Deep South, the trees would likely be bare already. In middle Georgia, it was only a little cool, not yet cold and not a snow flurry in sight. The planters still had a profusion of blooms that would have been long gone further north. He enjoyed the view and waited, hoping Beth would clear up the mystery soon.

"It's not easy to explain," she continued, wishing there was some less-awkward way to say it at all. "I had some ... feelings I needed to deal with," she admitted haltingly, her eyes kept firmly on the stroller.

"You might need to be a little more specific."

"For you," Beth said, blushing to her roots. "I'd started thinking of you as a little more than a friend, and then you were dating Ansley, and I ... I guess I was trying to stay out of the way," she said, furious at her own coloring for the flush of pink in her cheeks. It was too mild a day and too short a walk to blame it on the exertion. She took a couple of steps before realizing that Jamie had stopped completely, his mouth hanging open.

"What?" she demanded. "Please don't make this any more humiliating than it already is," she told him, pausing to wait for him to catch up. He fell into step beside her, grappling with words.

"Why didn't you just say something?"

"I was embarrassed," she admitted. "Besides, Girl Code."

"Girl Code?"

"I like Ansley. There's a code about these sorts of things. Besides, I already knew you didn't feel the same so what would have been the point except making us all uncomfortable?" she told him gamely, feeling some relief that the conversation was less awkward than she'd feared.

"How could you know that?" Jamie demanded. Beth shot a pitying look at him.

"The kiss, Jamie," she said, shaking her head.

"What about it?" he asked, trying to follow her train of thought.

"If you'd been interested, you certainly would have brought it back up or tried it again. You didn't so you weren't interested," Beth explained patiently. They got to the door of the coffee shop, and Jamie automatically went to hold it open, helping Beth maneuver the stroller inside.

"Did the two of you have a baby no one told me about?" Candace demanded at the counter.

"Nope," Beth said, while Jamie flushed. "Borrowed Lindy's." Candace had been working at Brews as long, if not longer, than Beth had been managing the bookstore.

Candace shook her strawberry blonde hair back out of her face where it had grown longer than the pixie cut she'd kept for years and asked, "What'll you have?"

"Lindy needs the biggest espresso you have," Jamie told her. "And let's do the assortment of mini muffins," he said looking at Beth, who nodded in confirmation. "What do you want?" he asked her. "Lindy's buying," he reminded her, holding up the card.

"Well, in that case—" Beth said with a laugh. "Get me a large toffee coffee."

"I'll take a mocha," Jamie said. "But just a regular sized one," he told Candace with a smile. "And something to carry them in." They walked out a few minutes later with all the coffee and Maya asleep in the stroller.

"I'm glad I finally told you," Beth admitted as they walked. "It was weird keeping something from you." She looked over at Jamie who was silent. "I'm sorry if I embarrassed you," she told him, a note of apology in her voice.

"No, it's not that," he replied slowly. "I think maybe you just misunderstood."

"In what way?"

"You thought I didn't think of you like that because of the kiss," Jamie said slowly.

"Well, yeah. I would have thought that was obvious," she said, rolling her eyes.

"But I thought that you didn't think of me that way because of the kiss. Because you never mentioned it," Jamie said slowly, meeting her eyes as she came to a stop.

Beth struggled to find any words, but none would come. She just looked at him and realized how much they'd misunderstood each other. Then she wondered what that meant for them now.

"Oh," she said shortly, resuming the walk.

"Yeah," Jamie agreed, wondering what it meant and what they were supposed to do now.

They walked the rest of the way to the studio lost in their separate thoughts, occasionally shooting glances at each other. They went inside and set the coffees down on the table, opening up the box of muffins for Lindy's approval. She came out of the back and headed straight to the caffeine. Already, she'd managed to make more progress than Beth would have thought possible.

"Why are you two so quiet?" Lindy asked suspiciously.

"No reason," Beth said with a shrug as Jamie stayed quiet.

"I've got to go run some errands," Jamie said quickly. "Talk later?" he asked Beth.

"Of course," she answered automatically, watching him head out the door with his coffee.

"What was that about?"

"I told him."

"Oh," Lindy said, watching him go and then looking speculatively at Beth who was watching him, too. "Did it help?"

"Yeah, I think it did."

"Huh," Lindy said thoughtfully. "Well, let's get back to work."

***

Jamie knocked at the door and waited. He wasn't sure exactly what he was supposed to do with this new information. He couldn't quite wrap his mind around it. He knocked again, and then remembered Dean's injury and waited impatiently.

"Hey," Seth said, opening the door. "Where's the fire?" he asked, in a slightly raised voice.

"Ha. Ha," Dean said loudly from the other room. "Who is it?"

"Jamie," Seth called back.

"Tell him to get his ass in here and stop knocking down the door!" Dean called out.

"You heard him," Seth said, stepping back to let Jamie in.

"What's your deal?" Dean asked, as Jamie came in. "Want a beer?"

"It's barely three."

"Hey, it's five o'clock somewhere."

"There lies the way to alcoholism," Seth deadpanned with a roll of his eyes.

"I've got meds, but there's beer if you want some. Tea or Coke if you don't."

"How are you feeling?" Jamie asked, grabbing a Coke and sitting down on the sofa, stretching out his large frame with a sigh.

"Apparently, better than you. I'm alright. Getting better. Taking less pain meds and doing rehabilitation a couple times a week," he said with a shrug. "Want to tell us what's up? I know you didn't come over here out of concern for my health."

"I just had a weird conversation with Beth."

"Well, if that's all," Seth began with a laugh. "Isn't every conversation with her a weird one?"

"Not like this," Jamie said with a sigh. "So get this," he said, sitting up and leaning forward on to his knees with a Coke in one hand. "She stopped hanging out because she realized she had feelings for me and thought that I wasn't interested." He sat back, waiting for the exclamations of surprise and not finding any. He leaned forward again, narrowing his eyes at them both as they exchanged a look. "You knew?"

"Well, yeah," Seth admitted, rolling his shoulders.

"We were just wondering how long it would take you to figure it out. Took you long enough. And she had to *tell* you."

"Huh."

"Did you tell her you feel the same?" Seth asked curiously, feeling a little empathy for his struggle. After all, he remembered the start of his relationship with Libby and how awkward it could be to discover each other.

"Yeah."

"And what did she say?" Dean asked curiously.

"Nothing. That's just it," Jamie told them in frustration. "What am I supposed to do now?"

"Okay, let me get this straight," Dean began as Seth grinned over at him. "She says she has all these non-platonic feelings for you. And you say you feel the same."

"I already went through this," Jamie said with an uncomfortable shrug, knowing that any advice from these two would come with the teasing they reserved for their closest friends.

"You'd think he'd know what to do when a girl likes him and he likes her," Seth said, shaking his head.

"I do. Just not when it's Beth," Jamie said miserably. "I already feel like I screwed everything up after that kiss."

"Wait," Dean said, struggling to sit up more. When Seth moved to help, he snapped, "I've got it." He maneuvered himself into position and continued, "What kiss? Why is this the first I'm hearing of this?"

"I don't know anything about it," Seth said with a shrug, turning his attention to Jamie. "Spill."

"It was just a joke," Jamie protested when they continued to treat him to the blank stare. "Under the mistletoe at Christmas."

"Wait—where was this mistletoe?" Dean asked, knowing he'd have remembered if it had happened at their house with the mistletoe handing in the center of the room for all to see.

"At Beth's." He briefly explained how she had been checking items off her holiday bucket list and had failed to cross off mistletoe. He'd had some in the truck and brought it out to help her complete the list.

"Right. To help her," Dean said, choking out a laugh.

"He carries mistletoe around in his truck. Man, that's bold," Seth told him, shaking his head.

"Anyway," Jamie continued with a roll of his eyes, "it was just a quick kiss, and then we never talked about it again."

"Okay, let me get this straight," Dean returned. "You kiss her, and neither one of you talks about it, and then you both think the other isn't interested."

"Yes," Jamie said, nodding.

"Got any more mistletoe in your truck?" Seth asked helpfully while Dean laughed.

"Why did I even come here for advice?" Jamie asked himself aloud.

"We were wondering the same thing," Seth told him, heading to the fridge. "Ready for a beer now?"

"Yeah, I could probably use a drink," Jamie admitted, sinking back into the couch cushions with a sigh.

Chapter 26

Libby was sitting downstairs curled into her favorite yellow chenille chair listening to Bing Crosby on vinyl crooning about a white Christmas when Seth came downstairs. She smiled at him as he walked toward her. He sank down on the couch with a sigh and reached over to take her hand.

"Well, that's one thing I don't think we'll get this year," he said, looking out the window at the overcast day with temperatures unusually high for winter.

"Hope springs eternal. Are you about ready to go?"

"Why are we having it at Lindy's house when I have to do all the cooking?" he asked, rolling his eyes to the ceiling in exasperation.

"It's your family tradition. And you love it."

"Yeah, I do. Besides, Dean is still laid up for a couple of weeks. It makes it easier for him, though he'd honestly rather have an excuse to get out of the house."

"I know he's tired of being cooped up. How's his rehabilitation coming?" Libby asked, standing up to join Seth on the couch, automatically curling into him and laying her head on his shoulder.

"Slowly. Slower than he'd like, anyway," Seth replied, wrapping an arm around Libby. "We could just stay home."

"Not a chance. But nice try," she said, nuzzling in.

"Fine," he said in mock exasperation. "Let's go then. Have you got all the gifts ready?"

"They're stacked up in bags by the door," Libby told him and hung back to wait for his reaction.

"I think we're going to need to take the car," he called back.

"We might have gone overboard."

"You mean, you did. I don't remember buying all of these," he said, nudging the load of presents. "We need a sleigh for all this."

"We could get you a Santa suit, pad it up a bit," Libby suggested, patting his stomach with a twinkle in her eye.

"If I don't start running with you again, we're not going to need to pad it," Seth said, looking down in dismay. He'd put on a few pounds over the last few months. He'd always run to a slightly broader build than Dean, but he was afraid he was bulking up a bit more than he was comfortable with.

"You're being silly," Libby told him with a laugh. "But you're always welcome to run with me. I like the company."

"You say that, but then you leave me in the dust," he said, bending to lift one of the bags of presents. "Did we get everyone weights?"

"No," she returned with a short laugh. "Need me to get that for you?"

"No, let's just get going—so we can hurry up and get back."

"You know it doesn't work that way with your family."

"We need a signal for when we're ready to come home, like in that movie we watched the other day," Seth suggested as he opened the hatchback of Libby's SUV and started loading up the bags.

"It's Christmas Eve," Libby reminded him. "We'll just make our excuses about Maya's first Christmas and leave it at that. I don't think a code word will be necessary." She considered for a minute. "But we should come up with one for my family."

Libby was close to her sisters, but her parents could be hard to handle at times. Their total disengagement from their lives could be a sore spot for Libby and Rachel in particular. They'd get there early to help Rachel out, but then they'd clear out not long after Libby's parents finally managed to remember it was Christmas and show up. "Eggnog."

"What?" Libby asked, quirking one eyebrow at him.

"Eggnog. Our code word."

"You don't even like eggnog. How are you going to slip that one in a plausible sentence?"

"Libby, I hate eggnog." He waited a beat. "Just like that. Short and sweet."

"Fine," Libby said with a smile, shaking her head at him. "But don't be surprised when my dad starts giving you his best eggnog recipe or my mom starts expounding on people's narrow-mindedness when it comes to holiday beverages."

"I'm never surprised at anything they say," Seth replied with a wink.

"You know, it's our first married Christmas," Libby said, changing the subject.

"I remember," Seth said smiling over at her as they pulled up to the curb near his sister's house. He looked up at the house that was once his grandparents, then his mother's, and now Lindy's, and looked over at Libby. "How does it compare to your first with Collin?" He had been jealous of Collin for far too long. Now he was just glad the guy had screwed things up so badly. If he hadn't, Libby would probably be married to him still and not here in Madison married to him.

Libby shot him a look. "I haven't been comparing it."

"But if you had to?" he insisted with a smug grin.

"I spent my first Christmas with him on a cruise, avoiding his monster mother, a fact that she blamed me for for the rest of our marriage even though Collin had surprised me with the tickets," Libby said, rolling her eyes. "So—it was a little more tropical but nothing like this." She leaned over and kissed Seth's nose. "I prefer this. Although I wouldn't object to a cruise with you."

"So noted," Seth said with a smile, getting out of the car. "Alright, let's join the mayhem."

***

Beth put on a jacket and shook her head. She had been hoping a cold front would come in with a welcome sprinkling of snow, but it was only warm enough for a light jacket. She looked down at Mr. Darcy in his Christmas sweater.

"Just for the walk over," she assured him. "Then I promise I'll take it off once everyone's seen it," she told him, leaning down to give him a quick cuddle.

At the sound of the doorbell, she called out, "Just a second."

She snapped on Mr. Darcy's leash, the seasonal one in red with jingle bells on it, and grabbed the large tote she used as a purse. It held her emergency reading material, not that she'd be likely to need it today, she thought. In fact, she considered, she was more likely to use it when she went to her dad's house than when he came to Keely's. Lindy's now, she corrected. Still, her dad had opted out of this year's festivities. He'd decided to go to his new girlfriend's celebration instead and had only half-heartedly invited Beth along, giving her the excuse she needed to decline without guilt.

"Hey," she told Jamie, flushing, as she opened the door. "I didn't expect to see you. I figured you'd be on your way to your parents' house. Want to come in?"

"Just for a minute," he said shyly. They hadn't really had much time to talk since her revelation. They'd been slammed with customers, and then the weekends had been filled with holiday activities. They'd met briefly at the Caroling by Candlelight festival in town, but Beth had volunteered as an elf in Santa's workshop, and Jamie had already left by the time her duty was done. "I just wanted to bring you this before I left," he said, showing her the box in his hand. "I'm going to be out of town for a week."

"That's longer than usual," Beth mentioned, casually, heading back in. Jamie leaned down to scoop up Mr. Darcy.

"Aren't you hot in this sweater?"

"He's just wearing it until we get there. It's too cute not to show off."

"It just so happens I brought him a present, too," Jamie said, reaching into a bag and pulling out a small gift bag and a Santa Claus squeaky toy with a ribbon on it. He removed the ribbon and sat Mr. Darcy down beside his gift where he happily sat on his haunches and squeaked it.

"Why does he get two gifts?"

"Well, you're welcome to share his pig ears," Jamie said, nudging the small gift bag her way. She wrinkled her nose.

"No thanks," she told him, going over to the tree and picking up a box. "Here's yours," she told him handing it over and picking up her own. They both sat at the breakfast counter and looked at their boxes.

"You first."

"Same time?" she countered. He nodded, and they began opening their gifts.

Tucked inside her box was a stack of books tied in ribbon with a sprig of mistletoe tucked in and a *Pride and Prejudice* themed tote bag. Beth smiled and leaned against his shoulder in thanks and then immediately began sorting all of her things from the old tote into the new one, adding one of her new books to her emergency reading supply.

Meanwhile, Jamie opened up his gift and looked through it with a smile. She'd packed the box full of things he liked—energy bars for the gym, a row of his favorite beer, a book she knew he'd like, his favorite candy, and a DVD of one of the classic horror films he'd been curious to watch. He grinned at her and then noticed something about the package.

He looked closely at the wrapping paper with its mistletoe theme and had remembered how he'd tucked that sprig of mistletoe into her own gift at the last minute, hoping to remind her of their conversation and break the ice about it. Clearly, she'd had the same idea, unless the selection hadn't been conscious.

"I feel like we should just get this out of the way," he said, turning toward her.

She moved at the same time with one eyebrow quirked in curiosity. He waited a beat and then moved in slowly, hesitating to make sure they were on the same page. She waited, and he closed the distance, his lips meeting hers and holding on. She moved closer, bringing one hand up to his chest before moving it up to wrap around him. One hand went to her hair, and his other cupped her face. He felt the sigh move through her, as she moved closer, practically moving into his lap. When he broke off the kiss, he rested his forehead against hers for a minute.

"Merry Christmas."

"Merry Christmas," she told him with a small, shy smile. They stayed that way for a minute before he pulled back.

"I've got to go. Can I walk you to Lindy's?"

"Sure," she said, easing back and turning to grab her purse.

"This one," he reminded her, handing her the new one.

"Right," she said with a smile, taking it from him.

"Do you have any gifts to take over?"

"I dropped them off yesterday," she said, grabbing her keys and shoving them in the pocket of her dress. She did love a dress with pockets, she thought with a happy smile. She looked over at Jamie, replaying that kiss and then blushing at the thought. It had been welcome but wholly unexpected.

"You're going to Keely's party for New Year's?"

"Of course."

"Go with me?"

"Okay," she agreed with a smile, meeting his eyes, and then looking over at Mr. Darcy who trotted along with his queaky toy firmly clutched in his mouth. "Maybe I should have left that at home. Think it will annoy everyone?"

"If it does, just put him out back with it."

"Will you let me know when you get there?"

"Sure," he said with a smile, wondering at the ways their relationship was changing. Slowly, but changing nonetheless.

"I'll leave you here. If I go inside, I'll never get back out."

"Be careful," she told him, standing with Mr. Darcy on the porch as he started to walk back toward her house.

"I will," he said and then turned and ran up the porch stairs quickly before he changed his mind. He kissed her, quickly but with enthusiasm. "See you later," he told her with a cocky grin and she waved with a bemused smile as he walked off.

***

"Was that Jamie I saw leaving?" Lindy asked as Beth came into the room with Mr. Darcy.

"Yeah," Beth said, flushing.

"Why didn't he come in and say hello?" Keely asked.

"Oh, he had to get to his family's thing so he didn't have time," Beth said, happy for an explanation.

"And he was too busy kissing Beth anyway," Dean added from his place over by the window, while Beth turned beet red and every eye in the room turned to her.

"What?" Beth demanded. "I'm going to go get a drink," she said, making her way to the kitchen.

"Don't embarrass her," Keely told Dean, exasperated. "We all wanted this. Now leave them be," she cautioned him, pointing one finger in his direction.

"So ..." Lindy asked, sitting down beside Dean on the sofa where his leg was propped up. "What kind of kiss are we talking about?"

"I can still hear you," Beth called from the kitchen to their laughter.

"What's all that about?" Seth asked in the kitchen.

"Nothing," Beth grumbled, holding open the fridge, ostensibly to look for something to drink but really to cool the flush of her face.

"She and Jamie were making out on the porch," Lindy said, as she came into the room. "Dean saw it."

"Is she serious?" Libby asked Beth, adding sugar to the tea, the most Seth would let her help with the family meal.

"That would be kissing and telling," Beth said primly, grabbing a drink at random and heading to the living room to sit by Layla with a sigh. She looked down and noticed the Dr. Pepper in her hand and rolled her eyes. She'd meant to grab a Coke.

"Want me to get you something else?" Layla asked sympathetically.

"Would you?" Beth asked, gratefully. "Anything but this!" she insisted, pushing the Dr. Pepper away from her on the table.

"I'll drink that," Presley said, snatching it up as Layla headed to the kitchen. "Don't let them bother you. They love you so they have to aggravate you."

"You must love *me* an awful lot," Layla commented to Presley as she handed Beth the soda.

"I must," Presley agreed, kicking back with a sigh and popping open the can.

"Would you like a glass for that?" Keely asked on her way to the kitchen.

"I'm good," Presley told her. "One less glass to wash."

"How's living together going?" Beth asked the sisters. "I always wanted a sister. You're really lucky to have each other."

Presley and Layla exchanged a look. "It's okay."

"Just—you know—different," Presley explained.

"I told you I don't want to cramp your style," Layla told her. "Not that you have any style to cramp."

"I know." Presley said rolling her eyes. "It's not like you have been. And I heard that. All I do is work lately. Now if you were preventing me from getting laid, I'd boot you out."

Layla rolled her eyes. "How much longer until what's her face comes back from maternity leave?"

"End of the month, I hear."

"Then maybe we can get you set up on one of those dating sites."

"Save me!" she pleaded to Beth in mock desperation.

"Actually, I did the speed dating thing with some friends, and it's entertaining anyway."

"Entertaining usually means awful in dating lingo," Presley pointed out.

"Well, yeah, but funny."

"I'm good, thanks," Presley said, deflecting. "Now about you and Jamie."

"Okay, I deserve that. Never mind. We should all mind our own business," Beth insisted, hoping to save herself from further embarrassment.

"Did you get any details out of her?" Lindy wondered, as she sank down in a seat beside Presley.

"Nope. We're not talking about it," Presley said fervently, dodging the question of dating. "So, how are you doing with Dean underfoot?"

"Ha! Surviving. I'll be glad when he's better so he's not so damn grouchy all the time," Lindy told them, rolling her eyes.

"You're one to talk," Dean said wryly, as he and Seth came into the room.

"You're getting around better," Presley noted.

"I'm okay. Where's your dad?"

"He ran home to grab the pies he forgot," Layla explained.

"Don't believe it. He probably just wanted an excuse to run home and get another chapter in," Keely said with a patient smile.

"Don't count on that pie any time soon."

"Libby knows all about that," Seth told them.

"What?" Lindy asked. "Are you writing something new?"

"It's nothing," Libby said, embarrassed. "I've just been jotting down a few ideas." She shot a look at Seth who shrugged in apology.

"Well, I'm sure it's wonderful," Keely said warmly. "Tell me, Layla. How are you enjoying the new job?" she asked, deftly maneuvering the conversation away.

"It's interesting. Everyone has been so welcoming," Layla said, pleased to have been asked. Presley had rolled her eyes when she'd heard she had a new job, but her dad and Keely had been pleased. It was only part-time, but with her internship experience, they were hoping to make it full time well before tax season.

"I'm so glad," Keely said, getting up when she heard Maya on the monitor and gesturing Lindy to sit back down. "I've got her. Lolly's coming!"

Chapter 27

"Are we nearly done yet?" Dean asked later that night as he looked around at the presents under the tree. It was getting late. The family had left about an hour before, and Dean and Lindy had immediately started putting together toys requiring assembly and placing a pile of wrapped gifts under the tree.

"Think we went overboard?" Lindy asked, looking around the room.

Dean took in the over-stuffed stocking embroidered with Maya's name and the pyramid of presents spilling out from under the tree. "For a kid who can't even crawl yet? Yeah. But I wouldn't have it any other way. We'll take lots of pictures to show her that her parents were crazy about her from the start."

"That's a good idea," Lindy commented with a sigh, sitting down beside Dean and leaning her head on his shoulder. "I had that after, with Mom and my grandparents."

"There aren't any pictures of your dad with you at Christmas?" Dean asked Lindy, realizing that if they existed he'd never seen any.

"He wasn't big on holidays, even then," Lindy said with a half shrug, biting back the disappointment that never quite left.

"Has he ever tried to contact you?"

"I don't think so. I don't think he ever looks back."

"Well, you can't know that," Dean said blandly. "Is that why you're waiting? Are you waiting to see if I'll stay or go?"

"What? No, Dean. No," Lindy said with a sigh, reaching up to stroke a hand over the short beard he'd kept the last few years. "At least, I don't think so."

"Is it my job? This accident?"

"No, actually, that makes me think …" She paused looking at

him. "When I got the news, it was such a shock. Accidents like that just don't happen here. Except they do. And they did. And I wished then that we hadn't waited," Lindy said, looking down. "But then I started thinking about it, and I didn't know if I could live with fear this big all the time. That you could leave one day and not come back home." Her voice caught, and she looked down.

"So what did you decide?" Dean asked her quietly, taking her hand in his.

"I just needed time to think. I guess I decided that I don't want to wait any more."

"Couldn't you have just said that?"

"I needed to be sure. I've never loved anyone quite like this. Seeing you hurt like that—it just broke something in me. I needed to be sure I was strong enough to handle this."

"You're the strongest person I know. Then you're ready? You'll marry me?" He leaned closer, taking her chin in his hand.

"I'm more than ready. I'd do it today. Tomorrow. Whenever you want."

"And you're telling me this now? We could have been married today and celebrating our first married Christmas."

"How about our first New Year?"

"You're not kidding? What about the big wedding you wanted?"

"I'm good with just us. Or whoever we can get to come at the last minute."

"Well, alright then," Dean said, kissing her and then leaning back with a sigh. "We have a lot to do."

"It'll wait," she told him, leaning back beside him and resting her head on his shoulder. They watched the lights twinkle on the trees, and Dean reached over to take her hand, stroking it softly.

"It's been worth the wait," Dean said quietly, thinking of all the years he'd wanted Lindy, never thinking he had a chance in hell. Mostly because she'd have told him the same, if he'd asked all those years ago, he thought with a smile. They hadn't expected this, and yet here they were. He turned in to her, and the kiss that started warm went molten.

The presents sat piled around the tree, and the twinkling lights illuminated their skin as they moved together. Outside, the temperature began dropping quickly. Seth and Libby were just going to bed, Seth's arm pulling Libby close as they drifted off to sleep. Around the corner, Beth was just bringing Darcy in from the cold, grateful she'd put his sweater back on before they'd gone out since it was so much colder than it had been earlier. Jamie was laying down in the twin bed that had once been his, while his cousin snored across the room, and wondered what Beth was doing. Presley was curled up with an old movie, and when Layla couldn't sleep, she came in with a bottle of wine and joined her, passing a glass over. Theodore and Keely were fast asleep, his finished pages neatly piled on the desk with a bee paperweight Keely had surprised him with holding them steady. Dean kept his eyes on Lindy's and watched the rise of pleasure—as the snow started falling gently outside, unseen.

***

Presley looked up from the book she was reading and wondered if there was any point in even going out on the date she'd arranged earlier in the week. After all, the last one had been an exercise in keeping her temper in check. She'd dressed nicely, taking time with her appearance, and he'd shown up looking like he'd just finished painting a house. He was several inches shorter than the height he'd listed online, and she hadn't even worn the serious heels but kept it to a modest couple of inches. He'd then ordered a drink for her without asking her preferences and then spent the next hour mansplaining politics and religion to her while she tried to find a polite way to get out of there.

To make matters worse, Derrick had come in with his work

friends as she was sitting there trapped. There's nothing quite like, Presley thought, seeing the one who got away when you were sitting with the one who would never go away. When Layla called, she had answered eagerly, not even caring that she was being rude after the monologue she'd been treated to. She'd acted like it was an emergency and made her escape without a backward glance.

Thinking of that night made her reluctant to try again. Layla flopped down on the couch beside her and closed her eyes. "That bad?"

"Some of these mandatory training sessions are such bullshit," Layla complained. "I did go to school for this."

"I thought you were done with training," Presley commented, putting her book down.

"I'll never be done with training," her sister said dramatically. After a pause, she asked, "Are you going on that date tonight?"

"I don't know. What's the point?" Presley asked with a sigh. She'd agreed, somewhat reluctantly, to the after-Christmas drink on a whim when Layla had signed her up for a dating app. The guy looked nice enough, but the last guy had looked that way, too.

"The point," Layla reminded her. "Is getting over Derrick." Presley, in a moment of weakness, had filled Layla in on the whole Derrick debacle—how he'd cheated on her with a colleague and even how he'd shown up while she'd been on the date from hell.

"I think there are some people you never get over," Presley said closing her eyes for a minute and breathing through that thought. She hoped, dearly, that she was wrong. She didn't want to spend the rest of her life in love with someone who didn't love her back.

"I guess," Layla returned with an equally deep sigh.

"Noah?"

"No. I mean, I thought I was in love with him, but then he changed. Or started being himself. I don't know. And I realized that I didn't even really like him. Still, he had his moments," she said with a roll of her shoulders to dislodge the anxiety that seemed to come up any time his name was mentioned. "But, no, I'm not in love with him. I don't even miss him. I just feel stupid, really," she admitted, shooting a look over at her sister. They didn't often talk this long or this honestly—at least, not since their mother had died when they were teenagers.

"We were all hoodwinked," Presley said honestly, remembering her own complicated feelings of attraction for her sister's boyfriend, a situation Noah had manipulated and encouraged. She'd never quite admitted that to Layla, but she had admitted that she'd thought he was a genuinely good guy. How wrong they'd all been!

"I'm glad it wasn't just me, in a way. It makes me feel less foolish," Layla said with a small smile. Then her smile evaporated. "I just hate that Naomi got hurt in the process. If I had spoken up sooner—"

"He still would have targeted her, or someone else."

"He's probably targeting someone else now," Layla acknowledged quietly, a chill creeping up her spine. "I have nightmares about that, someone else dealing with what I had to and not being able to stop it."

"You can't do anything about that. Naomi didn't want to press charges. Which I get," Presley commented. "The justice system is rarely kind to women in this situation. Take that Turner asshole and his short sentence."

"At least the judge got remanded on that one, although that's not much of a comfort to the victim." They'd both followed the Stanford rape trial coverage separately, but each had been incensed by the result.

"Naomi could still press charges."

"I get why she didn't. I just wish there was a way to stop him."

"Just don't let him have any power over you. At least he finally left you alone."

"I know. It's a relief. I was so sure he'd keep on."

"Yeah, me, too. But we were wrong about that, too. Okay, I'm going to get ready for this god-awful date," Presley said, rising to her feet.

"What are you going to wear?"

"Well, not something I could paint a house in!" she declared, and Layla laughed.

"Hey, maybe he'll be great, and you'll have a date for the New Year's Eve party at Dad's."

"Maybe," Presley replied, sounding unconvinced. "We'll see. Are you taking a date?"

"I doubt it," Layla returned dryly. "I'm not really up for dating."

"How about that cute guy who was training with you?"

"Oh. In a relationship. And the trainer was attractive until he started explaining, in great detail, how to turn on a computer."

Presley peeked out of her room. "That had to be entertaining."

"It might have been if it wasn't so boring," Layla said, rolling her eyes. It felt good just to joke around with Presley. They'd fought so often over the years. Since Christmas, something had relaxed in their relationship. She wasn't sure what it was, or why, but she sensed that Presley wasn't trying to overthink it either. "Text me if you want to come back here with him, and I'll go out for a while."

"Yeah, I don't know if it's going to go that well," Presley said with a laugh. "But thanks."

"Hey, far be it for me to cock block you."

Presley let loose a laugh in the next room. "Oh my God, shut up."

"We need a code for those sorts of things. I'm not dating now, but I don't exactly want to live like a nun forever."

"Yeah, okay. Well, you just let me know when I need to steer clear. I'm still on a couple of nights, so keep that in mind, too."

"Was it weird running into Derrick?"

"It would have been more weird if Amber had been with him. But that's happened a time or two. Anyway …" Presley stepped out of her room in a green sweater and slacks, putting small silver hoops in her ear. "How do I look?"

"Well, I don't know how you're going to paint a house in that. Looks good on you. The green is good for your coloring."

"Of course you'd say that since we have the same coloring. You want to borrow it, don't you?"

"Well, not tonight. Want me to do your makeup?"

"I'm wearing makeup!" Presley protested, affronted.

"I mean, you're wearing daytime makeup. At least let me give you smoky eyes."

"Fine!" Presley appeared to relent, although she'd been secretly hoping Layla would offer. Presley mostly went with a natural look while Layla leaned toward trendy and experimental. She had toned it down with Noah, but they all realized now that she'd toned it down because of the abuse and control within the relationship. Presley had to admit, to herself anyway, that Layla was much better with makeup than she was so she let Layla give her dramatic eyes before she went out.

"Hey," Presley came back in a few minutes later looking concerned.

"There's no way you've gone and come back already," Layla commented, pausing *Jessica Jones* on Netflix.

"My car has a flat tire. Mind if I borrow yours? I'm just going downtown," she said referring to downtown Athens with its mix of bars, restaurants, and music venues.

"Sure, keys are on the counter. What are you going to do about the flat tire?"

"I'll put on the spare in the morning," Presley said in frustration. They were brand new tires, and she couldn't think how this had happened.

"Okay," Layla said complacently, turning her attention back to the ass-kicking someone was about to get on the screen. "Have fun!"

When the episode wrapped up, Layla thought about the car with its flat tire. She didn't really know how to change it herself, although her dad had tried to teach her. On a whim, she decided to find someone who could fix it for Presley. After all, Presley was letting her share the apartment, even though she was notoriously introverted and liked having her own space. She'd even bit her tongue when she noticed a sink full of dishes that Layla had forgotten to take care of. She was trying, even if it wasn't always easy, Layla thought. She got out her phone and called around to see if someone could come change it.

Chapter 28

Jamie had only been back home a few minutes when Layla called. He shook his head and headed back out, regretting that he wouldn't have time to go over to Beth's first. He made it out in just under forty minutes and walked up to the apartment number Layla had given him.

"Hey," Layla said opening the door. "I know it's getting late so I appreciate you coming. I mean, I know it's dark out, but she is parked right by the street light."

"I don't mind doing it. Nice of you to want to help her out."

"Well, we're trying to mend fences. And I'm useless with cars. If you can get the spare on, she can go out tomorrow and get a new tire put on," she told him as they headed down to Presley's car.

Jamie checked it out. "Can it be patched?" Layla asked, hopefully.

"Not a chance. Looks like she ran over a nail. It's done for. Too bad though. It looks brand new."

"She's only had them a couple weeks. That's bad luck."

"Well, this should only take a few minutes," Jamie told her, opening the trunk to get out the jack sitting neatly beside the emergency car care kit Presley kept on hand.

"Why don't I grab you a drink? Want a beer or Coke?"

"Coke is fine. I've got to head back after I change this."

Layla ran upstairs and grabbed a soda from the fridge before heading back down. "I really appreciate this. Can I give you gas money or anything for coming out?" she asked, hesitant to be indebted to anyone.

"Don't worry about it. I'm happy to help," Jamie told her, already deep into putting on the spare.

"How's Beth doing?"

"I haven't seen her since I got back," Jamie admitted, shooting a look over at Layla. "Does everybody know?"

"Pretty much. Dean saw the kiss when you came over Christmas Eve and then proceeded to tell everyone."

"Well. I was afraid that would happen," he said, trying and failing to regret that impulse to kiss her before he left. He'd done it because he could now, and that knowledge had been difficult to resist.

"Do you mind everyone knowing? I mean, this is you and Beth we're talking about. We all kind of wondered."

"It just feels like a lot of pressure. What if things don't work out?"

"What if they do?"

Jamie laughed. "Okay, you have a point. Thanks for that."

"What if it does?" he asked himself, as he fitted the spare and double checked it. He stored the tools and the jack neatly back in the trunk. He gave Layla a brief hug and then got in his car to head out, while Layla walked back to the apartment alone pleased that she'd found someone to help. Presley would be so surprised when she saw it.

Jamie drove home thinking about what Layla said. He'd considered every worst-case scenario over the holidays, trying to caution himself against wanting too much, too soon. But he hadn't let himself truly think about what could happen if things worked out. He wasn't normally so pessimistic. He usually took relationships as they were, enjoying the surprises for the most part. But that was before Beth.

He had to admit that he'd nurtured a crush on her from the start. But she'd been so adamant about not dating that he hadn't wanted to be just another guy sticking around hoping to get lucky. He'd decided to enjoy her friendship and let the crush fade out or be his secret. He'd never thought anything would come of it. But now that things were changing, he let himself start to hope. He dialed her number and waited for her to pick up.

"Hey, Jamie. Did you make it home?"

"Home and then back out again," he said with a laugh and explained about Presley's car.

"Nice of you to help," Beth told him with a smile. It was just like Jamie to head straight out when he'd only just gotten home.

"I know it's late, but do you mind if I stop by?"

"No, not at all," Beth said, feeling both excited and nervous. "We're still up," she told him, exchanging a glance with Mr. Darcy who was stretched out in her lap. "When will you be here?" Beth asked, looking down at her silk pajamas with their flying books.

"Maybe five minutes?" He'd waited to call until he was close, hoping she might be available.

"Okay," Beth said with a smile. She didn't even bother changing out of the pajamas after she reminded herself it wouldn't be the first time he'd seen them. After all, they'd had pajama movie nights before, although not with all of this possibility floating under the surface.

"See you in a few." He saw the porch light flip on as he pulled to the curb by her house and got out of his truck. He took a deep breath. Everything was different, but some things were still the same. It was still Beth, someone he'd known for years now, his best friend. And a house he'd been to a thousand times. He tried to shake off the nerves and headed up the steps.

"Hi," Beth said from the door.

"Hey. Hey, Mr. Darcy," he said greeting the dog and relaxing some.

"Come on in," she told him, stepping back to hold the door open wider.

"Thanks." He took in her silk pajamas and the book sitting beside the recliner. "I've interrupted your reading."

"Life is an interruption of my reading. But I don't mind a break.

Have a seat. Want something to drink?"

"No, I'm okay," he said, sitting down and wondering why he felt like a guest when he had always felt at home here. She sat down, too, picking up a glass of wine and taking a large gulp of it.

"It's meant to be sipped."

"I'm a little nervous."

"Why is that?"

"You tell me. Is this going to be weird now?"

"Probably a little. But I'm hoping good-weird."

"Is good-weird a thing?" she asked him with her head cocked to the side.

"Well, you're good-weird," he reminded her, and she laughed.

"So—can we do something to make this less weird?"

"Well, we can pretend everything is like it was." She wrinkled her nose at him. "Except—when I put my arm around you, I don't have to pretend it doesn't mean anything," he finished, meeting her eyes. She continued looking back at him as a smile and accompanying blush spread across her face.

"Okay," She agreed, moving over to the sofa. Jamie got out of the chair and went to his usual seat beside her. She inched closer to him, looking up to see his reaction. He put his arm around her and kissed the top of her head as she leaned in. "Like this?"

"Yeah. Want to watch something?"

"Well, there was a Hallmark Christmas movie I missed the other night ..."

"Alright," Jamie agreed, smiling into her hair as he nuzzled it. "What's this one about?"

"Okay, so she's a high-powered executive but has to go home to help her dying father with his Christmas tree farm."

"Wait. Didn't we see that one?"

"No. That was a different tree farm," she told him with a laugh. "Just watch."

She settled back leaning against him and felt a pleasant jolt when he reached over and took her hand in his. After a few minutes, she curled her feet up under her and nestled against him on the couch. As the movie progressed, Jamie had stretched full length on the couch, and she was tucked in beside him, one well-toned arm tucked around her petite frame. She had reached over automatically and pulled the soft throw she kept on the back of the couch over them both. Mr. Darcy settled down near their feet, looking up in annoyance each time they shifted. When the credits ran, neither of them moved. Jamie kept his arm in place holding Beth close, and she kept stroking the arm wrapped around her wanting to stay in the moment as long as they could manage.

"Better?" he asked her softly. "Less weird?"

"Better. Only I want to ask you to stay, but I think that might be weird."

"Would you rather we took it slow?"

"Yes and no," she admitted, torn between wanting to be closer to him and wanting to savor this time between what they had been to each other and what they would be. She wanted to know him in the way lovers do, but she also wanted to enjoy the slow slide into it.

"I actually understand that," Jamie said with a short laugh. "So how about we take it slow, and any time you want me to pick up the pace, you say the word?"

She stayed still, enjoying the feeling of his arm around her and his body stretched full length against her own. She wanted to turn into him and feel his lips against her own but felt sure that if she did that things might escalate quicker than they had agreed. Instead, she kept making patterns on his skin, her finger tracing pictures over the muscles in his arm. He kissed the top of her head, and she felt his warm breath in her hair.

When she finally turned to him, his lips were already meeting hers halfway. He pulled her into sitting and wrapped his arms around her, as she found herself curling into his lap. She thought, distantly, that this position could be just as much trouble to their plan to move slowly when he pulled back and pressed his forehead to hers, taking a deep breath. This time, when he went back in to kiss her, it was slow and testing. She let herself enjoy it, a hand on the back of his head and then sliding down to his neck and over his shoulders, exploring him in a way she'd never had the chance to do before. And his hands were on her face and in her hair, moving down her arms and her back and back to her face and hair, careful to keep the touches just this side of innocent.

When he left later, Beth leaned against the counter with a sigh and looked at Mr. Darcy who was watching her curiously from his place on the recliner that he had retreated to when she and Jamie had been distracted. "Oh, I'm going to regret agreeing to take it slow," Beth told the dog ruefully. "It might just kill me," she said dramatically, feeling the heat of his mouth and skin on hers even now that he'd gone. The dog put his head down, and Beth practically floated to the bedroom to get ready for bed, her thoughts still replaying the warmth of those kisses and the fire they'd started.

Chapter 29

Dean stood leaning against the wall and talking with Jamie and his long-time friends Lucas and Allen while they waited for things to get started. He was glad he'd already had the good sense to buy a suit in black when he'd bought the charcoal one for Seth's wedding. He figured it couldn't hurt to have both options. Not that Lindy had discussed what she wanted exactly for their wedding, but he liked to think ahead. Particularly since he wanted to be ready at a moment's notice once Lindy made up her mind. He was glad now that he had, as Lindy had been as impulsive as he'd anticipated.

"The only problem with an elopement," Allen was saying, "is the lack of bridesmaids. Hard to get laid at a wedding with so few people."

"I don't know," Lucas returned, his eyes settling on Beth as she stood talking to Keely near the door. "It could happen," he said speculatively, smiling as he thought about the last time he'd seen her.

"I wouldn't be so sure," Dean said, noticing the way Jamie had stopped with a glass of water halfway to his mouth when he caught on to Lucas's meaning. His eyes had also been tracking Beth across the room, and now he narrowed them at Lucas, considering.

"Why not? She seeing someone?"

"Something like that," Dean said, shooting Jamie a look. Lucas put up his hands and backed away while he took in Jamie's linebacker build and set face.

"Hey, no harm no foul, man. Any other options?"

"I don't think so. Although Beth might have some single friends she could introduce you to sometime. Why don't you ask her?"

Lucas eyed Jamie, debating whether or not it would be a good idea to approach Beth to ask her anything with that look in his eye. "Maybe later." It was always interesting stirring things up.

"You ready for this?" Allen asked. "Got cold feet?"

"Have you seen Lindy? Of course I don't have cold feet. That's my baby mama!"

"Hey, that's my sister you're talking about," Seth said, coming in and giving Dean one of those man hugs with lots of back patting.

"And my future wife."

"She'd slap you into the next century if she heard you talking about her like that."

"She's feisty, but she's at least got a sense of humor," Lucas pointed out. "She'd probably only slap you into next week."

"No more dating for Dean Walton," Allen said in wonder. "Who'd have thought it? Guess it's left to me to comfort all those brokenhearted ladies out there."

"You're a good friend," Dean said wryly.

"I do what I can."

"Is she nearly ready?" Dean asked Seth, eager to get started.

"Almost."

"Are you ready?"

"Just about."

"Ready for what?" Jamie asked curiously.

"I'm the officiant. Dean asked me to get ordained online right after Maya was born. Just in case."

"This should be interesting," Jamie said with a grin, heading off to find Beth. If she had known, she hadn't said a word to him.

"Got the vows?"

"Oh yeah."

***

In the back room of Dean's cabin on the lake, Lindy stood looking in the mirror with Keely at her side.

"I'm sorry for Zeke sometimes, that he's missed out on all of this." Keely commented, squeezing Lindy's arm.

"I'm not. His loss. Besides, I'd much rather have you walk me down the aisle than anyone else."

"Your grandfather would have liked to." Keely commented, thinking of her own father.

"I know. Dean put his picture out so he could be here in spirit," Lindy said, examining her own reflection with satisfaction.

"Oh my God," Libby breathed, coming into the room for the first time. "Everyone's ready out there. Just look at you."

"It's something, isn't it?" Lindy asked smugly. She'd come across the dress online and knew that it was exactly what she wanted. The Brody Bodysuit and Stevie skirt had been the thing she'd been looking for without even knowing it. The top was all beaded black lace with a high neckline and racer back. Layered hemmed tulle in black made up the flowing skirt. It was bold and yet romantic with its sheer lace and contrasting skirt. She'd ordered it on a whim while helping Libby find her own dress.

"Does Dean have any idea?" Libby asked.

"Not a clue. Is he getting nervous?"

"Not even a little," Keely said with a smile. "He's such a handsome man. He's been asking all morning when we're going to get started."

Lindy rolled her eyes. "The man has no patience. Is everyone here?"

"Nina just came in as I was heading back," Libby offered, referring to Lindy's college best friend. "Is Marnie coming?" she asked, knowing that Seth's ex-girlfriend and his sister had stayed close friends.

"She couldn't make it, but I told her we'd take a video so she wouldn't miss it entirely. I'm ready. Where's Maya?"

"Theodore's got her," Keely told her. "Her little black dress could not be cuter!"

"Alright. Time to go marry her daddy. Tell Jamie to cue the

music," she said to Libby, who gave her a hug.

The song started playing in less than a minute, and Keely turned to give Lindy a last hug and kiss before they headed to the door. There would be no attendants, and the walk would be short enough—from one end of the little lake house to the front room where guests stood to the sides to give Lindy and Keely enough room to walk to Dean.

To the notes of Bruno Mars's *Marry You*, Lindy's eyes met Dean's and held as she walked toward him, the awe in his eyes starting tears in her own. Lindy stood beside him and at Maya's happy laugh, they both turned to glance her way where Keely now held her, standing beside Theodore. They waited for the music to finish, hands held and eyes never leaving each other's.

Theodore wrapped an arm around Keely who was already crying, Libby exchanged a smile with Seth, and Beth reached over and took Jamie's hand without even thinking. When the music finally stopped, Seth began the ceremony. When it came time to exchange vows, most of the room couldn't help but laugh. Lindy began.

"I promise to love you, respect you, support you, and above all else, make sure I'm not just yelling at you because I'm hungry," she said, while Dean grinned at her. He repeated it back, and then they finished with a Maya Angelou quote: "In all the world, there is no heart for me like yours. In all the world, there is no love for you like mine."

Seth pronounced them man and wife, but Dean had already started kissing the bride so he rolled his eyes and signaled Jamie to turn the music back on. After that, the crowded room turned into a party celebration. The New Year's Eve bash was later that day so they were only having a small cake and champagne, with the bigger celebration complete with fireworks to follow. Seth went straight to his wife where she was still drying her tears on a tissue she'd dug out of her purse.

"That was perfect," Libby said with a smile.

"It was something else." They walked over to Dean and Lindy and each wrapped them in hugs. "Now you're actually my brother," Seth said with a smile.

"Officially, anyway."

Keely joined them and said, "Only you," shaking her head. "What kind of vows were those?"

"Perfect ones," Lindy said cheekily. "He wanted me to promise to be sarcastic only when necessary, but we both agreed I'm not capable of doing that," she said with a half laugh, reaching over to scoop up Maya from Keely's arms. "My baby!" she said, kissing all over Maya's face and leaving a trail of lipstick.

"It was perfect," Keely sighed. "My boy," she said, pulling in Dean for a long hug. "Now you really are a part of the family."

"So Seth was saying," he said with a laugh, holding her tightly.

Keely Carver had been there for him when his own parents had been too busy fighting to really see him. She'd never suggested he spend more time at home. She'd simply opened up her home and welcomed him, any time of the day or night. He'd about eaten her out of house and home during his teenage years, and she'd never once complained. He'd spent his adult life being invited to every single family event without question, as if she assumed he'd come.

"I love you."

"I know you do. I love you, too," Keely said, patting his cheek.

"Stop that," Lindy said, tearing up. "You're going to ruin my mascara. And you already made me cry."

"What did I do? I was just standing there."

"That look. When you saw me. Best moment of my day."

"Who knew you could be so sentimental?" he said happily, pulling her in for a kiss.

"Right?" Seth asked. "Y'all stop that crying before you get me going."

"What did you decide about the names?" Libby asked with interest, admiring Maya's little black dress with the black rose headband.

"I'm keeping Carver," Lindy said with a shrug.

"Actually, we're doing Carver-Walton," Dean said with a grin, reaching for a glass of champagne. "Both of us," he said, watching their reactions.

"That's so sweet," Libby told him.

"Then you'll be a Carver, too," Keely said proudly.

"Your parents are going to hate it," Lindy reminded him with a laugh.

"They're already pissed that we got married without them, but it's not my fault they'd rather do their New Year's Eve parties rather than come out to this. Still, we got it on video. It'll have to do."

Across the room, Jamie stood in an awkward conversation with Beth and Lucas. Lucas had sidled up to Beth and hugged her, which made Jamie glower at him until Beth asked what his problem was. He'd smoothed out the expression on his face and tried not to feel annoyed. Lucas was chatting Beth up about introducing him to her single friends, and she was considering the options. All he wanted to do was leave and go get Mr. Darcy and head over to the party with everyone, but Lucas kept talking.

"Why are you being so weird?" Beth asked him when Lucas walked away.

"Was I?"

"Yes. Do you have a problem with Lucas?" she asked, and then it dawned on her. "Oh. Okay, never mind. You know that's ancient history, right?"

"Beth, that was a couple of months ago," Jamie pointed out, shifting uncomfortably.

"Yeah, but it's not like it was a regular thing. Besides, you were dating Ansley then. Don't tell me you weren't sleeping with her."

"I wasn't going to tell you that."

"Well, is there a double standard at play here?"

"No. Just tell me this: how comfortable would you be having a conversation with Ansley right now?"

She thought about it. "Okay. I'll admit it's awkward. But don't get mad. It was before—this," she said, waving her hand at him. "Whatever this is."

"I like whatever this is," he told her with a smile, bringing her hand up to kiss it.

"Yeah, me, too," she told him, stepping closer to lean her head on his shoulder.

"Save me a dance later?" Jamie asked against her hair.

"Absolutely," she told him with a smile.

"Maybe try not yelling at me this time?"

Beth laughed. "I'll see what I can do."

***

Layla sipped the drink Seth had unceremoniously dropped into her hand when she'd arrived. She'd looked at it at first with suspicion with its pretty layers of red, white, and blue. She inspected it closer and noticed the frozen blueberries and raspberries in the chunks of ice. He'd warned her about the alcohol content, saying that Libby had mixed it a little strong, before turning to greet the next guest. Everyone was in high spirits, and Layla felt out of sorts and out of place, a feeling that was sadly all too familiar for her. She sipped the drink and looked for someone to talk to.

She saw Presley standing with Jamie and Beth, looking a little run down after the extra shifts this week. Layla approached her hesitantly. After all she really needed to talk to her about the changes at work and wasn't quite sure how. She walked over, navigating the furniture in the farmhouse and the people milling about. They'd all invited friends. She'd invited Naomi. After all, Noah had made sure to do his level best to cut her off from her other friends months ago. She hadn't really been able to rebuild those relationships like she wanted, although Naomi had been an unexpected bonus out of the situation. Neither had thought that any good would come out of the whole thing, but they had built a pretty solid friendship from it all.

"I was just thanking Jamie for changing my tire," Presley told Layla when she walked up, trying to fish the blueberries out of her glass. "I still can't believe I had a flat that soon. The shop cut me a deal on the new one. I think they felt a little sorry for me."

"I was happy to help," Jamie said with a smile. "How's the drink?"

"Strong. I may just to have the one and then switch to something a little less lethal."

"I like it," Beth said gleefully, taking another sip.

"You might want to slow down," Presley cautioned, the sting of the warning softened by her smile. "You're on what? You second? Third?"

"Just the second," Beth said brightly. She looked over to check on Mr. Darcy who was still curled up in Theodore's lap across the room while he and Dean talked. Beth was looking forward to Dean and Lindy making the announcement and was trying not to tell anyone the big secret, especially now that the alcohol had loosened her tongue.

"Why don't we take Mr. Darcy out?" Jamie suggested, knowing that Beth was far too tempted at the moment and could use the fresh air.

"I'm glad they're going so I can talk to you a second," Layla said uncomfortably after Jamie and Beth walked away.

"What about?" Presley asked, finally giving up and taking a drink straight from the cup to catch the errant blueberries.

"My job has a branch in Madison, and they want me to transfer to the office here. The one in Athens is so much closer to your place, but I'm wondering if I should move closer so I'm not spending so much in gas."

Presley paused, turning it over in her mind. She'd gotten used to Layla, and they'd even started to get along a little. But she also missed having her own space. She thought about it for a minute. "Are you thinking about living with Dad?" she asked, looking over where Keely had joined Theodore and Dean

"I don't want to. I'm just not sure where else I can go."

"Go where?" Lindy asked as she passed with Maya who had just woken up from a short nap. "Somebody moving?"

"Layla's job is transferring her to Madison," Presley explained.

"I was thinking I might try to find a place near here, cut down on the drive. Anyway, there might not be anything, but I thought I could look."

"I might have an idea on that actually," Lindy said thoughtfully. "Give me a few days, and I'll see what I can do," she said, making a beeline for Dean and the others.

"Well, that was mysterious," Presley said with a grin. "Nice if she can help you, though."

"You don't mind if I move out, do you?"

"You're welcome to stay as long as you need to, but it does make more sense to be close to work. Maybe Lindy will come up with a decent place."

"I don't know. Everything around here seems so expensive."

"It can be. But not always. Hey, if you do have to commute, at least there won't be really any traffic coming in this direction. When do you make the transfer?"

"A couple of weeks. They're reorganizing that office, and someone from there is supposed to transfer up to Athens, too. Anyway, it didn't really sound like I had much of a choice if I want to keep this job, and they did say I could try to transfer back in the future when there were more openings if I wanted to," she explained, wondering why nothing could just be simple.

"Well, that works then. If you have to commute for a while, it wouldn't be forever. And if Lindy can find you something close, you can stay here and decide if you'd rather be in Madison or Athens. That's not the worst thing."

"I guess not," Layla said reluctantly, sipping her drink. "This really is good," she said with a smile. "Hey, there's Naomi. I'm going to go meet up with her."

Presley watched Layla and Naomi hug and shook her head. I bet that was something Noah never anticipated, Presley thought to herself. She was sure if he knew it would piss him off that the women who'd once been his victims were now fast friends. She was glad there were no repercussions to her outburst, but the whole situation still made her uneasy. Still, it was over, and she was hoping they could all move on now.

Chapter 30

Beth took a look around the room, satisfied. She had managed to gather all the potential players into the farmhouse, although a few had spilled outside into the garden even on a day as cool as this one. The usual New Year's Eve celebration was typically at what was once Keely's home and was now Lindy's, but they had decided to move it to the farmhouse in order to expand the guest list to include friends. Beth had invited Jill and Rebecca from book club. She knew Dean would invite his good friends Lucas and Allen, and Beth had run into Jonah in town and told him he and Emma were welcome to join them.

Although she and Jamie were still figuring things out, Beth had given Jonah a heads up. They had enjoyed a brief casual relationship, but he had taken the news easy enough. Still, she thought maybe she could introduce him to Jill. She thought Rebecca and Lucas might hit it off, too. She looked around the room and wondered how she could arrange it when Jamie came over with Mr. Darcy.

"Quite the crowd," he commented, looking around. He saw Lucas in the corner, eyeing Beth and tried not to scowl. He smoothed his expression and looked around to see who else had come in since his trip outside with the dog.

"I invited a few people," Beth replied with a shrug. "Hey, let me introduce you," she told him eagerly. "Jill and Rebecca, this is Jamie."

"Nice to finally meet you," Jill told him with a smile, shooting Beth a look that said she thought he was hot.

"We've heard a lot about you," Rebecca said smiling.

"And this," Beth said, snagging an arm out to ensnare Jonah who was passing by, "is Jonah," she told them. "We went to school together."

Jonah said hello and automatically reached out to shake Jamie's hand. It wasn't until Jamie recognized the assessing look on his face and the hard handshake that he realized Jonah and Beth had history. He glanced over at Beth who was nudging Jill.

"Emma was looking for Mr. Darcy," Jonah told Beth. "She went to the bathroom, but I'll tell her he's here when she comes back out."

"Emma is Jonah's daughter," Beth explained to Jamie. Jamie wondered how close she'd been to Jonah that his daughter was attached to her dog. He shifted uncomfortably and wondered why Beth would have invited an old—boyfriend/lover?—to the party. "She's just the sweetest," Beth said, turning her attention back to Jill who had gotten distracted by the approaching men.

"And this is Lucas, and that's Allen," Beth said, introducing them and wondering how to get Rebecca and Lucas talking so that Jill could talk to Jonah on his own.

"Hey, Beth," Lucas said, leaning over to hug her as he came up. He tried his best to hide a smile. He'd seen Jamie glowering at him and thought he'd give him a little push. After all, if things didn't work out between him and Beth, Lucas was confident he could give that another try.

"Jill, Rebecca, Jonah, and you know Jamie," Beth continued, laughing and stepping out of the hug. "I'm going to get a drink," she told them, waving and heading to the kitchen with a smile.

"Want to tell me what that was all about?" Jamie asked when they finally made it to the kitchen alone.

Beth turned around to tell him about her plan, and the smile slowly slid off her face. Jamie looked livid. She tried to think what he could possibly be pissed off about and forgot all about explaining her idea. "What's the matter with you? Are you feeling okay?"

"Is there a specific reason you threw not one but two lovers in my face tonight?" he asked her, keeping his voice low.

"That's not what I was doing at all!"

"So you don't even deny it. I knew there was something between you and Jonah."

"Well, yeah, but it was just a casual thing. And I ended all that when we ... when you and I ..." Beth wasn't sure how to continue. "Anyway, I ended that, and we're just friends."

"But you invite him to this party and don't even bother to give me a heads up?"

"I really didn't think you would care. I mean, why would you? I take it you probably see Ansley from time to time with work, and you've never heard me question that," Beth said, putting her hands on her hips and facing him, feeling her own temper rising.

"That's different. That's work. You brought them here to socialize! And you hugged them both."

"Did I?" Beth asked, shrugging because she was normally a hugger and didn't always thinking about it. Jamie took that shrug differently and spun out of the room, pissed off.

"What's your problem?" Seth asked, as he came outside.

"Your cousin," Jamie said shortly.

"Oh?" Seth asked, wondering what Beth could have done to piss him off so much. "So how did it go anyway? Her big plan?"

"What big plan?" Jamie demanded, wondering what else she'd been up to that she hadn't told him about.

"She invited a couple of single friends and wanted to introduce them to some guys she knows. I heard her talking to Libby about it yesterday. Of course, mum's the word on all that," Seth said, rolling his eyes. "Libby told her it might backfire, but I've been helping with the grill and haven't had a chance to peek in to see how it's going."

Jamie turned and looked back at the house where everyone was gathered. He hadn't realized that Beth had introduced everyone and then made her excuses to leave the room. It hadn't occurred to him that she was trying to set up her friends. He'd only thought about how it made him feel to be confronted with her past. He thought uncomfortably of how he'd acted and what he'd said. "I have been such an idiot."

"Probably. Better go find her," he suggested, heading back to the grill where Libby was watching with interest.

"What was that about?"

"Jamie did something stupid. He's going to find Beth."

"How'd the set up go?" Libby asked. "Any news?"

"Oh, I wouldn't even ask."

Inside Jamie went straight to the kitchen but couldn't find Beth. He walked all over the house and finally found her sitting in a window seat in the darkened library with Mr. Darcy. She looked over at him when he came in the room, but then she turned her attention to the window again, ignoring him completely. He sat down beside her and took a deep breath.

"I'm an idiot."

"Yes, you are," she agreed, still not looking at him. Mr. Darcy got up and climbed into his lap. "Traitor," she muttered to the dog, still keeping her gaze out the window. She was hoping the fireworks would start soon so she could make excuses and go home. After all, it seemed like midnight couldn't be all that far away, she considered.

"I'm sorry," Jamie said, waiting until she met his eyes. "I got jealous. I don't know how to handle this you and me stuff. It's never been a problem before. I don't care that you were with either of them before. I really don't. It just bothered me because I'm not sure what we're doing here. Or if you feel the way I do," he admitted, as her hand reached out to take his.

"You should try asking sometime. And maybe try trusting me."

"I do trust you," Jamie began, but Beth simply raised her eyebrows and didn't respond. He paused a minute. "Maybe I don't trust *them*."

"That's the same thing," Beth said with a shrug. "I'm going to go check on everyone," she said, releasing Jamie's hand and sliding out of the window seat. "I guess you just need to decide whether you trust me or don't because there's no need for this to go any further if you don't know."

***

Lindy unlocked the door while Dean maneuvered into the room. They'd left a few lights on, and Maya had fallen asleep in her carrier on the way home. After they got her settled, Dean shot a glance over at Lindy who was getting ready for bed.

"I'm sorry, Lindy. I couldn't even carry you over the threshold," he said, looking down at his leg. His recovery had been going smoothly, but he still had a ways to go before he'd be ready to go back to work. He was down to weeks rather than months, though, and counted his blessings.

"As if I'd let you," she said with a roll of her eyes. "I'm capable of getting through the door on my own. Besides, would you have wanted to wait until your leg was a hundred percent?" she asked him as she removed the makeup from her face.

"No. I like starting the year married to you," he said, leaning back against the pillows. "But we haven't even talked about a honeymoon."

"We might want to wait until you've healed for that. What'd you have in mind?"

"What would you say to Aruba?"

"Tropical paradise? I'd say yes." She shot a look over at the baby monitor. They'd tried settling Maya into her room a few nights a week to get her used to the nursery. "But not without Maya."

"Maybe we could talk your mom and Theodore into coming, have a couple of built-in babysitters on the trip."

"Couldn't hurt. But with all the work you've missed …"

"Hey, I told you I've been saving. We've got enough put back for a trip."

"What if we had another source of income?"

"What are you thinking?"

"Why don't we rent out the carriage house?"

"I don't know that I want to rent it out to a stranger. I mean, it would be someone living practically in our backyard."

"But it's a big backyard, and it wouldn't have to be a stranger." She explained Layla's predicament. "It'd be good to have someone we know right there, and she's got a good job. We could keep the rent low, but it would still be a little extra income to make up for the work you've missed."

"I've gotten hazard pay," Dean pointed out, and then continued. "But you have a good point. Let's do it! She's family anyway," he said with a shrug, as Lindy picked up the phone to text her. "Lindy's, it's almost 3:00 a.m."

"And at the time she left, she should just now be getting home."

"Not if they stayed at their dad's."

"Oops," Lindy said with a laugh. "Anyway, it's a good plan." She slipped out of her clothes and into a negligee. Dean watched her walking slowly toward him in bed. "So is Aruba," she told him, sliding in next to him. Moments later, the negligee hit the floor and Lindy smiled. She'd joked when she bought it that she would wear it all of two minutes, but it hadn't even made it past the thirty second mark.

Chapter 31

Jamie knocked on Beth's door and waited. She'd only left the party a few minutes before he did so she couldn't possibly be asleep yet, he thought. In fact, if she hadn't left in such a hurry, he was going to ask to take her home. He knew she'd gotten a ride, but he hadn't had a chance to find out with whom. Of course, he told himself, he trusted her. It wasn't about that. He just didn't want to start the year with this angry thing between them.

"What?" she growled when she opened the door. "Do you have any idea what time it is?"

"I need to talk to you," Jamie told her, crossing his arms.

"Fine. Talk."

"Beth, it's cold out here. Can I at least come in?"

"Fine. But be quick. I'm tired."

"I do trust you—"

"You have a funny way of showing it!"

"I said I was sorry about all that earlier."

"Yeah, I know. But then you spent the rest of the night glaring at Lucas and Jonah both. You barely danced with me, and I don't even think you'd have kissed me at midnight if you weren't set on guarding your territory from the two of them."

"Of course I would have! That didn't have anything to do with them."

"Oh yeah? Because the second you finished kissing me, you glared over at them," Beth reminded him. At that point, she'd stormed away, tired of being a pawn in whatever game he was playing. "You're not even my boyfriend! I don't know what this is, but I'm not going to deal with all of this jealous garbage."

"I didn't kiss you because they were there," Jamie told her, practically grinding his teeth together in annoyance.

"Well, that's a little hard to believe."

"Well, they aren't here now," Jamie said, advancing toward her. She took a step back, affronted.

"What do you mean they aren't here? Of course they aren't. Search the house if you don't believe me."

"That's not what I meant," Jamie said. He took another step toward her, and she started to understand.

"I'm not exactly in the mood," Beth told him warningly.

"Just one kiss, to prove my point," he said quietly, his mouth so close to hers she could feel the warmth of his breath on her lips.

"Fine," Beth said, closing the distance.

She was so angry that she'd spent what should have been a fun night dealing with Jamie's moods. He'd never been moody like that before. She thought that if dating him was going to be so damn complicated, she'd had enough of it. She put all of her frustration into the kiss and drew in a sharp breath when he lifted her up and sat her down on the counter. Her mouth was fused to his already with her arms fastened around his neck, and now she shifted to wrap her legs around him, too, as his hands tangled tightly in her hair and pulled it angrily. She gasped and then moved her body closer to his.

Jamie tried to break off the kiss a couple of times, feeling his point was made, but then she'd pulled his mouth back to hers, and he'd found himself lifting her up on the counter. By the time he took another breath, her skirt was inched up around her thighs, and the straps of the tank top she'd been sleeping in were down her shoulders. The fact that she'd managed to keep any clothes on at all was a wonder. He pulled back, not wanting their first time together to be in the heat of anger. He leaned his forehead against hers and tried to get himself under control.

"I don't want to do this the first time—I wanted it to be different," Jamie tried to explain, thinking how he'd almost fucked her right on the kitchen counter. He knew some men didn't know the difference between just fucking someone and making love, but he wanted to show her that he did. Besides, there'd always be another time for the kitchen counter. There wouldn't be another first time for the two of them.

"Okay," Beth said softly, drawing his mouth back to hers softly this time. She kissed him, holding his face in her hands and let the anger she'd been feeling drift away.

This time when he lifted her, he did it gently, scooping her up and carrying her back to the bedroom where he laid her down gently and started removing the clothes she still wore. She reached up to help him out of his, trembling with heat and arousal. "Are you sure?" he asked her. She nodded and pulled him down to her. "Protection?" he murmured. She gestured to the bedside table. "I'll bring some next time," he told her. "I wasn't exactly planning this." He smiled against her mouth.

"You seem pretty sure of yourself," Beth told him with a glint in her eyes. She liked the confidence, had always liked that about him. But now she was just curious. Their relationship was changing, and this was the part where it would change irrevocably. She thought she would be afraid. After all, this was her best friend. But she was only eager to know him in all the ways she could and to see what their relationship would look like after. She just wanted to be closer to him, she thought, as she let herself get lost in desire.

"You still owe me a dance. This doesn't count," he told her, as he twisted her hair around his hands and pulled her in closer. Beth opened her mouth to respond when her breath caught in a moan at the tug of her hair in his hands. She forgot what she was going to say and moved her body closer, intoxicated by the friction between them.

In the morning, Jamie woke up with an arm wrapped around Beth and his leg firmly entangled between hers. He thought about getting up to make coffee but then decided instead just to enjoy the time. He pulled her closer and felt her body relax into him as she sighed in her sleep. He stroked a hand down her pretty red hair and thought about how she didn't think he trusted her. He hated that he'd let her think that, even for a moment. Beth was the most loyal person he knew, he thought to himself, but he had just fumbled the entire situation. He'd been so insecure and jealous that he'd overreacted. Now he was going to have to show her what she meant to him and that he did trust her. He started to get a few ideas and then smiled when Mr. Darcy trotted into the room and looked at him steadily. He knew something that just might work.

***

Layla loaded up the last of the boxes on the truck and was grateful for the winter cold. January was usually not her favorite time of year, but she hated to think what it would have been like to try to move in the Georgia summer. As it was, she was exhausted. She didn't even own much, or so she'd thought, but apparently, she'd accumulated more possessions in her time living with Presley than she'd realized. She looked over at her dad, Seth, and Jamie who were securing everything to Jamie's truck and was grateful to have had the help.

"I promise I'm taking care of lunch for everyone when we get there," she told them, as she got into the car with Presley.

Layla's car had a few boxes in the back, but the bulk of her possessions were loaded into Jamie's truck. Presley was riding along with her and then getting a ride back with their dad later. She pulled the ball cap over her head and turned to her sister.

"Well, that was mostly painless," Layla said, as she started the white 2002 Ford Focus she'd bought used a few years back. She worried sometimes about how much longer it would last, but she put the thought out of her mind.

"Only because they loaded most of the furniture," Presley pointed out, fiddling with the radio stations. She found a classic rock station and settled back into her seat. It had been their mother's favorite music so she knew Layla wouldn't complain about the selection.

"Good thing, too. There's no way the two of us would have gotten that bed frame down the stairs."

"I don't know. We did get it up the stairs."

"Barely," Layla said with a small smile as they drove down 441 from Athens to Madison.

Layla thought about the last time she'd moved. She'd gone to the hospital when Lindy went into labor not realizing that she'd never return again to the apartment she shared with Noah. She had the clothes on her back and the backpack she used for school but little else. She'd left the hospital shell-shocked, not sure what she was supposed to do next. Her dad and Seth had gone by her old apartment to get her stuff and found most of it destroyed. They'd recovered a couple of textbooks that Noah had overlooked and a handful of clothes, but that was it.

She and Presley had scoured thrift stores and garage sales for a bed frame and dresser, and her dad had given her a mattress from his guest room. They'd struggled to get most of it in the house, but by the time she'd been at Presley's for a couple of weeks, her mattress was off the floor, and the clothes that weren't neatly hanging in the closet were neatly folded in the second-hand dresser they'd found. Presley had even added a lamp that she claimed she'd found at a yard sale but looked suspiciously new.

They'd moved in furniture and somehow made a start at mending their relationship. Layla wondered if this latest move would hurt it. She glanced over at her sister who was watching the farmland outside her window and singing along to the song on the radio under her breath.

"I was thinking," Presley began when the song went off. "Maybe we could start a regular thing like what Keely does with Seth and Lindy. Like a breakfast thing once a week or maybe a lunch."

"That would be nice. Keely does brunch on Sundays, right? Maybe we could do a Saturday thing, when you don't have to work."

"It doesn't have to be weekly. Maybe we could start with a couple of times a month and see where it goes." Layla smiled. It was nice to know that Presley, too, was thinking of ways that they could continue their relationship now that they wouldn't be living together.

When they pulled up at the house, they were surprised to see the reception party waiting for them. "Does this family make everything into a party?"

"It's kind of nice. Oh my God, someone ordered pizza!" she exclaimed, practically vaulting out of the car.

"What is all this?" Layla asked, as Keely, Lindy, and Beth approached the car.

"They've been helping me get the carriage house in order, and we went ahead and ordered lunch because you're probably all starving," Lindy told them. "Dean's inside with the baby. It's the first time he's been relieved to have an injury since the fire, so thanks for that." He'd been elated when he found out that he'd be exempt from helping Layla move and had happily volunteered to watch the baby instead and to spring for pizza and drinks for the crew.

"No problem," Layla returned with a smile. "I'm just grateful for the place to live. I'll try to stay out of your way while I'm here."

"Don't be ridiculous," Lindy said, rolling her eyes, and handing her the key. "I'll show you a couple of places you can hide a spare, too, and we can keep a key up at the house in case you ever get locked out."

"Thanks. It's so pretty," Layla told her, marveling as she walked through it. She'd agreed to move in, sight unseen on Lindy's assurance that she would adore it. Layla thought she was probably over-selling it, but now she corrected herself. If anything, she thought, Lindy had under-sold how great it was. "I can't believe I'll be living here."

"Nice digs." Layla shot her a look to see if their was an undertone of envy, but Presley was looking around in interest. "We may have to have our lunch thing, or whatever, here."

"I have a little bit of furniture still here, but if there's anything you don't want, we can move it up to the attic. Just let Seth know."

"No, it's all great," Layla said, walking around and touching the living room furniture. She hadn't been sure how she would afford to furnish the other rooms, and it was a relief to know that she didn't need to. "Thank you."

"Hey, we're happy to have you," she said, touching her arm briefly in passing as she went outside to give her brother a hard time. "Where have y'all been?" Layla heard her asking. "You drive like an old man, Seth Carver!"

"I was driving, actually. But there was plenty of back seat driving from this one," Jamie said, pointing at Seth. "So I had to go slower than usual."

"Technically," Seth defended himself with a grin. "I was in the front seat. And we all made it here in one piece."

"Was he really that bad?" Beth asked Jamie, as he started to unhook the straps from the boxes and furniture in the back. Beth had woken up a week before with Jamie in her bed and the dog nestled at their feet. They hadn't talked about the way things had changed, but she'd gotten used to him stopping by casually on his way home from work. He'd stayed over a couple of nights, but the other nights he'd made excuses to go home. She wasn't quite sure where it was going, but she was savoring the newness of the relationship that was unfolding.

"He was alright. I just have to give him a hard time."

"We have pizza."

"So I heard," he said, removing the last of the straps. "I just want to get this unloaded before I eat." He looked over at Beth in her vintage jeans and long-sleeve Jimi Hendrix henley. Her red hair was braided to the side, and she only wore the slightest bit of makeup. "You look pretty."

Beth laughed. "I look like a hot mess, but thanks." She thought about it for a second and then leaned over to give him an impulsive kiss before heading off to busy herself inside with the unpacking.

Jamie shook his head, as she ran inside. It was still so new, but he kept thinking that they really would have to talk about where this was going. Some time, he thought, as he started hefting boxes inside. "Just show me where to go," he told Layla, waiting for direction and wondering if she had a set of weights she'd packed inside this particular box.

Chapter 32

Jamie made excuses and left after he'd eaten half a pizza. Everything was unloaded and unpacked, and Layla was still getting used to it all. Theodore and Keely had gone inside to visit with Dean and the baby. Lindy and Libby had stayed in the kitchen drinking coffee and talking about their wedding photos, which had come in around the same time. Beth had stayed for awhile, alternating between holding Maya, looking through wedding photos, and making sure Presley and Layla were okay as Layla settled into the carriage house. They all seemed to be relaxing into the afternoon, but Beth was restless. She made excuses of her own and walked home.

Mr. Darcy was waiting eagerly at the door when she arrived, and she quickly adjusted his sweater, put on his leash, and grabbed a thicker coat before heading out to the dog park. She just needed to get moving, but the dog park wasn't close enough for a walk. She buckled Mr. Darcy's seatbelt around him, handed him his favorite toy and pulled out.

Traffic wasn't really an issue, although Beth could see that the downtown area was still busy enough, even on a cold January day. Naomi was handling the bookstore, and Beth thought about stopping by but then decided that she just needed a little air. It felt like everything was changing. Seth and Libby had been married only a few months back, with Keely surprising them all by getting married herself months before. Lindy's pregnancy had been surprise enough, and now they'd gotten married, too. Then there was Jamie.

Beth tried to wrap her head around what was unsettling her about the situation. They'd been best friends for years now, and she'd never expected their relationship to change. She'd sort of envisioned them continuing on the way they always had until Jamie got married or something. Of course, she'd never been able to quite imagine that scenario, but she'd tried. Her plan had been to stay single, take care of Mr. Darcy, and figure everything else out later. Now, it felt like the ground had shifted underneath her feet, and she wasn't sure what she wanted.

Or, for that matter, what Jamie wanted. He had stayed over a couple of days, but the other days it just felt like they were friends. She and Jonah had been friends with benefits. She wondered sometimes if that's how Jamie looked at their relationship. Was that all she was to him?

She parked the car and got out, sighing. It was getting colder, and she took the time to zip her coat all the way up to her chin. She pulled a beanie down over her red hair and pulled on the scarf she'd left in her car the last time. She unhooked Mr. Darcy's seatbelt and picked up the end of his leash to lead him over to the dog park. It was fairly deserted, but it didn't make her feel unsafe. She could see a couple of parents hanging out on the playground with their kids, a jogger had just waved as he ran down the trail nearby, and a couple of teenagers were hitting fly balls to each other on the baseball diamond. She let Mr. Darcy off his leash and went to sit down on the bench nearby.

"Where are you?" the text from Jamie read.

"Dog park," she replied. She waited, but no other texts came through. She thought that maybe he'd been planning to come over. Well, he'd just have to wait, she thought stubbornly. She needed some air and a little space to figure out if she could be okay with a casual scenario with Jamie.

She kicked her feet under her, as Mr. Darcy ran the length of the park and then slowly sniffed its perimeter. Beth thought about Jamie and how much had changed. How fast even. She didn't want to have the kind of casual relationship that meant he'd be dating other people, too. In fact, she should probably tell him right away that she wasn't going to share, she thought mutinously. They hadn't discussed the relationship at all so she had no idea how to bring up that particular point, but she was determined to make at least that one thing clear.

And if he didn't like it ... she paused, thinking. What if he didn't feel the same? She couldn't imagine just going back to being just friends, but at the same time, she wasn't going to just sit back and watch him date other people while he kept her on the side.

By the time Jamie pulled up to the park, Beth had worked herself into quite the mood. The argument in her head had escalated quickly, and she was nearly scowling when Jamie walked into the park. She was so irritated with him, for things he'd said in an argument he hadn't even participated in, that she almost didn't notice the leash in his hand or the little dog attached to the end.

"Who is this?" Beth asked, a little breathlessly. She'd been preparing to have it out with Jamie, but nothing could have prepared her for this. Even Mr. Darcy cocked his head and trotted over to stand beside Beth.

"This is Lizzie." The little red and white mini bull terrier sat down, practically on Jamie's foot, watching Mr. Darcy speculatively.

"She's yours?" Beth asked, cocking her own head to the side in an imitation of Mr. Darcy's that made Jamie's grin stretch wider.

"Yeah. She's from a rescue for bull terriers. I've been on a watch list for a while now, and they got Lizzie in last week. I was just waiting to pick her up," Jamie explained, watching as Mr. Darcy checked her out from where he was standing. Jamie reached down and unhooked the leash. "This is Beth and Mr. Darcy," he told Lizzie, stroking her soft coat. He stood up, and Lizzie looked back up at him before running off to stretch her little legs. Mr. Darcy took one look at her and hurried to catch up.

"You got a dog," Beth said wonderingly, plopping down on the bench. Too much was changing, and she didn't even know how to make sense of this. Jamie had never even said he wanted a dog. "Wait, Lizzie?" Beth asked. "Like from ..."

"*Pride and Prejudice*, yeah," Jamie smiled, glad she'd finally caught on.

"I don't understand what's going on here. You didn't even say you were getting a dog."

"Well, that's the thing," Jamie began, turning on the bench to face her and taking her hands in his. They were cold—she'd forgotten her gloves at home—and he put them in his own large hands to warm them. "We haven't talked about a lot of things lately. What this is. What we want. So I'm just going to tell you what I want, and see how it sounds to you," he told her calmly. "I just want you. You and me. Or us and them, I guess," Jamie said, nodding to the dogs who were chasing each other around the park. "Exclusive. Official. All of it."

"Are you asking me to be your girlfriend?"

"Something like that," Jamie said with a laugh. "Yeah, I guess I am. I don't want you seeing anyone else, and there's no one out there for me but you. You've always said you don't need anyone but Mr. Darcy. But maybe Mr. Darcy needs Lizzie." They both looked over at the dogs who were playing and smiled. "And maybe I need you."

It had all sounded great in his head, and he wondered if he'd rehearsed it so much that he'd failed to consider all the possible responses. After all, maybe she'd feel smothered by it since she'd been clear about staying happily single. He looked at her profile as she watched the dogs with a smile hovering around her lips. He thought then that maybe the dog had been overkill. It was clearly distracting her, he thought in exasperation. But he'd wanted a dog and thought Mr. Darcy could use a friend. The fact that he'd gotten a female dog had been a stroke of luck. He hadn't even considered any other name for her.

"Are you going to say anything?"

"I love everything that you just said. But maybe that's just because I'm in love with you," Beth said, leaning against his shoulder with a sigh.

"Are you?" Jamie asked, putting an arm around her and letting out the breath he hadn't realized he'd been holding. Beth nodded against his shoulder. "That's convenient. I love you, too."

"I know," she said turning and pulling his mouth down to her own. "This is going to change everything," Beth told him with a sigh. For the first time, she didn't feel like everything was moving too fast. In fact, it felt more like everything was settling into place.

"That's what I'm hoping," Jamie said, wrapping an arm around her and looking out toward the dog park with a smile. "So are we picking up Chinese food or Italian later?"

"Chinese. And it's your turn to pick the movie."

"I've got a couple in mind. We need to get Lizzie a sweater," he said looking over at his dog who was now following Mr. Darcy around the perimeter, looking for possible escape routes.

"I can't wait to show her Pemberley," Beth said with a smile.

Chapter 33

Across town, Theodore and Keely drove Presley home, the three of them belting out a little Clapton on the drive. Between songs, they talked about the day, and Theodore told them a little about the new book. Keely talked about some plans for the tearoom and how the book club was expanding. Presley caught them up on her work and amused them with stories of her most demanding and outrageous patients. They drove along and Presley thought about her mother, and knew, with absolute certainty, that wherever she was she'd be happy that they had healed their family. She'd have liked Keely, Presley knew. She'd have liked all of it, but especially the part where she and Layla found their way back to being friends again.

***

Dean and Lindy were sitting on the floor of the living room, hands clasped together, as they watched Maya finally crawl to them for the first time. When she made it to their laps, she gave a delighted laugh, and Lindy realized she was crying.

"I want another."

"Yeah, me, too," Dean told her, kissing her and then swooping to pick up Maya and toss her in the air, the sound of her giggles filling the house.

***

Seth and Libby sat in front of a fire, a couple of glasses of wine on the table and Chinese delivery opened on the table in front of them. Libby was writing in her journal, and Seth was on the opposite end of the couch reading a book with one hand and rubbing her foot with the other. He tapped her foot to get her attention and then waited until she was finished writing.

"I know it's too early to hope. But I still do."

"Me, too," Libby said with a small smile, moving across the couch to curl into his lap. "And if it doesn't work and the adoption does?"

"We're still a family, either way. Maybe they'll both happen. Wouldn't that be something?" he asked, kissing the top of her head and tucking an arm around her.

"You won't be disappointed?"

"With you? Not ever," Seth told her, putting down his book and holding her tight. "Not for any reason. You're my person."

"And you're mine."

***

Layla walked around the house. It was starting to get dark, and she'd turned on lights in most of the rooms. She'd have to be careful about that, now that she was solely responsible for the electric bill and on a tight budget. Presley had given her a hard time about leaving the lights on until Layla had experienced the first of the nightmares. Then she'd paid the electric bill without complaint, often leaving lights on herself when she left for work before Layla came on.

Well, I'll just have to get stronger, Layla thought. Braver. I can do this. After all, it was all done now. She hadn't seen Noah in over six months, and it had been at least four months since the calls and texts had come to an abrupt end. She took a deep breath and looked around her new place. For a small carriage house, it was surprisingly spacious. For the first time in a long time, Layla allowed herself to feel lucky.

A car pulled up next door, and the sweep of headlights in the room had Layla walking curiously over. She recognized the real estate agent's car pull into the driveway next door. One day, she hoped that she wouldn't jump at loud noises, check all the locks, and clock every car that drove by. She took a deep breath and walked over to the counter to pour a glass of wine, as the real estate agent got out of her car to remove the sign from the lawn.

***

Jamie whistled, and both dogs ran over, Lizzie circling around his legs before plopping down in front of him. Mr. Darcy waited patiently for Beth to fasten his leash, and they all headed toward the parking lot, Beth's hand tucked into Jamie's.

"I'll get the Chinese."

"Want me to take Lizzie with me?"

"No, she'll be fine in the car. I already called in the order on the way here."

"Confident, aren't you?"

"Actually, I was afraid I'd have to eat Chinese the rest of the week," he said with a laugh. "Glad I won't have to now."

"What if I'd wanted Italian?"

"You had pizza earlier. I figured Chinese was a safe bet."

"Did you think I was a safe bet?"

"Are you kidding me? I'd have asked you out the moment I met you, Beth Everett. You were anything but a safe bet," Jamie said rolling his eyes.

"I'm worth the wait," Beth assured him, getting Mr. Darcy into the car.

"I know," he told her, loading up Lizzie who was anxiously watching Mr. Darcy from the window.

"What are we watching tonight anyway?"

"I thought we'd go for a little *When Harry Met Sally*."

"That sounds perfect," Beth said with a smile, standing on her tiptoes to kiss him. "See you at home."

A Preview of

Waiting for the Girl Next Door

Book 4 of the Heart of Madison Series

"The world breaks everyone, and afterward, some
are strong at the broken places."
—Ernest Hemingway

Chapter 1

Layla Westerman kept one leg hanging over the side of the hammock, so she could occasionally make it swing. She glanced over at the baby on the floor, who had her entire fist shoved in her mouth, and grinned.

"I could get used to this," she said with a sigh, glancing over at Lindy who was lying on her stomach on the wide screened-in porch holding a toy out for Maya to grab. Maya kept ignoring her, pulling out her fist and looking at it before popping it back in.

"Why do I bother to buy her toys?" Lindy asked with a sigh, sitting up. "Get used to the baby or the hammock?"

"Oh, I'm not ready for a baby yet," Layla said with a wry smile, although her heartstrings pulled every time she looked over at Maya with her bright eyes and chunky cheeks. "This, the hammock, the whole thing," she sighed happily.

She was relaxed and being relaxed was still rare enough that she appreciated it. She didn't like to talk about the panic attacks she'd been having. Or the nightmares. In fact, her sister, Presley, only knew about the nightmares because they had lived together. She'd said she didn't remember them when she woke up. Of course, she was lying. She looked over at Lindy with her dark hair braided over one shoulder. She looked back at Maya. "She looks so much like you."

"Well, she's got Dean's smile."

"Dimples, too," Layla reminded her. "She's perfect."

"Isn't she?" Lindy asked. "You are perfect," she told Maya, leaning forward to kiss her nose. Maya started to giggle, her belly bouncing and her fist popping out of her mouth with a wet sound.

"Are you unpacked yet?" Lindy asked her.

"Yeah, it wasn't so bad. I didn't have that much really." They both paused, remembering why. When Lindy had been giving birth to Maya, Layla had been out in the waiting room breaking up with Noah. She'd finally admitted to her sister and their friends that he was abusive, and after she'd said the words, she couldn't imagine going back home with him. Her sister, father, and new friends had all stood with her when she faced him. Her new step-brother had helped escort him out. But of course, he hadn't gone peacefully. He'd burned most of her possessions. She'd even lost a few precious photos of her mom and a couple of mementos that couldn't be replaced.

It could have been so much worse, she reminded herself. After the breakup, he'd hung around her classes and called her phone repeatedly. She'd changed numbers and jobs, and he hadn't been around in months. She wasn't sure why, but she was grateful it all seemed to be over. Not the panic attacks or the nightmares. But the rest of it seemed to have settled back down.

She looked over at Lindy who had a smile on her face that mirrored her child's. She counted back. Maya was seven months. It was seven months since she'd left Noah. She'd lived with Presley for six of those, and they'd actually gotten along better as adults than they had as teenagers, though she sometimes suspected it was because Presley was worried about her. Still, it was nice. She hadn't been close to her family since her mom got sick. It was good to spend time with them.

Lindy was family, too, now. She'd invited Layla to come hang out with her over on the porch. It was the end of January, but it was still in the 70s. Typical Georgia weather, Layla thought. She laughed as Maya toppled over and then righted herself.

"Did you know the house next door sold?" Lindy asked. She watched Layla's body tense. "I met one of the owners. Nice enough guy. They said there might be some work being done in the next couple of months," she warned her.

"Nice to give you a heads-up," Layla said carefully, closing her eyes. She tried to remember how to relax her body the way they'd told her to in that one yoga class she'd agreed to attend with Presley. It wasn't working.

"I don't know if they're keeping it or flipping it," Lindy said conversationally, trying to lighten the mood. "But everyone mostly keeps to themselves around here," she reassured Layla. "If they're going to stay, I might invite them over and get to know them."

"Probably a good idea," Layla said absently. Lindy looked over at where Layla lay with her eyes shut and made a decision.

"Hey, can you take Maya for a minute? I need to run inside real quick." She picked Maya up and all but shoved her in Layla's arms for a second.

"Okay, sure," Layla said in surprise, looking up at the baby sitting firmly on her belly with her legs splayed in front of her. Maya looked back at her with a grin and leaned forward to grab handfuls of her hair. Layla remembered suddenly why Lindy had started braiding her long hair back. She smiled back at Maya. "Look, monkey, you're going to have ease up on your grip," she told her, prying the chunky hands from her hair and making sure to remove the stray hairs that came out in her hand.

Her own hair was nearly black and mid-length. It was curly where Presley's was straight, and she'd let it grow to just below her shoulders. Where Lindy's was more of a dark chestnut and midway down her back, Layla's was shorter, darker, and a riot of curls this morning in the humidity. She shoved it back over her shoulders and held Maya out of reach.

"Don't even think about it," she told her, as Maya opened and closed her fists in the direction of Layla's hair. She thought about sitting up, but wasn't sure she could manage it without toppling them both to the floor of the porch. She grabbed each of Maya's hands and patty-caked them together, which made Maya giggle.

"I thought I heard my best girl," Dean said in the raspy voice of the newly awakened. Layla looked up and felt her mouth go dry. Dean stood there in low slung, faded jeans rolled up at the bottom, and barefoot. He was wearing a plain black T-shirt and leaning on a crutch. Layla imagined she could just about make out a six pack under the shirt and averting her eyes to his well-muscled arms didn't help. He just smiled, used to the impression he made.

"Don't let Lindy hear you saying that," she warned him, turning back to Maya. Dean was pretty. God knows he knew it, she thought. But he was also Lindy's husband and Maya's father. Besides, Layla reminded herself, men were just trouble. Still, she liked to listen to his deep southern-fried drawl. It didn't have that twang of country found in some of the more rural areas of Georgia. It was definitely more Rhett Butler than Larry the Cable Guy. She shook her head at the thought and decided to enjoy the view.

"Lindy knows the pecking order around here," Dean said with an easy smile, shifting around on the crutch. He only used it reluctantly. He was still recovering from an injury he'd sustained in his job as a firefighter, and he was hoping to be back to work in the next month, if everything went well with rehabilitation. Still, it didn't affect his easy grace much. His blonde hair was carelessly mussed as if he hadn't done anything but run a hand through it when he woke up. He turned green eyes on Maya, and even Layla could see them light up.

"You want her?" she asked him.

"'Course I do," he said, leaning over to scoop his daughter up with one hand. The baby giggled, and Layla swung her leg over and sat up. "Where's Lindy?"

"You didn't see her inside?" Layla asked, her brow furrowing.

"I was getting more coffee," Lindy said, as she walked out, letting the door slam behind her. "It was an emergency," she told them.

"Maya kept us up a little last night. Teething," Dean explained.

"It was Dean's turn to sleep in, and I'm catching a nap with her later on," Lindy explained, sitting down on the floor beside Dean's chair and leaning her head against his knee. Maya turned and started reaching for Lindy's hair. She reflexively moved her hair out of the way and reached up to hold Maya's tiny hand.

"My turn," Dean reminded her.

Layla looked at the two of them and felt a stab of envy. She'd never even had a healthy relationship, much less the kind of love story that Lindy and Dean had. She'd thought Noah was the one. He seemed so unlike anyone she'd ever dated. He was smart. Like really smart, she thought. And he was in culinary school to be a chef. Plus, he had dark red hair and a dash of freckles. It's not that he wasn't handsome. He was. He just wasn't Layla's usual type. She'd gone for the blue-collar bad boy as long as she'd dated. Noah hadn't had any of those bad boy markers. He seemed reserved and a little sweet, almost a little nerdy even.

When she and Noah had started dating, he'd pulled out the stops with big romantic gestures. She closed her eyes briefly as she remembered how it had all been sleight of hand. He'd let her think he was one person, but he was really someone wholly different than the man she had fallen in love with.

It wasn't until she'd found out he'd been hurting someone else, too, that she'd had the courage to break away from it all. She'd started to believe what he'd told her, that she'd never find anyone else who would want her. She didn't talk about it to anyone but Naomi. After all, it had happened to her, too, and at the same time. No one else could really understand just how it was to be with someone who could be so sweet and so toxic in the space of a few minutes.

She envied Lindy and Dean their easy relationship. They both had assured everyone that it had been far from easy, but it looked easy from where Layla was sitting. She didn't realize she'd let out an audible sigh until she caught Dean and Lindy looking at her.

"Want some coffee?" Lindy asked sympathetically, guessing where her thoughts might have drifted.

"Sure," she agreed, not quite ready to go home yet.

"I'll get it," Dean said, placing a soft kiss on the top of Maya's head with its downy dark hair and handing her to Lindy. "How do you like it?"

"Sweet. Just pour the cream and sugar in."

"I thought you'd be coffee-black."

"Surprisingly, that's Presley. Although, she's more likely to grab a chai or a green tea these days," Layla said with a smile.

"One coffee coming right up," he said, heading inside. Lindy and Layla watched him go.

"Um, no offense or anything, but your husband is one beautiful man," Layla told her with a smile.

"I'm not offended. Just don't let him hear you say it. His ego is enormous enough as it is."

"I might have drooled a little when he walked up," Layla admitted with a laugh.

"Yeah, he has that effect. I was immune for years. Until I wasn't."

"Did you get glasses? Contacts?" Layla asked incredulously.

"I practically grew up with him. He was just Seth's bratty friend. Until he wasn't," she said with a shrug.

"That's pretty cute actually."

"Yeah," she sighed. "The guy before him was a real ass."

"He really was," Dean agreed, coming out with the coffee. "Are we talking about exes?"

"Not yours," Lindy told him decidedly. "We don't have time."

"She was dating this pretentious art asshole," Dean began.

"Hey!" Lindy said. "I mean, yeah, but ..." she nodded toward Maya.

"She's not exactly talking yet," Dean argued. "Okay, fine," he relented, holding both hands up after Lindy sent another significant look at the baby. "He was a super not nice guy. A real prick," he said in an exaggerated baby voice and then looked at Lindy. "She doesn't know what that means."

"He's not wrong. About the guy. He was kind of a tool," Lindy said with a roll of her eyes. "I mean, not like ..." She trailed off, a little embarrassed at their banter.

"Like Noah, I know. Continue." Layla waved off the embarrassment. She couldn't avoid the subject forever.

"He didn't think much of the fact that I went to art school only to open up my own canvas studio teaching painting to regular people," Lindy said with a shrug. "Though it seems like it ended for a bunch of reasons."

"And then she couldn't resist my charms."

"Um, that is not how it happened," Lindy said with a roll of her eyes. "If I recall, you followed me around like a puppy until I had no choice but to give in."

"Something like that," he agreed, picking up her hand and kissing it with a wink.

"Stop," she said, pulling her hand away and laughing. "He was a real pain in the ..." she glanced at Maya. "Anyway," she shrugged. "Now here we are." She gestured around them.

Lindy had once lived in the carriage house where Layla lived now. She'd moved in to the big house when her mom had married Layla's dad Theodore and moved in with him. Dean had moved in with her. After all, by then they were already pregnant with Maya. She'd thought the relationship with Dean would run its course, and he'd go back to serial dating. But it hadn't. He hadn't. They'd gotten married on New Year's Eve. She sighed happily and then turned back to Layla.

"Are you dating anyone?" she asked curiously, ignoring Dean's warning look.

"No. Not right now. I'm just getting used to the new job and everything." Layla had gone to school to be a CPA, and she'd taken a job at a local firm after her internship ended. The pay wasn't extravagant or anything, but she was doing okay, she thought. She enjoyed playing around with the numbers. Presley said tax law seemed boring, but Layla liked seeing how much she could help her clients get back. A lot of the families lived paycheck to paycheck, and it made her feel good to be able to help them get more than they expected. Plus, it was soothing just to focus on numbers for a while.

"How's that going?" Dean asked, changing the subject easily.

"I like it. It's different, but I think it's a good fit for me," Layla told them. Dean shifted Maya onto his shoulder, and she laid her head sleepily down, nuzzling against his neck.

"If she's ready for a nap, I'll take her up," Lindy volunteered eagerly.

"Give her a minute," Dean said, waving her away and snuggling in. He looked at Layla. "Just let us know if you need anything over there. We're thinking about putting security cameras up around the perimeter since we have Maya. It's a safe neighborhood, but it'll still be good to have. Make sure none of the kids TP our house come Halloween. Not that they would want to mess with Lindy if they did," he amended, shooting his wife a look.

Layla looked down, covering a sudden surge of emotion that might have been relief and gratitude. "You can never be too careful," she told them. "I think I'll go unpack those last couple of boxes. Thanks for coffee."

Lindy and Dean watched her cross the yard.

"Dean Walton, that was really sweet," Lindy told him.

"I am sweet sometimes," he said with a grin, while his wife rolled her eyes.

"Give me my baby back" she told him with a smile.

"If you remember, this is my baby, too," Dean reminded her.

"Yeah," she said, leaning up to kiss him soundly on the mouth before sliding Maya off his shoulder. "We're going to take a nap. Don't forget to put our mugs in the dishwasher," she told him as she headed inside. Dean smiled and grabbed the mugs. He wasn't going to forget, he thought. He thought a nap sounded pretty good himself.